What Really Happened to Wild Bill

Robert Emerson

Dream Catcher Publishing, Inc.

Published by

Dream Catcher Publishing, Inc.

P.O. Box 33883

Decatur, GA 30033

Fax: 888-771-2800

Web: DreamCatcherPublishing.net

ISBN: 978-0-9910308-0-4

Library of Congress Control Number: 2013951952

Many thanks to Sim Shattuck for his professional editing and to Marion Lea for her thoughtful suggestions.

Other Books by Robert Emerson

The Forty-Rupee Clock

What Really Happened to Wild Bill

CHAPTER ONE

1964

The light plane taxied up the runway, gathering speed. The engine gunned to quickly gain altitude over the tall pines at the end of the strip. Then the aircraft broke through into the bright sunshine, free into the blue sky. After a little over four miles, something was obviously wrong. The plane banked sharply to the left and headed back to the air strip. After a few gasping coughs, the engine stopped altogether. With only the sound of the air flowing over the wings, the plane began a long glide. It was losing altitude now, clipping the thin tops of the pine trees. The flaps came down in a desperate effort to go higher, but to no avail. The wings caught the solid trunks of the trees and the plane tumbled like a toy, making almost a complete flip before plunging to the ground in the woods and breaking apart. The cabin portion plowed into one of the small sloughs that crossed the area. All was quiet. The wreck was well out of sight of the runway. After a few minutes there was a sound of ignition as what was left of the cabin burst into flames. No one noticed the sound or the smoke.

***

1998

I'm trying to remember this place as home. I've come home lots of times. This is the last time I'll call this house home, and for some reason I feel less nostalgia this time than on many of the previous visits. Maybe it's because I'm old. Maybe it's because this is the last time, and I don't want to spend the emotion. Maybe it's because my parents are gone. I would like to feel something. I stare around the musty living room, trying to feel something of remembrance, even of loss. The smell of mustiness is faint. All houses have some sort of smell. Funny. When I lived here, I wasn't aware of the smell. Every time I came back, that smell would be there. Someone told me once that you become accustomed to odors, and after a while your nose rules out background smells. The people down river in Norco used to be that way. They lived next to an odious oil refinery, yet they couldn't smell it. As kids, when my family would drive by Norco on Highway 61 to New Orleans, we would try to hold our breaths as we passed by the refinery. I would get blue in the face. I think my father intentionally slowed down so we couldn't run the full gauntlet without inhaling.

Touching a familiar chair doesn't bring back memories. I lifted the chair, proud that I have kept in shape and was still strong. I could easily put it in the back of my pickup. But it's just a chair. I don't want it. I don't need anything here. The tenant has bought the house. He has graciously let me have a final tour and take what I want. He expects me to collect items as though they would remind me of the good times. They would not. My life was spent elsewhere--working, bringing up my own family. I do remember how excited I was--how eager I was--to come back here over forty years ago on leave from the Marines. Dad still had black hair; Mom, her energy. All that is gone. Home is not this place in Baton Rouge. Home is the latest house--the old farm house on Clear Creek near the Tangipahoa River, the one that I will spend the rest of my life maintaining, painting, and repairing. At least I am back in Louisiana. My earliest roots were the deepest. Ellen thought that retirement would be easier in familiar surroundings. Perhaps she is right; she usually is.

I hear Don and the dog in the kitchen and walk to the light. "Don, thanks for the offer. I won't be taking anything. I looked around, but the furniture just won't fit in our new place."

Don is a nice guy. He seems bright and ambitious, maybe to the point of going to law school if things work out right for him. He helped Mom when she was sick, and now he was offering to let me take things of sentimental value. He can keep the furniture if he wants it. "Sam, you know you are welcome to it. If you change your mind, please come back. I won't be throwing things away for a bit."

I shake his hand. "It's all yours now. I hope you enjoy it."

Backing out of the driveway, I take a last look at the old house. Everything seems about the same, except the shrubbery is fuller. Don has little signs in the yard to acknowledge his security system and to beware of the dog. The sign sports a menacing silhouette of a German Sheppard.

Baton Rouge is much bigger now than when I lived there. The traffic on College Drive is horrendous. Bumper to bumper all the way back to the Interstate. I get in the right lane because the exit is to the right. Unfortunately, cars pull out behind me, go up on the left to the front of the line, and some idiot lets them in. Our lane doesn't move much because the line is getting longer up front. I lucked out getting in the correct lane to merge onto Interstate 12. The traffic doesn't let up until I pass the Denham Springs exit. It's not like Denham Springs is a separate town anymore. Both sides of the highway are built up with commercial establishments filling in the old spaces completely. Once the traffic eases, I gun the pickup truck to seventy-five. The open highway lets me relax a bit, and I feel myself settle into the seat.

The drive back east to Clear Creek on Interstate 12 lets me think. The steady rhythm of sunlight flashing through the pine trees on the side of the road could lull me to sleep, but I drive on in an automatic funk. Are any other official duties left for me, or can I start on the mundane daily chores that will lead me to the end of my own life? A depressing thought. Retirement should be enjoyable, but I have no hobbies. The football watching season is upon us. It's probably too late to get LSU tickets, but that's a possibility for next year. Even though it was still September, they have won their first two games and beaten Notre Dame in a bowl last season. Maybe they'll be good again. I've started my jogging regimen already, but that doesn't take up much time. I need to find someone to play golf with. If I had a small boat, I could fish and go down the river to Lake Pontchartrain. Maybe I could go hunting with my old high school buddies. We had exchanged Christmas cards over the years, and I know they still get together. Some of them had visited us around football games. There are fewer of the old gang now. I tried to think of my Baton Rouge High School friends who had died, counting them as I recalled their names. I counted Wild Bill before I realized that he had not gone to school with us. I knew him as a boy in Franklinton, a drinking companion at LSU, and a roommate in Mexico; but we had not gone to high school together. I wondered if he had finished high school at Franklinton. There was no school in Oakville where he lived. "Wild Bill from Oakville. Never worked and never will. Wild Bill from Oakville, makes the girls on the window sill."

I realized that I had never been to Oakville proper, even though it was close to Franklinton. Maybe there was not a downtown Oakville. Some crossroads in Louisiana had town-like names, even though they boasted little more than a gas station. Wild Bill's family home was somewhere between the two towns. My father had been the camp commander at the CCC camp in Franklinton before the World War II, and Wild Bill's father had owned the nearby Chevrolet dealership. They were probably the richest family in town. They could afford not to live in Franklinton. I recalled going to Jenkins Chevrolet with Wild Bill to get spending money from his dad. His dad gave him money all the time, and Bill spent it all the time. Later in life his strategy was the same with friend or foe. He would buy things for them--dinner or a drink. He told me on one of our trips to Mexico that the best way to get the better of a romantic rival was to buy him something in the presence of their mutual girlfriend. He always reminded me of Toad from Toad Hall--full speed all the time, throwing money left and right. He told me that his favorite literary character was the Great Gatsby. He wanted to be a shooting star-- intensely bright for brief moment. Several times he had said that he wanted to have a young corpse. My stomach contracted for a second. I had promised him something that I had never done--a stupid symbolic something. He said that if he died first, he wanted me to pour a bottle of Scotch over his grave. Of course I would. It was a long forgotten promise, one for which I had felt no obligation over the many years. It was easy to ignore a youthful promise when I was many miles away. Where was my excuse now? My new home was less than 50 miles from Franklinton. What would be the harm in visiting the cemetery and paying my respects? Ellen would not understand. She always took credit for saving my life by keeping me away from Wild Bill. Again, she was probably right.

Bill had called me in Cleveland over 30 years ago. He had finally bought the light plane he had always talked about. Apparently, he was comfortable flying it already. He wanted to come pick me up to attend a friend's wedding in Louisiana. Mired in work, I still said yes. It was like my last shot at adventure. When I told Ellen of my decision, I could tell by her tight lips that she didn't like the idea. "No. Absolutely not. You are not getting in a plane with that madman, and that is that. Call him back right now and tell him that you can't go."

I resolved to do what I was told, knowing that Ellen was right again. I had the perfect excuse–it was time to write the evaluations for the men who worked for me. This was a formidable task–one on which their future and promotions were based. I realized that it was dead wrong to undertake a flight with Bill at the controls, especially now. Those wild days were over. I was married now, with another child to take care of. It took a long time to become responsible. I was a different man now.

When I did call, Bill was not at home, so I left my message with his wife. Oddly, I cannot pull up a picture of her in my mind. I remember that she was pretty. A week later, Bill's cousin called me to ask if Bill had come to Cleveland anyhow. He was missing. I took it lightly and told the cousin of some hotels that we had used in Mexico and that Bill was probably there. He was not. A few days later, Swifty called me from Louisiana. They had found Bill in his shattered plane just a few hundred yards off the runway in the heavy woods. Swifty told me there was no need to come, there was nothing I could do, and Bill was dead. "A classic case of drinking and driving." It was odd for Swifty to call. He owned a bar that Bill and I used to frequent when we were in college. He was also the one to contact Bill when we were in Mexico City five years before Bill's accident to tell us of another fatal accident. He had the same message then. Don't try to come back. Dennis was dead, and we could do nothing except hurt ourselves driving back through the Mexican desert. "A classic case of drinking and driving," the telegram read. The memories are coming back. Probably because of the sadness I was feeling then, the similarities between the two calls had eluded me at the time of Bill's death. I didn't even wonder how Swifty had obtained my telephone number or knew where I was.

I was coming up on the intersection with Interstate 55. That would be the fastest way to get to Franklinton. I had to make the decision now. I could go by my house in Clear Creek first and not drive many more miles. No, the Interstate would be faster, and I wouldn't have to explain my silly mission to Ellen. I was embarrassed by my intended gesture and the amount of time it had taken me to perform it. I tried to get in the right-hand lane to get on the exit to I55 North. The cars merging from I-55 were all trying to get in my lane and I was trying to get in theirs. Somehow we all made it without a collision. The interstate roadway north was rough, and the tires on my pickup went "whump, whump, whump" as they hit the creases in the concrete. I wished I had a map, but eventually I spied a sign for State Highway 16 going east. It was bound to go to Franklinton, and I took it. I had been on 16 for several miles when I passed 445. That would be the way that I would get back to Clear Creek on my return trip. Remembering my mission, I screeched to a stop at a little roadside tavern at the crossroads in Houghton. The early September sun was fierce outside of the car's air conditioning. How could I have ever driven all those years without air conditioning?

How do they play football in this heat? I put on my best redneck saunter as I walked inside the tavern. A heavyset man was standing behind the bar with one foot on a rung of a bar stool. He was sweating profusely in the hot air coming through the open door, even though a large fan on the floor was humming away. I tried to get my accent back. "Sure is hot."

"You're telling me. What can I do for you? Something cold?"

That sounded tempting, but I had work to do. "No. I thought I'd get a little Scotch to go. What's the smallest thing you got?" I tried to look past him at the bottle stacked up behind the bar, but it was all a blur. I'm too vain to wear my glasses all the time.

The man didn't look too interested. He showed me a bottle that he plucked off the shelf. "I got a half pint of Johnny Walker."

"That sounds just right." I said, pretending that I was familiar with Scotch. I paid him and walked hurriedly back to the car and air conditioning. I threw the bottle on the seat and continued on my journey. The road merged with 25 and then LA-10, and I could see signs I was on the right track. Just before Franklinton, I spotted a cemetery off to the right. It was large and within sight of the bridge over the Bogue Chitto River. Could this be the place? Might as well try before getting tangled up in Franklinton. I turned right toward the cemetery and crossed a little bridge over a dry gully that fed into the river. A cloud of dust followed me as I came to stop under a lone live oak. The oak must have been planted. Most of the trees around here should have been pines. I waited a minute for the dust to settle. Another cloud of dust drifted off to the right inside the cemetery. Someone was mowing the dry grass on a riding mower. I walked to the other side of the park to avoid contact. The cemetery was larger than I thought. Finding Bill's grave could take some time. I probably should have gone into town and made some inquiries. I stretched my legs as I walked down the rows, looking for headstones for the Jenkins family. The ground was uneven in places, so I had to watch my step as well as I perused the often faint writing on the tombstones.

Fortunately, most of the stones were in straight rows, so I walked up and down, like plowing a field. I recognized the old family names, Magee, Bickham, and Varnado. Lots of people with those names in Franklinton in the old days. No stone for a Jenkins. I stopped when I came to the Simmonses. We used to play with a Jimmy Simmons. There was a James Simmons. It might have been Jimmy's father. I looked at the dates on the headstone. No, it was probably Jimmy himself. Damn, I'm getting old. All those people in Franklinton had been living and dying while I was transferring around the country and around the world. It must have been comforting for them to live in one place all their lives. You got to know your town—where the best place to shop was, having the same doctors and lawyers, owning a home with no mortgage. No, I wouldn't trade my life if I could. Something about living in different places made me appreciate the differences in people and customs. It was a knowledge that should be kept to myself now. I sensed that people who stayed at home were offended by descriptions of other, more tolerant places. The man on the riding mower and I were getting closer to each other. I was sweating like a pig and needed some help.

He pulled to a stop at the end of the row I was searching. As I approached he stopped the idle and asked "C'n I help you with somethin'?"

"Sure. I'm looking for Jenkins."

"Which Jenkins? That's a pretty common name in these parts." He looked to be in his sixties, wrinkled and red and thin as a reed. He coughed a smoker's cough as he waited for an answer.

"Bill. William Jenkins. He's been dead for 30 years, but he would have been about my age."

"That wouldn't be Wild Bill, would it?

"Yes, it is." I was surprised at his knowledge, but I felt like this was leading somewhere.

"Well those Jenkinses wouldn't be here. They'd be in their own cemetery over in Oakville. If'n it's still there. Ain't nothing over there no more?" He looked at me curiously. "I don't seem to recall your face."

Strangers must be a curiosity in Franklinton–at least to this gentleman. I wasn't eager to tell him my silly mission, but if I seemed defensive, I'd not likely get the information I wanted. I extended my hand to shake quickly, so he couldn't see my hesitation. "Hi. I'm Sam Elliot."

He seemed surprised but wiped his hand on the back of his blue jeans and shook mine. "Pleased to meet you. "I don't remember any Elliots around here." His hand was rough and gnarly and his fingernails were long. The whites of his eyes weren't white. They were reddish yellow. His light brown irises did not contrast well.

I held his hand for a moment, hoping he would give his own name. He didn't. "No, I was only here for a little while--around 1944."

"Oh, that was before my time."

I was embarrassed. He looked older than I thought I did. Recent looks in the mirror always surprised me. I should look younger, but everyone calls me "sir" these days. A favorite courtesy in Louisiana was to call me "Mr.

Sam." I said, "But you knew Wild Bill?"

"Well, not exactly." He looked away and then back at me. "I saw him and I heard a lot about him, but you couldn't say I knew him. You know what I mean?"

"Sure. I know what you mean." It was likely that a lot of people had heard about Bill and his wild escapades. I looked up at the blue sky, hoping he would continue the conversation, because I didn't know what to say next.

The man sniffed his nose and spat, politely, on the other side of the mower. "I mean, like, I was probably the last person to see him alive."

I was taken aback. How could I have been so lucky as to hit on this piece of history on my first stop? This information was a little out of my mission, but I was curious. I said the magic words to evoke a response, "No kidding?"

He hunkered up to spit again, but couldn't find enough to make it worthwhile. "Yep. I was working the town airport that day. You know he died in a plane crash?" He searched my face as if the truth were there.

"Yes. I heard about it, but I wasn't--" I started to say something else--"in these parts when it happened. So you actually saw him and talked to him?" That had to provoke more explanation.

"Yep." He smiled self-consciously as though he was proud of what he had done. "He gave me ten dollars."

I wondered if Bill had done that because he liked this guy or disliked him. It would have been like Bill either way. "That was a lot of money back then. Why did he do that?"

"Well, to tell the truth..." He looked both ways as if he didn't want the dead to hear him. He then leaned forward and lowered his voice. "I think he was just trying to get rid of me."

"Why would he want to do something like that?" I tried to get a little indignation in my voice to show how implausible it was that anyone would try to get rid of such a fine character.

"I think he just wanted a little privacy to talk to some foreign kid."

"A foreign kid at the airfield? How do you know he was foreign? Did he have an accent?"

"Nooo. I can't say that exactly." He scratched his chin in thought. "I don't exactly know if I heard him talk much. But he was dressed different."

"Like?"

"Like he wore a hat and sunglasses and had on a shirt with some fancy stitching that wasn't tucked in. Mr. Bill was like that sometimes, wearing funny clothes and doing strange things and all." He stroked his own denim shirt to emphasize the difference from the local dress.

I got the idea that "foreign" could mean anyone not from Franklinton. "Oh. I see. Boy! You really have a good memory to remember things like that after so many years." Nothing stirs the conversation like a good compliment.

He smiled the self-conscious smile again and looked away briefly in modesty. "Yep. A lotta people 'round here tell me I got a good memory."

I didn't know how to keep it stirring. "So he just gave you ten dollars?"

"No. He gave me the money to go get him a sandwich at the golf course on the other side of the runway."

"So you brought him a sandwich."

"Well, yeah, but he took off before I got back. I seen him taxi past when I was at the golf course."

"And the foreign kid?"

"He dug out in a big black car back towards Franklinton."

"And that's it?"

"That's it. You got to remember, that was a long time ago. I never seen either one of them again. A kid shouldn't have a fancy car like that. I never did."

"Who else was in the car besides the kid?" I knew not to ask a question that evoked a "yes" or "no" answer.

"I dunno."

"But you saw the kid get in and dig out."

He scratched the whiskers on the side of his face. "I'm trying to remember. I don't exactly recall seeing him get in the car. I just saw it peeling out. The car was going one way, the plane the other. I had just about crossed the fence to come back, so they both took off before I had gotten very far."

"But this kid and Bill were just talking?"

He cocked his head and bit his lip. "More like arguing, if I remember right. I couldn't hear very good, but Bill must have owed the kid something. I know Bill gave him something—I couldn't see what. The kid put it in his pocket and kept on talking like it wasn't enough."

I tried to visualize the body language that would convey all that to an untrained observer, especially to have remembered such an impression after so long a time. "Well, that was very interesting. Thanks for taking the time to tell me about it." I stuck out my hand to shake again, trying to think of a way to end the conversation. "Can you tell me the way to Oakville?"

"Sure. Just take that main road straight through Franklinton. The first paved road past the dairy, take a left. You can't miss it. But there ain't anything there no more—and all of them Jenkinses are dead and gone." He pointed back to LA-10 with his left hand as he shook mine with his right.

I wish I had a nickel for every time I heard that you can't miss it. I summed up the incident as I started to turn away. "I guess ole Bill was just too drunk to pilot a plane that day."

The man looked puzzled. "You know. He sure didn't look drunk to me."

"No?"

"No. But he musta been. The talk was that he had been drinkin', and they found a bottle of gin in the cockpit. Or so I'm told."

I hurried back, got in the truck, and hastily got the air-conditioning going again. Bill rarely looked drunk even when he was. I understand that is common with alcoholics. He used to put away a lot of liquor, but I don't remember him staggering or slurring his speech, with the exception of a couple of times before accidents. He sure did some crazy things though. As I crossed the bridge over the Bogue Chitto River, I looked down stream to see the tavern on the bank. It was gone. Nothing but woods there now. Commercial Franklinton began just a block away. All new stores in what used to be woods. I stopped at the stoplight and noticed that they had built a new courthouse. Franklinton deserved a big courthouse because it was the seat of Washington Parish. The artesian well fountains were no longer there on the corners. A sacrifice to progress maybe? The light changed and I pulled away. Then I looked over at the bottle of scotch on the seat and quickly pulled to a stop in a parking place by the courthouse.

Wild Bill never drank gin. He couldn't. He said he must have been allergic to juniper berries or something. Gin caused him a reaction that made his breathing difficult. It was an affliction that he abhorred because he desperately wanted to drink martinis. I think the Great Gatsby drank gin martinis, but Bill could not. He once told me a story about wanting to walk on an island beach in a white suit with a treasure map in one hip pocket and a bottle of gin in the other. Then he changed the liquor to rum, acknowledging his affliction. Maybe the man in the cemetery was mistaken. There must be a way to check it out. I was getting interested. Maybe this would be a good short-term project for my retirement. After all, I had been an investigator in the Public Health Service. The problem back then was that, because of confidentiality, we rarely used public sources when they required us to disclose the reason for our inquiries. We had to protect our sources. This was different. I could do anything I wanted. Accident findings should be public records. Maybe verifying the gin aspect was insignificant, but I never did find out the details of Bill's accident and that prospect seemed challenging now. To hell with pouring scotch over a stupid grave. Maybe I could do something more constructive. I could resolve this gin thing. I might be able to clear his name about the drinking and find out what really happened to Wild Bill!

I circled the courthouse and headed back to the bridge. I was exuberant. I had a mission, albeit a small one. As I crossed the bridge, I took the bottle of scotch and threw it back over the car toward the river. It missed, hit the side of the bridge, and shattered. I muttered under my breath, "Shit. I'd better get out of here before someone notices and I get pulled in."

My thoughts raced as I drove home. Was I giving too much importance to a minor discrepancy? I didn't want to look silly. Somehow the finding of a gin bottle had to be verified. The guy in the cemetery easily could have been mistaken. His memory sounded amazing, but that could be because he didn't really remember and just was saying whatever came into his head. How much should I tell Ellen? Everything. She could help. A dark thought crept in. Was there some connection between the deaths of Bill and Dennis? Right now, Swifty's involvement looked suspicious. My most traumatic contacts with Swifty were strangely similar. When he telegraphed Bill in Mexico to tell us about Dennis's death, he specifically told him not to come back to Louisiana. There was nothing we could do, and driving Mexican highways at night was dangerous. He told me something similar when he called about Bill's death. He also put the blame strictly on alcohol for both deaths. I never thought much about how Swifty got my telephone number–maybe from my parents.

Bill and I had discussed Swifty when Bill called me that time in Cleveland. I had tried to make conversation after agreeing to fly back with him for our friend's wedding. Bill said something about Swifty embarking on a new business. I told Bill that I had always thought of Swifty as something of a criminal. I remember talking to Swifty's wife one late night long ago and noticing that her pupils were fully dilated. That wouldn't have meant much except that I had seen *The Man with the Golden Arm*, and Frank Sinatra had fixed pupils when he was on heroin. I think I mentioned that to Wild Bill as part of my suspicions. Did I somehow get Bill in too deep with my accusations? I hate conspiracy theorists. They seem paranoid to me. I would be no different if I jumped to conclusions with so little evidence. Best not get in too deep. There had to be a point where I would not pursue this concern too openly. I decided that the first thing I should do is to find out if Bill's accident was thought to have been caused by gin specifically. If not, I should drop it right there. Good. I had a partial plan to begin with.

My planning occupied the entire trip home. Some of my best schemes were hatched while I was driving. That was the way I composed and practiced my speeches. I was happy to see the lights on in the old farm house. I parked out back and made little noise as I went in the side door. Ellen was over the sink in the kitchen, making a salad. I walked up behind her and patted her on the bottom and kissed her neck.

She did not turn around but whispered loudly. "We better hurry; my husband could come home at any time."

I reached around her and picked up some carrot wheels to munch on.

She glanced at me briefly and went on with her chopping. "Oh, it's you. How did you make out in Baton Rouge? Did you bring anything back?"

I leaned against the counter and crunched carrots. "No. We already had the books and photographs that I wanted. Everything else was either too big or too shoddy. You said you couldn't think of anything you wanted."

She carried the salad over to the counter where the rest of the dinner was materializing.

I folded my arms and watched her. A little plumper than when I married her. A few more wrinkles. She was still sexy, and I loved her. "I went by Franklinton on the way home."

"Franklinton isn't on the way home."

"I know. But it isn't that far out of the way. I thought I would see Wild Bill's grave."

"And did you?"

"No. It was too far to go and I changed my mind.

But I did have an interesting conversation with a guy at the cemetery."

"I thought you said the cemetery was too far."

"It was. This was a different cemetery. This was on the near side of Franklinton, and Bill is probably buried in Oakville on the other side."

She remembered the sayings about Bill. "Never worked and never will."

"Right. This guy at the cemetery said that he didn't think that Bill had been drinking the day he crashed. He also said that they found a bottle of gin in the plane. Bill didn't drink gin."

"So where is all this leading?"

"I'd like to find out what the official investigation of the crash found. I'm not sure just how to do that."

"There's bound to be a government agency that keeps that kind of record. You can find anything on the Internet."

Ellen was right again. After just a little searching, I found a web site for the National Transportation and Safety Board. They have a wonderful site that makes available final reports on fatal accidents. Unfortunately, the internet database begins in 1983, so there was no record of Bill's crash. I keyed in some search information for a recent crash in Hammond and found it right away. My only recourse was to write the Board and ask. I hate writing letters. It's so much easier to send e-mails. I messed around with the site a little and found some hypertext that purported to have information on earlier accidents. It popped up with an e-mail format. I filled in everything that I remembered and hit the send icon. That might not be enough information for people to find the report. Nothing to do but to sit back several weeks and wait. I had made my plan already. If gin wasn't mentioned in the report, I probably would drop it. I had plenty of time. As one of my friends would say, "What's time to a hog?" I'm retired and there are lots of things to do around the house. I would just forget about this mystery for a while.

To my surprise, I got an e-mail back the next day. It listed six accidents in Louisiana, but not the names of the parties involved. It was easy to pick out Wild Bill's accident. It was the only one in Franklinton. The format suggested that the document was fill-in-the-blanks from some kind of filing program.

2-0197 64/5/29   FRANKLINTON LA   BELLANCA 14-13   CR- 1 0 0 MISCELLANEOUS - STUDENT, AGE 29, UNK/NR
TIME - 1900   N86783   PX- 0 0 0 FERRY
TOTAL HOURS, UNK/NR IN   **DAMAGE**-DESTROYED
OT- 0 0 0
TYPE, UNK/NR INSTRUMENT RATED.
NAME OF AIRPORT - FRANKLINTON
TYPE OF ACCIDENT - COLLIDED WITH: TREES
PHASE OF OPERATION - LANDING: FINAL APPROACH
PROBABLE CAUSE(S) - PILOT IN COMMAND - MISJUDGED ALTITUDE   **MISCELLANEOUS ACTS, CONDITIONS** - ALCOHOLIC IMPAIRMENT OF EFFICIENCY AND JUDGMENT

That was it. Nowhere near the detail of the more recent reports on the web. The Hammond accident was several pages long. If they did find a bottle, the kind of bottle probably never made the official report. I was prepared to drop my inquiry if gin was not mentioned, but the absence of evidence is not the evidence of absence. How could I find out? I could go back to Franklinton and try to find someone who participated in the recovery. I could search the local newspaper archives. Maybe that would be better. I was still a little embarrassed to confront people about such a trivial point. Most newspapers have been reduced to microfiche. I've done searches like that before, looking for contacts to communicable diseases. Maybe there was an autopsy report. Surely they had checked Bill's blood alcohol content. The report would not have said anything about alcoholic impairment without evidence. This was going to be more work that I expected. I talked about my plan with Ellen that night as I snuggled up to her back in bed. She was supportive. "Sure, get it out of your system. Maybe there is someone else to talk to in Franklinton. There has to be a coroner's office and records."

I ran my hand up her abdomen and touched her breast. She sat up and slipped her nightgown over her head. God, I love that woman.

CHAPTER TWO

The next day after breakfast, I headed back to Franklinton again. According to a man at the gas station, the airport and golf course were easy to find. I took a right at the courthouse and headed south out of town on Highway 16. On the way, I passed a former family friend's house that since had been converted into a lawyer's office. The large stream and gully that ran by the house back in the forties was just a trickle now. Was it my memory distorting the size of things, or had the topography changed over the years? Farther down, I almost missed the turn to the left on highway 1072 because the sign for the Franklinton Country Club was small and past the side road. The paved road ran through dairy farms where black and white cows contentedly chewed their cuds on small rolling hills that didn't exist just a few miles south in the delta country. I spotted the golf course and what looked like an airstrip in the open country about a half mile before I reached it. The runway came up almost to the road just before the turnoff for the golf course. Unfortunately, there was a fence, and I couldn't get into the airport from there, so I had to go back to the main road again. I turned around in the entrance to the golf course, cursing all the way to the highway and took a left again. The airport was clearly marked by a sign with a silhouette picture of a big airliner on it. I thought to myself, *Looks like the Franklinton International directly ahead.*

I turned left again and drove a few hundred feet through desolate fields with practically no vegetation. Then I parked in the gravel by a corrugated metal building. It was the only structure on the property besides a small hangar less than a hundred yards away. A beat-up old Ford pickup was the only other vehicle in the area.

Inside, the main room had no ceiling but ran all the way to the roof from which was suspended a single fan dangling over a desk. A window air-conditioning unit struggled to fight the heat, but it and the fan were losing the battle of the large area. A soft drink machine stood against the far wall. No one was around in this part which seemed to be an office with files, but I could hear some metallic banging noise behind a low plywood wall that separated the office from the major portion of the building. I went through the only door in the plywood wall. A balding man in his late thirties was pounding with a small sledge and a screwdriver on an engine hanging from some chains. He stopped pounding when he saw me and wiped his hands on a grease-streaked rag. He was sweating profusely. "What can I do you?"

I thought better of shaking hands. "Sorry to bother you. You look like you were enjoying yourself."

He looked back at the motor. "I'm just about to give up. I don't think I can get that bolt off without drilling it out." He paused to let me answer his first question.

"I really just want some information. I'm looking for anyone who might have been around when there was a plane crash here back in the sixties."

"Well, it wouldn't be me. I wasn't even a gleam in my daddy's eye back then." He looked down in thought. "I might know somebody who was here then. Joe Varnado was the main mechanic here before me, but he's been retired for about five years. I can find his telephone number if you want."

"I'd appreciate it. I just wanted to talk to him for a few minutes. Do you know if he still lives around Franklinton?"

"Yeah. He has a place up by the Fairgrounds. Come on in the other side, and I'll get his number." He put the rag in his back pocket.

I followed him through the door. "That's kind of you."

"No trouble. I was looking for an excuse to get away from that damned engine."

He went to the desk and leafed through a Rolodex until he found the card he wanted. He pulled it out and handed it to me. A grease-smeared surface revealed a name, telephone number and address. I copied the information down on a Home Depot receipt I had in my pocket.

The mechanic watched me. "You can call him on this phone if you want." He unlocked a drawer and lifted out an old rotary instrument with the receiver on a cradle. "Bet you haven't seen one of these in a while."

"You're right. I dialed each number and let the rotary spin back. The numbers were barely legible and had letters above each number from the time when telephone numbers included alphabetic prefixes. I remembered that my mother's phone was on the Dickens exchange.

The mechanic volunteered information while I was waiting for a connection. "We lock up the phone in the drawer to keep people from using it when there's no authorized people around. One time someone snuck in here and ran up a long-distance bill."

A man answered after five rings. "Hello."

"Mr. Varnado?"

"That's me. Who is this?"

"My name is Sam Elliot. I'm down at the airstrip in Franklinton now and I wondered if you could give me some information about a plane crash that happened here a few years ago."

"What crash?"

"The one in which Bill Jenkins was killed."

He paused for a while. "That was a long time ago. What is it you want to know?"

"As much as you can tell me. Were you here when it happened?"

"Yes, but I can't tell you very much. He took off without a flight plan or nothing. Been drinking, you know."

I was afraid he might cut me short. "Look, I'm going to be up by the Fairgrounds in about two hours. Is there any way I could talk to you in person?"

"Les see. It's about nine now. That would make it about eleven. You know where I live?"

"I've got your address, but I would appreciate some directions." Years of investigating had taught me that addresses were not anywhere as helpful as directions in the country, and his address had five digits in it. He gave me the directions which sounded straight forward enough, and I thanked him.

I hung up and thanked the mechanic. "Could I buy you a drink?" I nodded toward the vending machine. "I could use one too."

He gave his hands one last wipe with the cloth. "That sounds good, if we can get it working."

I was hoping the drink machine was the same vintage as the phone, but it wasn't. It took dollar bills. Things have changed a lot since I lived in Franklinton. Cokes were a nickel then. They must have cost five cents for most of their history. Pepsi cut into their market by offering twice the volume for the same price. "Pepsi Cola hits the spot. Twelve ounce bottle, that's a lot. Twice as much for a nickel too. Pepsi Cola is the drink for you.

Nickel, nickel, nickel." I sang the jingle for the mechanic, but he didn't seem amused. The cans slid down with a rattle. I hoped they hadn't shaken to the point of fizzing over when we opened them. I changed the subject as we sipped on our drinks. "You know, there must have been a coroner's report on that accident. I wonder how I could get a report like that."

The mechanic finished off his can with his head thrown back. "Your best bet is to ask up at the courthouse. Thanks for the coke, but I need to pound on that engine some more. I'm afraid I'll have to take a chisel to it at least."

I thanked him again and headed back to town.

At the courthouse, a nice lady referred me to the sheriff's office across the road. That spot had been occupied by the post office in the forties. The sheriff's secretary took me down into the jail area to talk to the investigators. The two investigators were very polite and professional. No, records from the sixties didn't exist because of the fire in 1972. I asked what role the sheriff's office would have played in an accident like that I described.

They took turns answering. First, they would address the safety of any surviving passengers and the public. The area would be roped off to prevent further accidents and looting. The coroner's doctor would be called. Only that official had the authority to pronounce someone dead and to take charge of the body.

I asked if the coroner was a physician. The investigators looked at each other. Not today. The coroner ran a grocery store and gas station on the Bogalusa road. They gave me directions. This job was getting more complicated than I had thought. I looked at my watch. Still plenty of time to see the coroner and make my appointment with Joe Varnado.

I hadn't planned on yet another stop, but that had to be. The coroner was helpful as well. No, the coroner in Washington Parish had never been a physician as far as he knew. Whenever he needed a physician, he used Dr. Brumfield. That physician would perform autopsies at the hospital. The physician that was used in the sixties? That would have been Dr. Brumfield's father. Dr. Brumfield junior had taken over the old man's practice about fifteen years ago. Luckily, Dr. Brumfield's office was close by. I still had time to see the doctor and make the Varnado appointment.

The doctor's office was above the bank on the main road through town.. A small elevator led to the second floor suite. The waiting room chairs were plush. A large aquarium dominated the far wall. The receptionist was pretty and polite. "Dr. Brumfield is just leaving to make his rounds at the hospital."

This didn't help. I tried to look respectful and perplexed at the same time. "Would it be possible to talk to him on the way downstairs?"

A distinguished-looking man came out of an interior door behind the receptionist and handed her some small pieces of paper. "Sherry, would you answer these calls for me. Call me at the hospital if anything sounds serious. And call me if Mrs. Simmons's test comes back from the lab."

"Dr. Brumfield?" I stuck out my hand.

He shook it tentatively and searched my face for recognition.

"My name is Sam Elliot, and I'm looking into an accident that happened back in the sixties. I understand your father would have done autopsies in fatal accidents back then."

"He did. What's your interest in the case?"

"The deceased--Bill Jenkins--was a very good friend of mine, and I couldn't get back for the funeral or to talk to the family or find out the particulars or anything." My excuse was sort of lame. I should have thought about what I was going to say beforehand.

Dr. Brumfield shuffled his feet. "I have my father's old records, but even if your friend's chart is here, I'm not sure whether I can let you look at it."

"I understand. But I was hoping that since your father's involvement was in his public capacity, his notes might have been public property. I'd really appreciate any thing you could do for me."

Dr. Brumfield scratched his chin. "I've never run into this before, and I've really got to get over to the hospital. Tell you what. Let me have Sherry look for the record. If she finds it, she can read some of the pertinent information. Sherry's pretty sharp in these matters, and I don't think she would read or show you anything that might be objectionable to the survivors. Would that be all right?"

I was relieved. He could just have easily said no. I stuck out my hand again. "Thank you. I'm grateful."

He turned to his receptionist. "Sherry, you heard this. Do you know what to do?"

"Yes sir. The sixties records would be in the old filing cabinets, right?"

"You'd know better than I do. Have at it." He rushed out the door.

I looked at Sherry and smiled as I nodded toward the door. "Nice man." I wanted to be pleasant. Sherry held the power.

"He is. Bill Jenkins?" She smoothed her slacks as she got up. Her bottom was larger than I expected. People eat well around here.

"Yes. William, I guess. The accident was in 1964."

"That's helpful. The records are alphabetical within the year the chart was closed. We put them up if we haven't seen a patient in three years." She walked to a back room full of file cabinets. Through the open door I could see her put a clenched hand on her chin while she ran the other hand up and down the fronts of the cabinets as she read the labels. "Here they are. Jenkins, Jenkins." She leafed through the tops of the folders. "Sure are a lot of Jenkins. Oops! There's more than one William."

"This one would have been about 29 in 1964."

She looked in the tops of the folders and pulled one out of the file. "Bingo. Born in 1935." She brought the folder back to her desk and sat down. "Please have a seat." She motioned to a chair where it would be difficult for me to see the record. "Now, what would you like to know?"

I thought quickly. "Well, whatever you can tell me about the accident and the cause of death."

She skimmed through the record and summarized as she went. "Plane crash. Plane flipped over causing massive injuries." She read some more. "Boy, he was really torn up. Everything looks broken. He must have died right away. The doctor thought he was dead before he was burned."

I was a little surprised. "There was a fire?"

"An intense one apparently. The body was badly burned."

That wasn't very helpful, but I didn't know what else to do. "What does it say about alcohol?"

She turned the page and leafed through laboratory reports. "Alcohol blood level of .001." She looked up at me to see if I had any more questions.

I got up and thanked her. I guess that answered my questions. Bill had been drinking. That wasn't unusual. As I rode down the elevator, I cursed myself. I should have used Dr. Brumfield's phone to cancel my appointment with Joe Varnado. Never mind. The fairgrounds were not far away and the drive around town would allow me to see some of my old haunts. I got in the truck and headed north for about twelve blocks. The entrance to the fairgrounds looked just like it did sixty years ago. The biggest county fair in the U.S. went down there every October. In the forties, I watched Jimmy Davis on the big stage, singing "You Are My Sunshine." He was either governor or running for governor. I hung a right just before the entrance down a paved road that was gravel back then.

Joe Varnado's place was easy to find. It was a neat white house, just about ready for repainting, with a picket fence and a brick walk. The house was elevated on concrete pillars, like many of the houses in this area. Joe was sitting on the porch in a rocking chair. He wore a white shirt and blue jeans and what little hair he had was confined to just above his ears. I got out and paused at the gate. "Mr. Varnado?"

"That's me. Come on in." He stood up and walked over to the steps to greet me. His face was red and wrinkled, and his hand was rough. He looked like he had spent a lifetime doing hard work. His square jaw and large forearms gave me the impression that he was still a strong man in spite of his age. He opened the screen door and motioned me inside. "Let's go in where it's a little cooler." The door squeaked when it opened and slammed shut with a bang thanks to a long coiled spring that ran from the door sill to near the inside handle.

"Thanks." I tried not to look around in order not to

appear judgmental. I couldn't help noticing a row of porcelain pitchers sitting in bowls on the mantel of the false fireplace. "That's a fine collection. They must be antiques."

Joe smiled. "That's my wife's work. She used to travel the countryside working for the welfare department. Anytime she'd see one of them jugs, she'd offer the owner a few dollars for it. Most of the time, they'd accept. With running water, there's not much call for pitchers and wash basins anymore. They are pretty though. Look. There's not much more I can tell you about that accident. It happened a long time ago."

I tried to be calm. "Did you see the crash scene? I needed to ask some questions to make the visit seem worthwhile.

"Yes. Some kid found the plane. The sheriff's office called me in because I knew a lot about planes and there wasn't anybody to do a proper investigation. I was there when they pulled young Mr. Jenkins's body out. He was an awful mess. I wouldn't have recognized him."

I leaned forward to engage him. "You said that he had been drinking?"

"Yes. They found a bottle of gin under the seat. Somehow it wasn't busted up too much."

"What do you think caused the accident?"

He jerked as though that was already settled. "Why, he was drunk, I guess, and came in too low and clipped the trees."

"But he had just left the airfield, right? So he was coming back to try to land?" Why do you think he turned around so soon?"

Joe looked down at his gnarled hands in his lap. "I think the poor guy realized he was too drunk to fly and just tried to get back and didn't make it."

"What happens to the plane in cases like this?"

"Well, the family gave me the engine. The insurance company didn't want it. I tried to get it running again. But I couldn't." His head sank lower and I could see a tear coming down his cheek. He turned away and brushed his cheek with the back of his hand.

I doubted whether the tear was because he missed Bill. I remembered patients who acted the same way when they had difficulty talking about something. If you didn't address it at the time, they would avoid the issue. I automatically did what I had done with the patients and acted as though I knew what he was thinking. "There's something more that you want to tell me." It wasn't a question.

Joe looked up at the ceiling and both eyes were brimming with moisture. "I checked all those engines at the air strip. They were always in good working order, or I wouldn't let anybody take 'em out of the hangar."

I looked him in the eye. "But there was something wrong with that engine."

He turned his face away. "There was some kind of gunk in the gas line."

That statement surprised me. The blood left my face for a second. "Enough to cause the engine to conk out?"

"I think so."

"What kind of gunk was it?"

"I don't know. When things get mixed with fuel, they change. This was just sticky." He was shaking.

I didn't want to lead him too much, but I felt sorry for him and wanted to take him off the hook somehow. He must have been worrying about this all these years. "So whatever was in the engine got there after you had done your inspection?"

31

He blinked, trying to stem the tears. "That's the only thing I can think of."

I stood up, put one hand on his shoulder, and offered him my right hand to shake. "Look. I appreciate you talking to me. I know this might be difficult. Would you take my card and give me a call if you think of something else?"

He shook my hand and took the card. "Sure." He seemed relieved that I was leaving.

"I heard the plane caught fire. Why didn't anybody see the smoke right away? A plane like that must have carried a lot of fuel."

Joe cleared his throat. "The whole plane didn't burn. I don't think the tanks ever caught. Bill had some five-gallon cans in the cockpit that must have gone up in flames. The cockpit ended up at the bottom of a slough that had a little water in it. I know he had talked to me about building in some auxiliary fuel tanks to increase the range of the plane."

I stopped at the door on the way out and turned to him. "This wasn't your fault. You're not in any trouble."

I was numb. I tried to find out more about Wild Bill's death, and I had. I really didn't expect to find anything new, but somehow I had. The new information didn't prove anything, but now I had a suspicion--a suspicion that couldn't go away. I had to find out more. I was driving in a blue funk, going home without thinking. As I passed the courthouse, I pulled over to gather my wits. Was there something else to do before leaving Franklinton? Better thank Dr. Brumfield. He could be helpful later on, and he should know what was in the record. I looked both ways before crossing the street and let an old pickup clatter by. An old pay phone was in the lobby. Luckily, a telephone book dangled beside it. Only one hospital in town. Was it an imposition to summon a doctor while he was on rounds? Might as well give it a try anyhow.

A young lady answered the phone after two rings, and I began apologizing right away. "This isn't an emergency or anything, but would it be possible to speak to Dr. Brumfield?"

"Sure, he's right here by the desk. Who shall I say is calling?"

"Sam Elliot."

The phone went dead for a few seconds as if a hand was over the mouthpiece. Then the lady's voice again. "Here's Dr. Brumfield."

"Mr. Elliot?"

"Yes. Sorry to bother you at the hospital. I just wanted to thank you for letting me look up my friend. It's been bothering me all these years."

"Was Sherry able to find anything?"

"Yes. She was very discreet, but she read me a few things that were probably public knowledge at the time. My friend had a blood alcohol level of .001. I'm not sure what that means."

"Ordinarily, not very much. He could have been drinking the night before or had a small drink recently."

"You mean that a person is not impaired with that level?"

"I don't think so. Different people react differently, but the legal definition for intoxication in Louisiana is .01. This reading is much less than that. You're not with insurance are you?"

"No. No. I'm really just an old friend. Thank you again. You and Sherry have been very helpful."

I hung up the phone and rested my chin on my

upper arm a while as I leaned on top of the instrument. "What to do now?"

CHAPTER THREE

Ellen was either interested or wanted to appear interested as I related my latest story. I tried to get a positive reaction. "It sounds less like an accident now, doesn't it?"

"It may sound less likely than it did before, but where is the majority of the evidence--accident or not?"

"Probably accident."

"You are the one who hates the conspiracy arguments. If you think this was a murder, doesn't it put you in the same league with those fringe groups?"

"Probably. But I'm the only one with this information. No one would ever question the accident if I don't do anything.

"So, what is your plan?"

"I don't know. I was hoping you would give me some ideas."

"How about painting the porch?"

"Not that kind of idea. I mean, how would I go about proving or disproving the accident- slash-murder?"

"Well. You started with two accidents. You appear to be at a temporary dead end with Wild Bill. How about looking into what happened to Dennis Dawson? You said that Swifty informed you about both deaths in a similar way."

"Yes. And it seems like there was something suspicious about Dennis's accident too--like he was alone when he hit the tree, but someone was with him earlier. I'll bet Tommy Freeman could help. He knew Wild Bill and Dennis--and he and Dennis were both lawyers. "

"Have you talked to Tommy since his accident?"

"No. I just sent him that get-well card. I understand

that he has been despondent since he lost his legs."

"Wouldn't you be despondent?"

"Yes, I would. He still lives in Baton Rouge. This might be a good excuse to visit him."

"Sam, don't let him think you're wanting to see him just about Bill. You and Tommy were good friends. That ought to be reason enough."

"You're right. Tommy has had it tough enough."

The next day I called information to get Tommy's telephone number in Baton Rouge.

Unfortunately, there were three Thomas Freemans listed. The robot operator would only give me a number for one. I picked the wrong one and had to call information back again. It seems like this process was easier when you got a real operator the first time. The second time worked and Tommy answered the phone.

I was glad to hear his voice. "Hey, Tommy. It's Sam Elliot."

"Sam. Where are you? Are you calling from Atlanta?"

"No. I'm retired. Ellen and I are living in Tangipahoa Parish."

"I'd heard that you might be moving back to Louisiana. What's up?"

"Well, I'm less than 60 miles from Baton Rouge, and I'd like to come by and see you some time."

"When?"

"Almost anytime you say. I don't have many obligations any more--just enjoying retirement."

There was a pause. "You know I can't walk."

I didn't want to dwell on that. "Yes. When do you think I could drop by? You tell me the time."

"Can you come by Friday?

"Sure. Just give the directions."

Friday. This was Wednesday, so I had a couple of days to do some things on my own. The porch painting crossed my mind, but I put that aside quickly. I could look into buying a small boat and motor. I took the morning paper and a cup of coffee and went out to the back porch to read. The porch was screened and kept out the bugs, but let in whatever breeze there was. I could see past the garage to the drop-off to Clear Creek. The Hammond paper had lots of boats for sale. I was amazed at how much they cost. What I needed was something small anyhow, small enough to navigate the trickle that was Clear Creek to get out to the Tangipahoa River. I looked through all the ads but didn't see anything that met my needs. I remembered seeing some "for sale" notices posted on the wall in Walter's store and thought about paying him a visit. I liked talking to Walter anyhow, and time was something I had plenty of. Funny, after all those years of running around with work, now I was trying to think up things to do.

We had found our house by looking in the Hammond paper. Before I retired, I had given some thought to teaching part-time at Southeastern Louisiana University in Hammond. The chairman of the History and Political Science Department had talked to me about doing a unit on public health for some graduate students. Unfortunately–or maybe fortunately–he found a better job at another university not long after we had closed on the house, so the only involvement I had with SLU was a unit outline that, most likely, nobody ever read. I was fine with that. Hammond was far enough from Baton Rouge and New Orleans that we had no obligations to see old friends, but could do so on special occasions.

The house we bought had been for sale by an elderly

couple who were moving to an assisted living facility. The old man had spent some energy in showing me Clear Creek, which, at the time wasn't too clear, but running deep enough to get to the Tangipahoa River. What he didn't tell me was that the creek was high enough to be navigable only after a substantial rain. Otherwise, it would take an inflatable raft with no draft to get down to the river. The "clear" part of Clear Creek was intended to describe the stream in normal times. It was a pretty little stream, with a sand and gravel bottom and several small pools where a few sun perch lived until the raccoons and moccasins got them.

Still, we were happy with the house and especially the price. The house was off a small side road and fairly remote. Coming from the highway, we had to turn right just before a little bridge over Clear Creek. The creek ran diagonally across the back corner of the property behind a barn that had been turned into a two-car garage and workshop. A small loft over the garage afforded plenty of space for the accumulated junk we couldn't fit into the main house. The workshop and creek are what sold me. I needed a place for all my tools and had spent the first few days at our new home building solid benches to house the power tools. I kept going back and forth to the hardware store in Hammond if Walter didn't have what I needed. I used the trips to get some calling cards printed with my new address, thinking I still might run into some part-time job to keep me busy.

The house was raised and white, with an open front porch and a screened-in back porch. An ancient pecan tree dominated the front of the house, and azalea bushes ran around the sides. Both the house and garage had shiny metal roofs, which seem to be the norm for all the older houses in the area. The former owner told me the house was originally one storied, but the large attic had been turned into two bedrooms and a bath. One reason the old couple was moving was to avoid the stairs to the second story, but we looked at the climb as an enforced way to get daily exercise. I was used to exercise and missed the jogging areas around our old neighborhood in Atlanta. The house looked as though it had been well-maintained although the paint on the porch was peeling a bit. I wasn't too happy with a large yard to maintain, but the old man threw in a riding lawnmower that would help considerably.

Another plus was the presence of Walter's store, which was only a half mile down the road. Walter was an older man (probably close to my age) with a full head of white hair which I envied. He had been in the same spot for many years and served the scattered houses and farms around the town of Robert. He had a little bit of everything–groceries, tools, beer, rugged clothes, plumbing supplies, and advice. Today, I was in the market for advice. I wanted to buy a boat and didn't want to shop around too long. I got in the truck and took off dustily for the store. No one was parked in the gravel parking area in front of the store.

I got out and jumped up to the raised porch in front of the store to avoid the steps. I hoped the leap was athletically youthful, but I suspect not. My footsteps were noisy on the wooden planks, so I knew Walter would know someone was there. I scanned the space on the wall where the notices had been, but no boats were posted. People were selling things that were hard to sell–a dilapidated trailer home, several old cars, and unwanted pets. I went inside to talk to Walter. He was stacking a new supply of blue jeans on a table and turned around as I walked in, squeaking floorboards as I did. The store had a pleasant smell to it, evoking memories of other old stores long ago. I think it was the odor of chicken feed and Royal Crown Cola.

His blue eyes focused on me as I emerged from the sunshine of the open door. "Ah, Mr. Elliot!" There was no special respect in the "Mister," just Walter's way of greeting people. "What can I do for you today?"

I thumbed through some flannel shirts next to the blue jeans. "Actually, I just wanted some advice. I'd like to buy a small boat and motor, but I don't know where to get started."

Walter went back to marking tags on the jeans. "You don't happen to want to go down your section of Clear Creek, do you?'

"Probably not. I haven't seen it high enough to float a boat down to the river. Since there's so much water around elsewhere, I thought there has to be a place to put in near here."

Walter leaned his right hand on the table, put his left on his hip, and looked me in the eye. "Yeah, there's a few places. How big a boat are you talking about?"

"Oh, maybe a fourteen or fifteen-foot jon boat with a fifteen to twenty-five-horse outboard motor."

Walter rubbed the short white stubble on his chin. "Seems like I saw something like that near the crossroads in Goodbee. A guy was filling up his truck at the service station and was pulling a short metal boat with a 'for sale' sign on it. I think--I'm not sure-- that his motor was more like a nine. If you just want to fish in the rivers that might be good enough. I wouldn't want to take it far out in the Lake. The wind can really kick up out there sometimes."

He was talking about Lake Pontchartrain, of course. "I hadn't given it much thought, but I was really thinking about fresh water fishing in the bayous and rivers. Should

I ask someone at the service station about the owner of the boat?"

"That would be a good idea. I think the guy with the boat was one of the Hudson brothers. They have a brush clearing outfit around Goodbee and sometimes pull a Bobcat around on a trailer. They operate out of one the brothers' houses. If you take a left on 1077 at Goodbee, you could probably spot their sign and maybe the Bobcat in the yard not more than two miles north where you turn off of Highway 190."

Goodbee wasn't very far down 190. I decided not to stop at the service station and go north on 1077. Within two miles, an oak tree near the road sported a crude sign announcing brush clearing and a telephone number. I turned up the gravel driveway and crossed a cattle guard bridge over the ditch. The Bobcat wasn't there, but the boat was. It was sitting on a trailer that had its tongue propped up on a cinder block. A silver Chevy was parked under a flimsy carport to the rear of a raised wooden house. I stopped near the front door and went up the steps to the house. A woman drying her hands on her apron answered my knock. I shielded my eyes from the glare so I could see her better through the screen door. She looked to be in her thirties, plumpish, fairly attractive, but with stringy hair. "Hi. My name is Elliot. Is that boat for sale?" I pointed to the boat which had a clear "For Sale" sign taped to the side.

The screen door opened with a screech, and the woman came out on the stoop. "Yes. It belongs to my brother-in-law, Frank. He and Doug are out working right now. Are you interested in buying the boat?" She wiped some perspiration off her forehead with the back of a hand.

I backed up to give her room. "I'm interested in buying something like it. Do you know what horsepower motor is on it?"

She came down the steps and walked with me toward the boat and trailer. "I think it's a 15, but I'm not sure. Frank doesn't live here, but he left the boat where I could be around it. He's already bought him a bigger boat, so I know he wanted to sell this one." She looked at the back of the motor. "Yep. It's a 15. It runs real good. I've been out in it a couple of times. The tires are good on the trailer, and it comes with a trolling motor and battery." She lifted up a small motor from the floor of the boat to show me. Apparently, she had been entrusted with showing off the boat.

"How much does he want for it?" I said as I walked around the other side of the trailer.

She looked at me as if to assess how much I could afford. "He's asking twelve hundred for the whole thing, just what you see here, gas can, anchor and everything."

That was a good price. I could pay that much for the motor alone. "Do you think he'd take a thousand for it?"

She looked like she was finished with her duties. "I don't know. You'd have to ask him. I can get him on the cell phone if you want." She pulled a cell phone out of her pants pocket.

"Sure. Give him a call. I could meet him back here when he finishes work."

She opened her cell phone and said "Call someone." Then she said "Frank." In a few seconds, Frank apparently answered. "Frank, this is Maureen. There's a feller here asking about your boat for sale. Can you talk to him?" She handed the phone to me.

I agreed to meet Frank in about an hour when he broke for lunch. I didn't have enough time to go home and eat, so I drove to Minnie's restaurant and had a bowl of gumbo and a Barc's root beer. I got back to Maureen's just a little before Frank did. He looked younger than Maureen and in good shape. He hauled out an apparatus that looked like ear phones and attached it to the shaft of the outboard. He hooked up the apparatus to a garden hose and started water running through the shaft. The motor started on the first pull and spewed water from an opening at the top of the shaft.

Frank shouted over the noise of the motor. "I've only had this for three years and haven't had a bit of trouble with it. The only reason I'm selling it now is that I bought a bigger boat that can take me out to the Gulf and I don't need this one."

"I shouted back. "Would you take a thousand for it?"

He frowned a bit and hit the kill button on the motor. The silence was deafening. "I really need to sell this." He paused. "I'll take eleven hundred if you can give me cash."

"I could go to my bank in Hammond. What do we have to do to get it registered in my name?"

Frank turned off the water and unhooked the ear phones. "I've got all the papers. The trailer and the boat are separate licenses. I've got a friend in Goodbee who's a notary who can sign them over to you, but you'll have to go to the Motor Vehicle Bureau to get the trailer registered. You can use the old ID numbers on the boat." He pointed to the decals on the boat.

We agreed to meet back after he finished work, and I went home, elated that I had done a good day's work.

Ellen was working a crossword puzzle on the kitchen table. I kissed her on the cheek. "I found a boat.

I'm going back this evening and close the deal."

She looked up. "Where are you going to keep it?"

I hadn't thought about it, but spoke quickly as though I had. "I thought I'd back in into the space beside the garage. I could put it in the garage, I suppose. I rarely put the truck in there."

Ellen filled in another word on the puzzle. "You surely wouldn't want the boat to get wet. Did you eat something?"

"Yes. I got a bowl of gumbo at Minnie's. Actually, I shouldn't wait around here too long. I have to go to the bank in Hammond and get some cash for the boat. Do you need anything while I'm out?"

"I can't think of anything right now. I'll run over to Walter's in the Camry if I need to."

The bank and the notary went smoothly. I asked Frank if I could have the cinder block for the trailer tongue, but he showed me a wheel on the tongue that cranked down to support the trailer and could be used to pull everything around. It seemed easy enough to move–especially on flat ground. We hooked it up on my ball hitch and plugged in the lights to a receptacle on my bumper that I wasn't sure would fit on the trailer plug. Fortunately, Frank told me the turn signals, running lights and brake lights were working when I tried to use them in the truck. I pulled out into the road and headed for home. The boat wasn't very visible in the rear view mirror. I figured I need another mirror or something high enough on the boat to see it.

The boat pulled great as long as I was going forward. When I got home, it was a different matter backing it up. Ellen came out of the house to laugh at me as I attempted to guide the trailer in the space by the garage. Several tries were in vain. Finally, when I got close enough,

I unhooked the hitch, cranked the wheel down, and muscled the trailer close to where I wanted it.

CHAPTER FOUR

Tommy had given me good directions to his house. He used the names of landmarks I didn't remember, but I found his place easy enough. His house was in a newly developed subdivision southeast of anything I had known of Baton Rouge before. The developers had carved a road through swampy territory crossed with erosion gullies. Tupelo and cypress trees stood silently in the moist soil along the route. Everything looked damp. The road paralleled the gullies whenever possible, but just before the settled area, a thin bridge crossed a deep ravine. The bridge was at an angle to the road, and the neighborhood wasn't apparent until I braked and made the turn. An area just before the bridge to the left had been cleared away, an obvious attempt to let cars turn around before committing to the subdivision. An upscale sign proclaimed this was private property and had no outlet. I didn't expect to see large homes and manicured lawns in such a setting. About six houses were spread out over what amounted to an island seized out of the swamp. Tommy's house was a large brick structure that spoke of money.

His wife wasn't at home, and he came to the door in a wheelchair. He shook my hand warmly and led me to the living room. Most of our visit dwelt on old times. Tommy seemed to know what our mutual friends were doing even though he didn't see them very often. He offered a drink, which I declined. I waited for a good segue to a discussion of Bill, but none presented until he asked me what I had been doing.

I told him my full story, including my suspicions about Swifty and the connection with Dennis. "Maybe this is a wild goose chase, but on the way over, I was thinking that a lot of notables in Louisiana have died in plane accidents: Jesse Webb, the mayor of Baton Rouge; Hale Boggs, the prominent congressman; Bo Rein, the LSU football coach; Jim Croce, the singer."

Tommy added "Don't forget Chep Morrison, the mayor of New Orleans."

I hoped that was a signal that Tommy was interested. Our conversation up to this point had lacked animation. "That's right. I had forgotten. He was killed in a plane crash in Mexico, wasn't he?"

"Yes, and Boggs, Rein, and Webb were all killed in plane crashes outside of Louisiana." Tommy was silent for a minute. He looked down at the space where his legs had been. "There is something that may be related. You know Swifty was murdered in the parking lot of his bar? Also, I had a client about that time that I've often wondered about."

I was stunned. "No. I didn't know about Swifty. Why did you wonder about your client? Do you think he killed Swifty?"

"No, but maybe the other way around. This guy worked for an oil company and flew bigwigs around to meetings, but somehow got mixed up with Swifty. He was facing indictment--maybe twenty years ago. No, more than twenty. It was probably 1964. I know it was around the time that Bill died. He wanted to turn State's evidence against Swifty about something and get a lighter sentence in his narcotics case. He was not familiar with the legal system and wanted me to help him cop a plea. Unfortunately, he never got a chance. Apparently, he was involved in a car accident before he could testify, but they never found his body."

"How could that have happened?"

"They think his brakes failed on a curve by a river, and his car went into some deep water. The police searched and searched but never found any trace of him. He either washed away or the gators got him. The kid had told me when we met that he hadn't said anything to Swifty about his plan to talk to the authorities. I had warned him against speaking to Swifty about this, but I've often wondered whether he said something anyhow and had his car sabotaged. You know Swifty owned a car repair place, and some of the hoods who worked there used to hang around the bar at night. There was some talk that Swifty ran a chop shop."

"Chop shop?"

"A place where they cut up stolen cars for the parts or make them look different to sell them again. At any rate, there should have been plenty of expertise around to damage a brake line. The other thing that could have happened is that Swifty's crew disposed of the body because of some incriminating trauma and just pushed the car into the water."

"Where was the repair shop? I don't seem to remember that aspect."

"It was way out Hooper Road in North Baton Rouge. The building is still there on a hill in an otherwise empty field just past a seat cover store."

I breathed deeply. What I was hearing seemed to strengthen a case for foul play, but no one had considered these incidents were related. Three accidents and a murder. "Tommy, I never knew about Swifty's murder or your client's disappearance. Doesn't putting all this together make Bill's death less like an accident?"

"It might. But, Sam, all this happened a long time ago. What could you do if you could prove it? Swifty's gone. Nobody cares anymore. Besides, if you're messing with the mob, you could be getting in over your head."

"Mob? Who said anything about the mob?"

"Swifty's murder looked like a professional job. Nobody was ever charged, but the talk is that it was a mob hit."

"Maybe the mob's all dead too."

Tommy looked me in the eye. "Organized crime seems to go on for generations. Any institution like that doesn't dissolve when the boss dies. I wouldn't be surprised at anything around here."

The evidence was building. I would definitely need some help now. "Tommy, could you help me?"

"Help you do what?"

"Investigate these deaths."

He looked up at the ceiling in minor anguish. "What can I do?" He gestured weakly at the spaces where his legs had been.

It wouldn't do to answer the question directly. "Would you like to find out what really happened?"

"Actually, I'm not too interested."

"What are you interested in?"

He took out a cigarette. I guessed he did that to kill time to think of an answer. He gestured at the cigarette. "Do you mind if I smoke?"

"No. Go ahead." I hate smoke. Ever since I quit myself, tobacco smoke seems to choke me, and I avoid it whenever I can. Thank goodness most people in this country don't smoke in public places.

Tommy lit up and took a deep drag. "Interested? Nothing interests me much anymore. I like to eat." He coughed and patted a small pot belly.

"You used to read a lot. Do you still read?"

"No. I don't read much except the newspaper."

"I wouldn't have guessed that. You probably read more than any of my other friends. In fact, you introduced me to a lot of good literature--good music too. All of my first exposures to classical music came from my visits with you. Surely you listen to music these days."

He seemed a little perturbed. "No. I don't listen to music either." He turned his head and looked off into space. "Everything's changed."

I wanted to break the mood. "I just thought with all of your connections--you used to know everyone--that you could help me get some of the facts."

Tommy seemed definite. "I wouldn't know where to begin. Besides, there's no way I can get around anymore." He didn't look at me directly.

That sounded like a final "no." I changed the subject. "I haven't met your new wife. What's she like?"

"Well, she ain't new anymore. We've been married off and on for close to twenty years."

Somehow that didn't seem like a good subject either. "How are you making out for money?" I looked around the well-appointed house. "Do you have a steady income?"

"That's a bright spot. My dad invested wisely, and after my mother died, everything came to me. Thank goodness, I had the sense to set up an annuity. We have more than we need. I can't find enough things to spend it on, housebound like I am. Then too, my wife Evelyn pulls in a little. She's a receptionist in a doctor's office." He paused. "I think she works just to get out of here." He paused for a few seconds. "Sam, there's one more thing. I'm dying."

"We all are eventually. What exactly do you mean?"

Tommy gestured vaguely at his abdomen. "I have

colon cancer."

I was sorry I had seemed flippant before. "Are you taking treatment?"

"No, it's a little late for that. They removed a section of my colon a few months back, but either they didn't get all of the cancer or it had already spread."

I tried to sound reassuring. "Tommy, they can do some marvelous things today. Have you really researched this thing?"

"Yes. We've been through all that. Anything they would do for me would just make me feel worse with little hope of even prolonging the inevitable. Even my oncologist seemed to agree no treatment was the best treatment."

"Have they given you a prognosis?"

"Months, probably less."

I'm at a loss in situations like this. "Are you feeling pain?"

He sighed as if to test his damaged organs. "Some days are better than others, but it is surprising that it doesn't feel any worse than it does most of the time."

"Is there something I can do?"

"No. I'm glad you dropped by. It's been a long time."

The visit ended with us talking about some old acquaintances, and I drove home discouraged, both by Tommy's condition and my failure to enlist him in my investigation. Ellen was right. My friendship with Tommy was worth more than that. She seemed genuinely sorry to hear about his condition.

The next day, I got up early. After breakfast, I put on my running clothes. Ellen and I had quit the gym when we left Atlanta, and hadn't found anything yet to completely replace the weight training. I called out to Ellen from the bathroom. "Honey, I'm going over to the school and run."

"Jog." She corrected.

"Jog. Do you want to go?"

"No. I'm going to do some shopping today."

I looked in the bathroom mirror. I look older than I feel. Lines crease my face around my mouth, and my hair is thinning. There are hollows under my cheeks. I could either get fatter or stay gaunt, but I'm trying to stay under 190 pounds. At 6 feet tall, that didn't sound like too much weight, but I'm getting a little pot belly. I sucked in my gut. There, that looked a little better. I drove over to the school and started my regimen. My route was less than two miles, but I felt like I could stay in shape if I could stick to it. Besides, this was a good time to think and plan. I tried to imagine what it was like for Bill on the day he crashed. He must have known he was about to die moments before it happened. Did he feel pain? I hoped it was quick. Two coeds approached me from the opposite way. I sucked in my gut and quickened my pace. They gave me little condescending smiles as they passed. I let out my gut and slowed down, hoping I wouldn't pass any more pretty coeds soon.

Two days later I got a call from Tommy. Happily, he sounded excited. "I found out a few things."

"About what?"

"About what we talked about. Are you getting so old that you don't remember?"

"I just thought you weren't interested."

"Well, I still can't get around, but there is one thing that I can do that doesn't involve mobility. I forgot to tell you that I can surf the internet. It's about the only thing I can do around this place to keep me interested."

"What did you find out?"

"I looked up Hale Boggs and Chep Morrison. Funny thing, just about everything on their deaths was in the same database."

"And what was that?" I asked.

"The Kennedy assassination."

"Oh, no! I don't want to go there. I never believed in any conspiracy, and that whole thing was well investigated. With our meager resources, we couldn't touch it. My idea was just to look into the local thing."

Now it was Tommy that was pushing. "Look, information is information. Shouldn't we take advantage of what someone else has found?"

"Of course. What in the world would those two have to do with Kennedy?"

"Well, for starters, Boggs was on the Warren Commission."

"No kidding? I never knew that."

"There were only seven members of the Commission, and Boggs was one of them. But that isn't the reason for his connection in this context. Apparently, Boggs was having some second thoughts about the conclusions of the Commission. At least, that's what *Argosy Magazine* was claiming just before Boggs' plane went down in Alaska."

"What context are you talking about?"

"I'm looking at a list of suspicious deaths connected to the Kennedy assassination. Gosh, there must be thirty to forty of them."

"But why would Morrison be on the list?"

"Hugh Ward was killed in the same crash."

I searched my memory. "Hugh Ward doesn't ring a bell. Should I know him?"

"Probably not. I keep forgetting you weren't around

when Jim Garrison was making a fool of himself in the Clay Shaw trial. Hugh Ward was a private investigator working with Guy Bannister and David Ferrie, two of the people that figured prominently in Garrison's accusations. You do remember hearing about Garrison and Shaw, don't you?"

This was good. Tommy was needling me. It was like old times. "Of course. Garrison was the DA in Orleans Parish and actually brought Shaw to trial for conspiring with Oswald to kill Kennedy."

"Right. And some people thought Garrison made up the whole thing to throw people off the trail of Carlos Marcello and the mob, who may have had better motives for getting rid of the Kennedys."

I was feeling a little uncomfortable with the way this was going. "Tommy, you're right about taking information where we find it. I just don't want to get sidetracked with this whole Kennedy thing. Anything else in that list that might be connected with our case?" This was moving up a notch, saying "our case."

"I'm looking right now." I could tell he was scrolling down a list on his computer. "Here's another plane crash. John Crawford was killed in a private plane in 1969."

"What's his connection?

"Nothing much. This says he was a close friend of Jack Ruby's and that he gave Oswald a ride on the day of the assassination."

"Oh, great! What else?"

"Nothing much. Unless you want to count Sam Giancana, who was murdered when he was slated to testify to a Senate Committee about CIA and the mob cooperating in death plots. Also, but not in this data base was the case of Barry Seal. He was connected with some of the guys in the assassination stories. He was arrested several times flying drugs around and linked tenuously to Oliver North when Seal's old plane was used in Iran-Contra. He was gunned down in Baton Rouge much later--maybe 1986. "

"Tommy, thank you. I didn't mean to sound negative. I just was having trouble getting started and I didn't want to get sidetracked. Does this mean that you're willing to spend a little more energy on the Wild Bill case?"

"I guess so. I'd probably still need to be a bit more mobile to do any good, though."

"Tell you what. I'll do the next piece. Maybe a crime reporter at the newspaper can tell me how to get information that far back. I'm sure they have a little routine to go through when they investigate things."

Tommy's voice had a twinge of disappointment in it, as though that was something that he could do too. "You'd probably have to have some good dates and names. I never knew what Swifty's first name was, and I don't even remember what year he was killed."

"I remember a bit, but I didn't even know about Swifty's death. We can come up with some approximates. We're dealing with four people really. Dennis was the first to go because Swifty sent Bill a telegram about the accident when Bill and I were going to summer school in Mexico City. That would have been in June or July of 1958. Swifty was still active when Bill crashed because he and I discussed Swifty on the telephone when I was in Cleveland, and that was the end of May 1964. And Swifty was the one who called me about Bill. Your client went into the drink before Swifty was killed. Since Swifty was murdered, his date might be a little easier to pin down. And you think your client would have to have died right around the time that Bill did?"

"Sounds like a good start. Let me know what else I can do."

"Well, one thing you could do is to e-mail me everything we've talked about, including info about your client and your suspicions about Swifty. All this is too much for me to remember. And Tommy?"

"Yes."

"Thanks. It was good hearing from you--like this." As I hung up the phone, I was feeling a little smug. You never know when you really are getting through to someone. This had happened to me before several times. My arguments had seemed to fall on deaf ears, but reasonable people would reflect on logic and sometimes change their minds. If nothing else came of this inquiry, at least it got Tommy interested in something. That alone would make it all worthwhile. His commitment shone through when his e-mail came in – it was three pages long.

The crime reporter sounded like a good idea because they must have to do a lot of investigation like this in their normal work. I called the newspaper in Covington and asked to speak to whoever covered police work. The lady who answered said that nobody specialized that way for their paper, but connected me with someone who might help. After I explained what I wanted, the second lady wanted to help but didn't have a handle on the procedures in Baton Rouge. "Here in St. Tammany Parish, we just go to the Clerk of Court's office and use what they call the Public Computer. Anyone can go in there and look up anybody who has died. Then, with the date of death, you could come to the newspaper office or the library and look up the obituary."

I called the Clerk of Court's office in Baton Rouge, but they didn't have such a computer or records that I could access without knowing the dates of death. Then I called the information operator for the telephone number of the *Baton Rouge Morning Advocate*. The operator said no such organization was listed. I insisted that the newspaper still existed, and she reluctantly looked up newspapers and found a listing for the *Baton Rouge Advocate*. The *Advocate* people were very accommodating as well. I talked to a young man in the library who took the names and volunteered to look them up in the files. Later that day, he called back and said he had nothing. If the people had been prominent, the paper most likely would have made a record, but that apparently wasn't the case. He suggested that I call the State Archives and find the date of death and then come to the newspaper or the Goodwood Branch Library to try to find obituaries or articles on the deceased individuals. I had looked up articles on microfiche before when I was investigating syphilis contacts. It was dull work. This whole thing was taking a lot of time, and I was getting nowhere.

I called the State Archives, but they had closed for the day. Exasperated, I just gave up on this path for a while.

CHAPTER FIVE

1953

I lost touch with Wild Bill from the time I was nine until I was eighteen. My family had moved around a bit and then came to live in Baton Rouge when I started junior high school. I don't remember ever visiting Franklinton again in all those years or even thinking much about my old friends there until college. Quite by accident, I renewed acquaintances with Wild Bill when I started LSU in the fall semester after high school. I was standing in line at the bursar's office in the Campanielle, waiting to pay my tuition. Someone tapped me on the shoulder as I was handing over the $27 required to register for a semester back then. I turned around to see a friendly, but unfamiliar face topped with blond, curly hair. He was dressed in a cord suit, which seemed out of place on a warm day, the boy seemed to know me. "I say, old chap. I heard you give your name. Are you the same Sam Elliot who used to live in Franklinton?"

"Why, yes." I still did not recognize him, and the British accent threw me off.

"I'm Bill Jenkins, your old comrade."

"Of course, Bill. It's been a long time." We shook hands.

"Since we were nine. How about we go somewhere and have a toddy?" He offered me a cigarette from a flat box.

"Well, sure. I'm finished here. Aren't you going to register?"

"Oh that. I can do that any time. Let's have a drink."

Somehow, most of my recollections of Bill after that

were having drinks. I noticed that he held his cigarette between his teeth. I really didn't have anything more to do after I registered. Buying books would come after my first classes, and having a drink in the middle of the day sounded different and good. I agreed.

Bill led me outside to the circular road in front of the Campanielle. He had a new Chevrolet that was blue on the bottom and white on the top. It had a Jenkins Chevrolet frame for the license plate and was parked in a no parking zone. Bill must not have been there long because he didn't have a parking ticket yet.

"Nice car." I said.

Bill slid in behind the wheel. "Part of the package to get me out of the house. I didn't work out selling cars. I know a little tavern not too far from here."

He did, and the air conditioning was welcome. The place was dark as our eyes adjusted, but we found a table away from the juke box. I was used to sitting at a bar but Bill wanted to get waited on. A lady dressed in a white uniform came from behind the bar and asked us what we wanted. I was hoping she would be pretty, but she was older and had a crooked nose. I ordered a beer and Bill ordered a rum and tonic.

While we waited, I tried to make conversation. "Never heard of a rum and tonic. Guess it's like a gin and tonic?"

Bill crossed his legs and leaned back. "Except for the rum. Can't take gin, dammit. Makes my nose run and gives me the hives. Actually, I don't want anybody to know about my allergy and I really shouldn't have told you. Promise me you won't tell anybody. They might think I'm a hypochondriac and ruin my reputation."

That sounded like a lame excuse, but I promised.

Bill was sounding a trifle eccentric.

He changed the subject. "What fraternity are you pledging?"

"I've been to a few houses during rush season, but it doesn't make much sense for me to join. I'm going to stay with my parents here in town, and I don't need a place to stay. Besides, they sound expensive."

"You ought to join us at the Sigma Omega Tau house—we're the sots, you know. He grinned at the association, and I knew the nickname probably fit.

"How come you're in a fraternity already?"

"Because I started in the summer semester. My parents wanted me out of the way, I'm sure. And besides, I like the idea of no responsibility."

"Isn't there some responsibility to study and make good grades? I asked.

He smiled as he accepted his rum drink from the crooked nosed waitress. "We'll run a tab, if you please." He clicked his glass against my beer and said "Cheers! No, not much responsibility at all. I found that I could just show up for finals and still make C's and D's."

I took a swig. "That won't keep you in school, will it?"

"Probably not. I'll see how it turns out this semester. I would miss the fraternity though." He leaned forward. "And the girls. You'll love the girls here. High school girls are a curious mixture of giggle and serious. I think they all want to get married and have children. It makes me shudder. I can't think of a situation that would tie a man down more. There's so many women here it's like a candy store. You treat one like a lady and she melts."

We didn't have much to share about our times together in Franklinton, so we filled each other in on our lives since then. Bill had barely gotten out of high school in Franklinton but had aced the entrance exam for LSU. His nonchalance toward school belied the fact that he seemed to be well read. He was especially fond of quoting English and Southern authors. He had continued to see movies at our old theater in Franklinton until it shut down and became a furniture store. As we continued to talk, I began to recognize the old Wild Bill. He was more mature looking now with a square jaw and a futile attempt to grow a small mustache. He was trying to be the experienced fraternity man with only a summer semester behind him.

His cord suit didn't go with his white buck shoes. He saw me looking at them and straightened up to glance down. "Damn things are too new looking." He rubbed the sole of each shoe against the top of the other. "Have to dirty them up a bit."

His skin was pale and didn't look like it had been exposed to the sun very much. He wore an expensive-looking ring on his left hand. When I remarked about it, he said something about his cash reserve if he needed it. After we had drunk more than we should have, I declined his offer to see the SOT house, and he drove me back to my car. We exchanged telephone numbers and promised to keep in touch. The sun was blinding.

CHAPTER SIX

1944

Bill always had a fascination with guns, not to take them apart or collect them--to shoot them. One Saturday when we were nine, his dad dropped him off at my house on his way into the dealership. Bill, Jimmy Simmons, and I always went to the Roxy Theater on Saturday mornings. We and almost every other kid in town got to see two cowboy movies, at least one cartoon, and a serial. The movie cost nine cents; popcorn, five. The theater must have had two entrances. The white kids sat downstairs. The black kids sat in the balcony. I would get so engrossed in the movies that later on, I would forget that some of my secret playmates were probably sitting above my head. I often thought they had the best seats, but I didn't know how they got there. If you walked down to the stage and turned around, you could just make out the balcony when the screen was bright.

This Saturday, Bill brought his BB gun to my house. It was a Red Ryder with a lever action. The kind of gun that I could only dream about. How could he get such a thing during the war? It was hard as heck just to get a bicycle to get to school on. Jimmy was at my house already and wanted to shoot the gun. Bill would have none of it. I don't think he cared about wasting BBs. He just wanted to see someone squirm. Kids are like that sometimes. Bill went out back and set up a target on an oak tree that was growing sideways. He would shoot and then send Jimmy to go to the target and see where the shot had hit. I got tired of watching and walked around toward the front of the house. I stopped just before rounding the corner of the porch.

Something large was in the gum ball tree --several large something's. It was the family of Ivory-billed Woodpeckers. My mother told me that this must be one of the last of the breed living, that most people thought they were extinct. We had a large bird book, and my mother had written in her fine hand beside the article on Ivory Bills, "Pair seen in Franklinton, LA, 1944." I thought the birds were the most wonderful things I had ever seen and felt privileged to be a witness to such rare creatures. I crept slowly backwards, keeping my eyes on the birds. The mother and father must have been teaching the three young ones something. They were all perched on limbs instead of their usual position on trunks. The male was resplendent with his red topknot. The female's head was a blue-black, and both adults were huge.

As soon as I was out of sight of the birds, I ran back to Bill and Jimmy. I whispered, "Come quick. It's the most marvelous sight you have ever seen." I motioned them to walk stooped over as I did to the corner of the house and to be quiet. At the edge of the porch, I pointed my finger in a jabbing motion to the top of the large gum ball tree. The birds were still there. I smiled in triumph to be the instigator of such a rare showing. My smile turned to a look of horror as Bill steadied his Red Ryder on the side of the porch and took a sighting on the magnificent male. I leaped sideways and knocked the gun up. Not satisfied with disturbing his aim, I grabbed the barrel of the rifle and wrestled Bill to the ground. I was furious. How could he think of harming such a rare and beautiful creature?! I would take the gun from him and destroy it if I could. Bill was equally intent on protecting his property and would not let go of the rifle. We rolled over and over, much to the delight of Jimmy, who yelled encouragement to first one and then the other of us. My mother came out on the porch and ran down to separate us. She didn't seem to realize that there had been a fight. She was more concerned that we were dirty and it was time to go to the movies. She brushed us off with her hands and told us to go inside and wash our faces. She pointed to Bill's rifle. "And you leave that thing here. Your dad says you can't take it to the theater."

Bill said "Yes'm" and meekly handed over the Red Ryder. Bill always said polite things to women. Mother held the gun with her forefinger and thumb as though it was dirty and went back to the kitchen to stand it in a corner.

We walked the quarter mile to the Roxy on the Bogalusa Highway. There was no sidewalk. We stirred in the grass along the side of the road in our canvas tennis shoes, hoping to scare up a snake, but they were all holed up in the ditches during the warm part of the day. I brought a dime and a nickel and had a penny left, even after the popcorn. We walked down to the front of the theater in the dim light during the credits for the feature and groped for seats. The kids cheered at the title. It was a *Red Ryder* movie. I elbowed Bill in recognition of his air gun's namesake. Wild Bill Elliot played Red Ryder and Bobby Blake was Little Beaver. This crooked sheriff framed Red Ryder. The crooked sheriff got killed and his son thought Red Ryder had done it. Halfway through the show, Jimmy leaned over Bill and told me that he had to get out. "I got to pee," he said.

"Not so loud!" I whispered. Saying "pee" in front of other people was embarrassing. I turned my knees so he could slip past me. "I think the restroom is in the front of the theater."

He stepped on my feet anyhow as he stepped sideways with his eyes fixed on the screen. "I'm not going to miss anything. I'll just pee up by the stage."

I was horrified. How could he think of exposing himself in front of all those people? I looked in back of us to see if there were any girls sitting nearby. "Don't!" I whispered desperately. It was to no avail.

Bill got up. "I'm going too." Bill wouldn't let anyone be more daring than he was. I doubt if he really had to pee, he just wanted to be in on the excitement. I couldn't stop them. I scrunched down in my seat so no one could see that I was with them. In a few minutes, they both returned, but I wouldn't speak to them. When the feature and the serial and the cartoons were over, the feature started again for the second time, and we worked our way back up the aisle and out of the theater. I'd get so engrossed in the entertainment that sometimes I'd forget where I was. I'd still be living the movie. I could tell that my friends were the same way. We walked with a swagger as though we were all cowboy heroes. Nobody better mess with us when we were feeling tough like that!

The daylight was bright as we walked out of the theater. We blinked at the sudden change and milled around groggily a bit before striking out for the Bogalusa Highway. We talked about the movie on the way home. I had mixed feelings. "I thought Little Beaver was okay, but Wild Bill Elliot didn't make a good Red Ryder. He plays himself in a lot of the movies, so he can't play Red Ryder too!"

Bill often disagreed. "What do you mean 'played himself'? He plays other people all the time."

I tried to think of an example. "He played himself in *Bells of Rosarito*.

Bill was contrary. "Everybody played themselves in *Bells of Rosarito*. I thought Wild Bill Elliot was great!

Besides, you ought to like him. He's got the same last name as you."

Jimmy said, "Let's play cowboys and Indians when we get to your house." We always played cowboys and Indians whether there were any Indians in our fantasies or not. That was just the name of the playacting. That year, during WWII, some of our favorite villains were Japanese. It seems as though we all need people to hate. Sometimes it just takes someone else to tell us who those people are. The news and the movies helped us decide who the enemies were.

Jimmy was excited. "I'm going to be Bob Steele. Who are you going to be?"

"I think I'm going to be the Cyclone Kid," I said, naming a character I had made up for a previous episode. Lots of heroes were known as Kids.

Bill was practicing his quick draw with imaginary pistols and shooting Japs off the telephone wires. "I'm going to be Wild Bill. In fact, you can call me Wild Bill all the time. Nobody takes chances like I do." He somersaulted in the snake grass beside the road to prove his point.

When we got home, Bill retrieved his air rifle from the kitchen, and we went out back to play. We pretended we were riding horses, loping along and slapping our rumps, when the Japs attacked. We holed up behind the bent-over oak tree and began shooting. Jimmy had a pine knot stick with a right angle in it that looked more like a ray gun than a pistol. I had a pistol made out of glue and sawdust painted black, and Bill had his BB gun. Every once in a while, a Jap would leap over the oak barricade and we would wrestle around on the ground with him.

After we had shot about a hundred Japs, Bill stood

up. "This is boring."

I agreed. "You're right. Why should we be fighting Japs and hostile Indians most of the time? How come we don't play like we're the Indians and shoot the cowboys?"

That arrangement was unthinkable, and they ignored me. Bill gestured with his open hand in the air. "I mean this doesn't seem real enough. We ought to be shooting at real people. Jimmy, you play the bad guy, and we will shoot at each other."

Jimmy didn't like the idea. "Why should I be the bad guy? I'm Bob Steele. I'm always the good guy."

Bill didn't hesitate. "Okay. I'll be the bad guy. You two goodies go out in the woods and try and get me out from behind the oak tree."

This was a new game for us. We went into the woods and hid behind the pine trees. I called out, "Wild Bill, throw down your rifle, or we're coming in to get you!"

Bill knelt down behind the trunk and yelled, "You'll never get me alive. Come and get me, Rangers!"

We wheeled around and came out firing, dodging from tree to tree and rolling on the ground to the next cover. "Pow! POW! Pow!"

Jimmy stood up and took aim with his pine knot. "Psst! Smack!" A BB hit him right in the eye. He went down holding his hand over his eye and crying. I ran in the house and got my mother. "Jimmy's got his eye shot out! Come quick!"

Mother hustled us all into the '38 Chevrolet and sped downtown to Dr. Bateman's office. Dr. Bateman was very patient. I didn't like the office. I was remembering the pain when he sewed up my foot after I had stepped on the broken bottle. Bateman got a light on Jimmy's face and pulled his hand away from the eye. Then the doctor slowly opened the eyelid. I couldn't look. The BB fell out and bounced on the wooden floor. Dr. Bateman looked pleased. "He'll be just fine, but he'll have to keep that eye covered for the next few days. It may look bruised, but that's just temporary."

I think I remember that day so clearly because of the excitement about Jimmy's eye.

CHAPTER SEVEN

1944

The house we lived in in Franklinton when I was nine had a small front porch with no railing and was raised about three steps off the ground. A gravel driveway dropped down off the Bogalusa Highway about fifty yards before it curved in front of the house. I think another small house was at the end of the driveway, but I forget. There must have been some reason for the driveway to curve. I know there was a field of weeds right across the driveway and before the highway. A beaten path led from the driveway to an oak tree that had a swing hanging from one of its large horizontal limbs. I was so proud of myself because I could climb straight up the ropes of the swing with one hand on each rope. I wanted to be able to sit on the limb and see up the hill to the left, but I couldn't seem to get over the side of that big limb. The limb was too big, and I'd have to let go both hands at the same time to pull myself up and over. It was a little scary up high like that, and I didn't want to take chances. If I was by myself and fell, no one would be able to see me because of the weeds in the field. A stout wire fence with a strand of barb wire on the top ran diagonally up the hill from the place where the driveway flattened out. Actually, my mother called it "The Hill" and hinted that there was something mysterious up the Hill that might be dangerous. I never figured out what that might be. One day I tried again unsuccessfully to reach up around the oak tree limb and realized that I would just have to see what I could hanging from the top of the swing ropes. I couldn't see very far up the Hill, but I was pleased to see that the blackberries looked ripe on the other side of the fence. I had been waiting for this ever since my mother told me that the white flowers on the thorny bushes in a neighbor's yard would turn to berries. The fence didn't make sense. Why would it be open where it met the highway at the end of our driveway but still run as far as I could see up the Hill? A dirt path paralleled the fence on the other side. Someone had to use that path.

I shimmied down the ropes and dropped off in the powdery dust under the swing. Most of the time, I didn't wear shoes in the summer, and the cool dust felt good on my feet. Avoiding the stinging nettles, I tiptoed over to the fence, hooked my fingers in the squares formed by the wires, and leaned my forehead against the wire to look through. Yes, the blackberries were ripe. Their bushes formed a border on the other side of the dirt path that led up the Hill. I considered walking back to the house and going around the end of the fence on the driveway, but that was too long. I climbed the fence instead. Predictably, my short pants caught on the barb wire. I couldn't go back down the way I had come, and the wire fence hurt my bare toes, so I just dropped off the other side and tore my pants. Darn it. No matter, my mother never got angry about anything, and the blackberries were huge. Someone had obviously been picking on them because there weren't as many accessible as I had thought. But they were delicious! I could see more ripe ones inside the bushes, but the thorns were too thick to reach them. I would pick a jewel, blow it off, and pop the whole thing in my mouth. Slowly, I worked my way up the Hill.

It was joyous work. The bushes were lush and green and the berries were velvet black. Every now and then, I would encounter snake spit--tiny foam bubbles hanging like clear miniature grapes from the blackberry bushes. Bill had told me about the snake spit, but my mother said they were insect eggs. Still, I didn't want to take any chances. As I neared the top of the Hill, I was surprised to see two boys eating their way down the slope. Two *black* boys. None of my friends were black, and I was curious. They didn't see me, so I announced first. "Hi!"

They were startled and turned as if to run back. The older boy pulled up sharply and grabbed the smaller boy by the shoulder. "Hi." He obviously tried to make his voice sound deeper.

I guessed the bigger boy was about my age and the smaller one about two years younger. I walked up to them and stuck out my hand to shake. "My name is Sam Elliot."

The older boy hesitated a second and then wiped his palm on the back of his bib overalls and shook my hand. "My name is Gerald, and this here is my brother Vincent." We both stood there, shifting our feet in nervousness. We were all barefooted.

I jerked my thumb back over my shoulder. "I live in that white house down at the bottom of the hill."

Gerald went up on his toes to look over my shoulder in the direction I was pointing. "We live past the top of the hill. You want to play?"

The hot sun was making me thirsty. "Yeah, but I'm awful thirsty."

"We got some water up to the house."

"Let's go." I looked back to see if my mother was in sight.

When we crested the hill, I could see three or four unpainted houses. The path went up to the end of a gravel road that came in from the other direction. The houses looked old. There was a heavyset woman sitting on the porch of the first house. She was wearing a thin dress and was barefooted. She got up when we approached and dusted off her ample rear. Gerald ran up to her. "Maw, this here's Sam. He's thirsty."

Maw smiled at me kindly. "Howdy, Sam. I think we got just the thing for you over at the well."

A well. An honest to goodness well. I'd never seen a real well before, but I had seen them in picture books. Wells were made out of brick or stone, had a little roof, and had a crank that lowered and raised a wooden bucket. This well had none of those things--it was just a pipe in the ground. I had seen hand pumps before. There was one at Peter Pan near where we swam. This was different and I was disappointed. "Is _that_ the well?"

Maw said "That's it. The sweetest water you ever tasted." She grabbed a rope and pulled up a metal container that just fit inside the pipe. The container looked like the long, slender buckets that were filled with ice cream down at the drug store. Gerald held out a tin dipper and Maw poured out some water from the heavy container. "Go ahead. Drink it. It's good."

I gulped down the water from the dipper. She was right. The water was cold as ice. "May I have another, please?"

Maw tilted the container again. "You shore can. Drink as much as you want." They all had a swig from the dipper and Maw let the bucket down the well again. She looked at the back of my short pants. "Lordy, chile, you done ripped your britches."

I tried to look behind me, but even at that young age, I wasn't flexible enough to see my rear end. Maw put her hand on my shoulder. "You want me to sew up your britches?"

I didn't know what that might entail, but as I

thought about it, a little mending might be in order. My mother would ask questions about my torn pants, and I'd have to tell her about climbing the fence and everything. That didn't seem like such a good idea. "Yes 'Mam."

Maw started up the steps of her house. "Well, you take off your britches and I'll get some thread."

Oh no! I hadn't thought about removing my pants. I couldn't let a strange woman see my underwear! I looked at Gerald. "Do I have to?"

Gerald was laughing. "You do if you don't want a needle in your butt." He made sense. I removed my pants and sat down on the top step real quick so as to minimize my exposure. This was embarrassing. I didn't want her to see my underwear.

Maw came out with two spools of thread and a needle and sat on the porch beside me with her feet crossed on the step below me. She held both spools against my pants and selected one. "I think this is the closest. Gerald, why don't you get some cornbread for Sam? You do want some cornbread, don't you, Sam?'

"Yes, ma'am." I tried to put my elbows in my lap so she couldn't see.

Gerald and Vincent both rushed up the steps to go in the house and knocked each other down. Maw took a swipe at Vincent and said, "Didn't I say Gerald?" Vincent sat down obediently.

Gerald came out with a frying pan filled with cornbread. One piece was gone already. He pried out another wedge for me. It was golden brown with little black semicircles where the surface had been burned. I tried to accept a piece without exposing myself unduly. The cornbread was thinner that the kind my mother made. It was also crunchier and better tasting. This was a pretty good trip--and not far from home either! Maw worked quickly and expertly on my pants, pulling long strands through and knotting the thread back on itself. I remembered my manners. "This cornbread is very good."

Maw bit off the thread with her teeth and held up the pants for inspection. "Well, I'm glad you enjoy it, Sam. You'll have to come and have a full supper with us sometime."

I looked at her crossed feet. The bottoms were almost white. Her palms were real light too. I never thought about black people having light palms and soles. I motioned for Vincent to come over. I held out my palm and compared it with his. His wasn't all that light when I could see it up against mine. It was just the contrast that made it look so light. Maw watched me intently with a little smile on her lips. ""You don't play with colored children very much, do you Sam?

"No, ma'am."

"Does your momma know where you are?"

"No, ma'am."

Gerald broke in. "He lives at the bottom of the Hill, Maw."

Maw patted me on the back. "Sam, your momma might be missing you. You best be getting back, don't you think?"

"Yes, 'Mam." I was trying to pull on my pants in a dignified manner. I turned away as I buttoned my fly. "Thank you for the water and the cornbread."

Maw stood up. "Come up anytime you want, Sam. You're a real polite boy, and I'd be proud to have you play with my boys." She hugged Vincent. "Maybe a little of that might rub off on them." Vincent swung back and forth as he hugged her leg and smiled a shy smile.

Gerald followed me part way down the hill. "Next time, maybe we can play pitch and catch."

When he stopped, I waved goodbye. "Thanks. I'll be seeing you."

When I got home, my mother wanted to know what I had been doing for so long. I told her I had been playing on the swing. It wasn't a lie.

I snuck back to play with Gerald and Vincent whenever I could, but I never stayed very long. My mother still had that notion that there was something mysterious and dangerous up the Hill, but I wasn't afraid as long as Gerald was there. He seemed to know everything about the Hill. He taught me to play pitch and catch with a red rubber ball. I was very awkward at first. Gerald was amazed that I had never played ball before. I was better at pitching than I was at catching. Vincent would back me up and run down the balls that I would miss. He said he was playing "pigtail." We had to be careful that the ball didn't go over the side of the cliff at the back of his house. It was steep and overlooked the Bogalusa Highway. I think they cut through the hill so that the highway could be flat. Sometimes when we were tired, we'd sit on the edge of the cliff, dangle our feet off the side, and watch cars on the road.

One time after the BB gun incident, Wild Bill came over to my house to play. This time he had another weapon. He explained that his father wouldn't let him bring the air rifle back to my house. His new toy was a one-piece clothes pin with a thin strip of rubber inner tube tied securely to the round top. At the other end of the elastic strip was a pouch made out of the tongue of an old shoe. Bill would pick up a small piece of gravel and place it in the pouch. Then, with right hand firmly holding the clothes pin, he would pull back on the pouch until it reached his nose. Sighting across the tip of the pin, he would release the pouch, sending the rock a remarkable distance through the air. It was pretty accurate, too. The small rocks would make a whizzing sound as they shot through the air. We would take turns shooting at distant objects. Sometimes, we could even hit the telephone lines, which responded with a pleasant twinging sound. Bill was looking for small birds, but they were really hard to hit in the air. I glanced back uneasily at the gum tree, praying that the ivory bills didn't return.

I thought Gerald would really like this new toy. It looked like something we could make ourselves. I told Bill, "Let's take this sling shot up the Hill and show it to my friend, Gerald."

Bill was game for anything. "Sure, but it's not a sling shot. A sling shot has two strips off of a fork. This is a spook shooter. That's what you call them when there's only one rubber band. A sling shot is even better than a spook shooter. You can aim it a lot better and it goes farther." He searched around on the ground and found a rounded piece of white rock. "This is perfect! This will shoot as good as a marble because there's no friction."

I studied the rock. "Is this what you call a spook?"

Bill looked at me funny. "Yes. See if you can find some more."

I couldn't imagine anything more deadly than the spook shooter. It was much more powerful than the Red Ryder. I told Mother that we were going to play by the swing. Bill liked the idea of sneaking over the fence. As we got up to the top of the hill, he put his hand on my shoulder to stop me. "Wait a minute. Colored people live in those houses."

"I know. Gerald is colored. I want him to see the spook shooter. You're not afraid, are you?"

Bill frowned. "I'm not afraid of anything. Tell you what, though. Let's not call this thing a spook shooter in front of Gerald. Let's call it a sling shot."

I didn't understand, but it didn't make any difference. "You just told me different, but whatever you say."

Gerald and Vincent were delighted with the new toy. We could send rocks all the way across the highway. We shot so many times that we ran out of rocks and had to go back to the gravel road to get more. Eventually, the string that held the leather pouch tore through the hole, and we had to stop. Bill wasn't upset. "No matter. It's easy to make another." He threw the contraption on the ground.

Gerald picked it up. "Can I have it?"

Bill acted like it was of no consequence. "Sure." Gerald put the spook shooter in his pocket.

An uncomfortable period ensued after the demise of the sling shot. Gerald suggested that we play pitch and catch, but Bill wasn't up to it. We had never played with a ball before, and I could tell Bill didn't want to do anything that he wasn't good at. He began looking around on the ground and picked up an L-shaped branch. He aimed it at the sky like a pistol. "Let's play cowboys and Indians."

Gerald looked confused. "What's that?"

Bill seemed more confident. "That's when we pretend like we're cowboys and fight off the bad guys."

"How do we do that?"

"We shoot them with our play guns or knock 'em out with our fists."

"Like in the movies?"

"Just like in the movies."

"Do we rassle with 'em?"

"Yes."

"Let's rassle." Gerald assumed a wrestler's crouch.

Bill went on the offensive. "Okay." He leapt at Gerald as though to throw him to the ground.

Gerald deftly stepped aside, tripped Bill, sat on his chest, and pinned his arms over his head. Bill squirmed, but couldn't get loose. He started to whine. "That's not fair! I wasn't ready. Let's do it again."

Gerald let him up. Bill started circling Gerald, looking for an opening. Suddenly he lunged, but the result was the same. Gerald was sitting on Bill's chest. Bill kicked and squirmed, but he couldn't get up. "That's enough."

Gerald wanted complete victory. "Say 'Uncle'."

"What's 'Uncle'?"

"That means you give up."

"I can't breathe!"

"Say 'Uncle'."

Bill struggled a bit more and gave up. "Uncle, uncle. Let me up!"

Gerald let him up again. Bill dusted himself off. He was breathing hard. "That's not fair. You're bigger than I am. How old are you, anyway?"

"Seven."

Nine-year old Bill didn't answer. He had been humiliated.

I've often thought that my mother sheltered me too much during this time. I didn't even play softball until I was ten and we had moved to Florida. It was several years later that I realized that "spook" was a derogatory term. Then I wondered about the connotation with regard to the sling shot. Did it mean that black people used it instead of the forked instrument? That might make sense if the prevailing feeling in my white culture always relegated inferior instruments to the poorer blacks. The worst case would be if the word related to the intended target rather than the missile for Wild Bill's sling shot. I would have been mortified if I had said anything that would have offended Gerald.

CHAPTER EIGHT

1944

Summers were great fun during the 1940's in Franklinton. Some days we would take off from home with nothing but a canteen of water, a fishing line, and a sandwich. We would stay out all day. We would wear short pants--no shoes, no shirt. Many times we would have no particular destination. It was more fun that way–like exploring. But most of the time we would end up on one of the many small streams that crossed the area. These streams were mostly clear, with sand and gravel bottoms. Our favorites were the ones where the water had carved deeply into the clay banks. There were two levels--the larger, semi-dry flood plain where we could walk unimpeded, and the perennial creek bed where the water was clear and deep. Sometimes the sides were cut so sharply that the little stream was as deep as it was wide. A boy could be in the water and hang onto the side of the bank just like a swimming pool. Those stretches were where we would catch the colorful sunfish and, occasionally, a small catfish. Jimmy, Bill, and I would catch a bug for bait or use a bit of baloney from our sandwiches to bait the small hooks. A bit of a stick could serve as a cork. We didn't need poles. The excitement was intense when the stick would move around as the fish nosed the bait before biting. The water was so clear that we could easily see the bright gold and blues of the sunfish as they rose to explore our offerings. When the mood struck us, we would swim in the cool water. I say swim, but Bill and I couldn't really swim. We rarely got into water over our waists. Sometimes we would get trapped on one side of a stream and have to find a log to cross over, but the streams were usually shallow enough to ford. Jimmy could swim. He would show off in the deep pools, but we knew he was faking it most of the time, because his hands were touching the bottom in his overly graceful strokes.

The prettiest spots were the old gravel pits. We never knew exactly how deep these tranquil holes were, but the water was so clear we could see the bottoms. Large bass patrolled these deeps. But our lines were not long enough to reach them. We were also extra careful not to fall in, so there were only a few spots where we could approach the edges. We never kept any of the fish we caught. We didn't really know what to do with them. It was more fun to watch them shoot away when we released them. The worst thing to me was when the fish would swallow the bait. I knew we seriously injured the little fish when that happened. Also, the dorsal fins were stiff and sharp, and getting the hook out was sometimes painful to us as well. At times we would spot the many water moccasins we shared the streams with. Once, we saw one saw one with a catfish in his mouth. He stayed just below the surface of the water, swaying in the current and waiting for us to leave him in peace.

On weekends, a truck with wooden slats on the sides would come downtown and pick up all the white kids and take them out to what I called Peter Pan. I found out later that the stream was actually Hayes Creek. The shallow part that we played in was called Peter Pan, and farther downstream was a deeper swimming area known as the Blue Hole. Nearly every kid would bring a sandwich. My mother would usually make tuna fish. We didn't get to eat our own sandwiches all the time, but contributed them to a large pile on one of the outdoor tables where anyone could select them. Two rustic log cabins by Peter Pan were used by the Girl Scouts for overnight stays. A hand pump for a water well was in the center of the complex. You could stop up the spigot with your palm and, with the help of a friend to pump, create a water fountain through a small hole in the top of the cross pipe. Mothers would come ahead of the truck and prepare even more food. They would make a large stainless steel bucket full of peanut butter and jelly stirred together so that the mixture was a homogenous spread for yet more sandwiches. It made me think that some kids didn't contribute a sandwich. In big glass jugs, the mothers would make a lemonade-type drink known as bug juice. I think the bug name came from the little bits of fruit that floated on top of the liquid. The juice was good and sweet, and we drank it out of small paper cups shaped like triangles.

One day after a big rain, Bill and I arrived at Peter Pan and climbed over the railings of the truck before they let down the gate in the back. We put our sandwiches on the table. Bill stripped off his short pants to reveal his white swim trunks with blue and red stripes on the side. He ran to the bank to jump in the water. Bill always wanted to be the first one in the water. I lingered a bit to see if I could identify my sandwich among the others in a growing pile on the table. I liked the tuna fish, but sometimes I would get someone else's sandwich that I didn't like. Pimento cheese--ugh! Still not sure that I would be able to get my sandwich back, I followed Bill to the kid-made slot in the bank that led down to Peter Pan. When I got to the bank, I pulled up short. The creek was swollen to five times its usual size and flowing swiftly. I didn't see Bill. He surely was hiding along the bank, trying to scare me into thinking he was underwater. I looked both ways, but he wasn't there. What should I do? I wasn't bold enough to cry out, especially if Bill was playing a joke. That would be too embarrassing. But if Bill was underwater? Just then, three teenagers came up to the water's edge. The girl jumped in and started swimming to the sand bar on the other side of the creek. I grabbed one of the boys by the arm. "I think my friend is under the water. He can't swim." The boy just smiled.

The girl came out of the water on the sandbar in a low stooping run and yelled back to the teenage boy as she pointed back at the creek. "Sonny! Somebody grabbed me under the water!" She was tugging at a strap on her swim suit.

Sonny went into action. He looked angry. He dove in the water and disappeared. In seconds, he came up with limp body of Bill and deposited him on the clay shelf below me. The other boy jumped down and began giving Bill artificial respiration. After a while, Bill rolled over and groaned. He sat up but was obviously exhausted. The boys looked him in the eyes, asked how he felt, and stood up as Bill waved his arm weakly in dismissal. Bill propped himself up on one arm, and I could see that his thin back was heaving with large breaths. I scrambled down the bank and tried to help him up, but he didn't want to stand. He sat in the mud with his knees drawn up and rested his head on his knees. When he recovered, we climbed back up the bank. One of the mothers came up but obviously didn't realize what had happened to Bill. She called out to the girl who, by this time, had swum back across and was dangling her feet in the stream. "Come out of the water. No swimming today, the water is too high!"

We washed off the mud by the well pump and ate our lunch mostly in silence. That afternoon, as we rode back to Franklinton on the truck, I asked Bill if he had been afraid. He didn't look at me when he answered. "Naw, we all got to die sometime."

I didn't believe him. No one in his right mind wants to die if he is in good health. His outward indifference must have been part of his bravado. He obviously enjoyed life and surely could not have taken a near miss so lightly at only nine years of age. I also resolved to learn how to swim. The near-tragedy lingered on my mind. I had never known anyone who had died. Being close to someone who had almost died was very disturbing. We rode back on the truck to Franklinton, hanging on the wooden slats on the sides, both of us nearly dry by now. I had to ask him: "What were you thinking when you were sinking to the bottom, not knowing that anyone could save you?"

Bill looked serious, finally and hung his head. "I thought, here I am, nine years old. I've never done anything special and I'm going to die.' Now that I'm out of this, I'm never going to let that happen again."

I thought I understood. "You mean you're not going to jump into deep water again?"

He looked at me as though I had missed the point. "No. I'm going to experience all there is to do before I kick off."

That sounded awfully far-sighted to me. I never thought about anything more than what I was going to do tomorrow.

CHAPTER NINE

1998

The next Monday after my visit with Tommy, I got a call from him. He sounded excited. "Come over. I've got something to show you."

"What is it? Have you solved our mystery?"

"Something better."

"You're not going to tell me, are you?"

"That's right. You have to see this."

I was curious, but I couldn't break loose just then. "I can't come over this afternoon or tomorrow. I've got a man coming to give me an estimate on replacing the gutters on the house. But I could come over the next day in the morning."

"Good enough. Think about where you want to go for lunch."

I had premonitions about how to get him and his wheelchair in my truck, but I couldn't refuse. "Okay, but it's an hour's drive, so I can't get there before, say, about ten."

The gutter man wanted too much money, so I decided to do it myself. First, I had to buy a ladder. Not too bad. Home Depot in Covington had a ten-footer for about $150. Picking that up cost me about two hours. The old rotten gutter was attached a lot better than it looked. It was screwed into the soffit with two heavy bolt-head screws and wired at each attachment to keep it from tilting over. It took me the rest of the day just to get the damn thing down.

The next day, I still wasn't finished with putting up the new gutter when it was time to go to Tommy's. Ellen came out to laugh at me while I cursed the work. "How much have you saved so far? " I phoned Tommy to let him know I wouldn't be there until noon.

The swamp around his house had a more pleasant appearance with the sun directly overhead. I could imagine that wood ducks called the shallow pools home during the winters. A large van was parked in Tommy's driveway, and I wondered if we had a mutual friend as a lunch companion.

Tommy answered the door but told me to go out to the driveway. I didn't see anyone behind him in the house. He maneuvered his chair to the van and pushed a button on a contraption in his hand. The horn beeped once, the lights flashed, the driver's door opened, and a lift came out and lowered to the concrete. Tommy expertly rolled upon the lift, pushed another button and began to rise. "Come on! Get in the other side."

I was amazed. When I got in the passenger's seat, Tommy was comfortably situated behind the wheel. I felt the obviously new dashboard. "When did you get this?"

"Day before yesterday."

"But how can you drive it?" I regretted the way I said it, but I was truly interested.

Tommy grasped the gear shift between us. "It goes into park, reverse, and drive just like any other car, but I have hand controls for the brake and accelerator." He pointed to the aforementioned. "I spent all day yesterday learning about it and driving it around. The guy who delivered it spent a lot of time showing me how it works and making sure I was comfortable with it."

"Where in the world did you find it?"

"On the internet. A place near Lafayette modifies vans and has a website that explains all about their products. I wanted it right away but had the sense to have them come here for a demonstration. I was really pleased after I tried it out and settled the deal on the spot." He looked in the rearview mirror to make sure I was parked in the street and not behind him.

"Where do you want to go for lunch?"

"Lord if I know. Baton Rouge is all strange to me now—and bigger. Where do you want to go?"

Tommy backed the van out of the driveway. "I know a spot near here. Could you go for a shrimp po'boy?"

"You bet. I'll even buy."

We didn't drive very far to a rather noisy place that was obviously a hangout for kids from LSU, which was a mile or so farther down Highland Road. The girls were pretty and the boys all wore baseball caps. Blue jeans and tee shirts were the uniform of the day. Tommy and I found a table that he could access with the wheel chair and ordered po'boys from a waitress who looked like the female customers. Two television sets were showing two different sports events. I moved my chair so I wouldn't be distracted. Tommy gazed at the beer pitchers that were being delivered, sometimes two at a time, to the kids at the tables. Trays of crawfish arrived with equal regularity. The smells were delicious in themselves.

Tommy seemed amused. "Remember when we acted like this crowd?"

"It all seems a long time ago. I don't think I could drink that much beer again."

"They all seem so confident. Look how they kiss everybody as they greet them. I don't remember doing that. A kiss really meant something when we were young. I'd like to drink a beer, but I know I shouldn't. I'm a driver again. I need to be more responsible."

"Well, we do have some serious business. Ellen says

that if we are stuck on Wild Bill, maybe we should pay some attention to Dennis Dawson. Got any suggestions?"

"You tried the papers. Maybe someone who knew Dennis well. From my lawyering days, I seem to remember that he was a partner in Tyler, Dawson, and Reed."

"Do you think that's Johnny Reed? He's a few years younger than we are. Maybe he's still practicing. Johnny was a cub scout when I was a Den Chief. I'm pretty sure he became a lawyer, but I didn't know him very well after that."

"Yes, the partner was John Reed. Seems like he had some health problems a while back, but that might be a place to start. Another thing. We have been talking like Swifty and his crew were behind these three deaths. That's not a very good perspective. It can bias how we look at things. What if we try to be completely objective and let the chips fall where they may?"

"Good idea, but it is going to be hard to disregard Swifty with the connections we have already."

When we got back to Tommy's house, I looked up attorneys in the yellow pages and found a John Reed in the firm of Tyler, Reed, and Smith. I called the number and asked to speak to Mr. Reed. Miraculously, I was connected right away.

"Mr. Reed?" I inquired of the voice at the other end.

"This is he."

"You may not remember me. I'm Sam Elliot. I believe I was your Den Chief when you were in the Cub Scouts many years ago."

"Actually, I don't. I was never in the Cubs. "

"This isn't the John Reed that lived in the South downs area in the early fifties?"

"No. But my father lived there as a boy."

"Sorry about that. Is your father around?"

"Not around here. He retired a few years ago and moved to Florida."

"Good for him. Actually, I'm inquiring about a member of your firm who died some time ago, Dennis Dawson."

"Yes, I remember stories about Dennis. Killed in a car wreck, I believe."

"That's him. I'm trying to talk to anyone who might have known him well at the time—surviving family maybe."

"Gee, I don't know. Old man Tyler is still living, but I'm afraid he couldn't help much. Had a bad stroke a few months back and can't even speak. I don't think anyone else in the office goes back that far. Wait a minute, though. Mr. Tyler kept a scrap book of the firm's highlights in his office. Maybe there's something in there. Hold on, I'll go over there and transfer you to his phone."

Silence for a moment. Then the other phone kicked in, and I had a mental picture of him holding the phone against his ear with his shoulder while leafing through the scrapbook.

Wrong picture. "Gotcha on the speaker phone. I've got the scrapbook. What year did Dennis die? The book looks chronological." His voice sounded like he was down a well.

"June of 1958, I believe. I really appreciate you going to all this trouble. I know you're busy."

"I wish I were busier." I could hear him leafing. "'57, '58. Gee. He kept every little tidbit. Most of this doesn't even pertain to the firm. Here we go. An obituary for Dawson from the *Advocate*. It's very short. You want me to read it to you?"

This might keep me from perusing the hated

microfiches in the library. "Please, if you don't mind."

He read it, but the article didn't say very much. The survivors might be helpful. Besides his parents, there was a younger sister, Rose Dawson Larsen, who was married to a Kenneth Larsen. I thanked Reed and hung up.

I turned to Tommy. "Well, I got one lead. Dennis had a sister named Rose, and we know her married name. Let's see if they are still together after all these years." The telephone book revealed that a Kenneth Larsen lived in Denham Springs, just east of Baton Rouge. I dialed the number and a woman answered.

"Mrs. Larsen?"

"Yes."

"My name is Sam Elliott. Did you have a brother named Dennis Dawson?"

"Yes I did. Why do you want to know?"

I smiled at my good luck. "I was a friend of Dennis's, and I wanted to ask you some questions about his death, if you don't mind."

Rose didn't speak for a few seconds. Her response was unexpected. "Can you prove you were a friend?"

I fumbled a bit. "Verify our friendship?" I stalled and looked at Tommy. "Well, we had a mutual friend in Bill–Wild Bill–Jenkins. Dennis had planned to visit us in Mexico City when Bill and I finished summer school down there. Dennis died before school ended."

"What did Dennis like to drink?"

I felt like I was losing this opportunity, and the conversation was getting strange. "That was a long time ago. Let's see. We used to frequent a tavern in downtown Baton Rouge called the Three Coins. I seem to remember all of us drinking liter steins of draft Lowenbrau."

"That's not what I was thinking of, but that sounds

reasonable. I remember Wild Bill and the plans for Mexico, and Dennis did hang around the Three Coins. I'm sorry to be so suspicious. Look, I'm leaving the house right now. I've got to pick up my granddaughter at school and drop her by my son's house. Where are you now?"

"I'm in South Baton Rouge, but I'll be heading back on Interstate 12 toward Hammond and will go right by Denham Springs if we could talk a bit."

"Well, our house is well off the highway. Suppose I meet you at the Pancake House close to I12. There's a big sign. You can't miss it. I'll just have a cup of coffee, and we can talk."

"Sounds good. Oh. I'm an old guy with thinning white hair, and I'm wearing a blue shirt. I'll be driving a grey Toyota Pickup."

"I'm wearing blue jeans and a red blouse. See you in about a half hour."

I hung up and rested my hand on the phone. Tommy leaned forward to hear the results. "I'm meeting Rose Larsen at the Pancake House in Denham Springs. This doesn't sound like much, but we'll be able to cross it off the list."

Tommy crossed his arms in his lap. "It does sound promising to me."

"Why so?"

"First of all, from this end, she sounded suspicious. She may be afraid of something or else she wouldn't have asked you to verify your friendship with Dennis. Secondly, the fact that she agreed to meet you at all means she thinks she does have something to say or thinks that you know something that she doesn't. She has more than a passing interest. She's smart. She arranged to meet you in a public place rather than her home. I'd be really careful with her.

Don't scare her off or take her lightly."

"Tommy, you sure assumed a lot from a conversation that I was having over the phone."

"Sounds like you could really use my astute analytical abilities. I wish I could go with you."

That didn't sound practical, and I didn't know if he was serious or not. He clearly wanted to be more involved. "Well, you just said we shouldn't scare her off. I wouldn't be surprised if she didn't show, or wanted to look me over before we meet. Besides, I can keep on going back down I12 when we've finished. Do you think you know everything about your client who was killed, or could you work on that for a bit on your own?"

"I could dig a little deeper. I still have access to records at State Police headquarters." He sounded encouraged.

"By the way, who was your client?"

"His name was Lindsey Scott. Does that ring a bell?"

"No. Not at all. Was he from around here?"

"No. I think he was from Gonzales or someplace down river toward New Orleans."

As I pulled out of Tommy's driveway, I felt encouraged too. Tommy was interested in something and he had found a way to be more mobile. If nothing else came out of our little investigation, Tommy's quality of life may have been enhanced.

Traffic on I12 was crowded, and most of it seemed to exit at Denham Springs. The Pancake House was easy to find, and I pulled into a parking space near the front door. The smell of pancakes was strong as I entered the building, but very few customers were present at this hour. I looked up and down the booths but could see no lone woman or anyone fitting the description that Rose had given me. A woman in a striped uniform standing behind the counter said I could sit anywhere. I chose a booth next to the picture window in the far left corner and sat down. A young girl brought me a menu and asked if I wanted something to drink.

I glanced at the menu. "Actually, I'd just like a cup of coffee. I'm waiting on someone. Do you have decaf?"

"We can make some." She tucked her order book in her apron. "Do you want me to leave the menu?"

"It wouldn't hurt."

I had practically finished the coffee and wondered if I should wait longer, when I spotted a woman in a red blouse in the parking lot. She was carrying a manila folder. She stopped in back of my parked truck and copied down the license number in the folder. She saw me right away from the doorway and came to my booth.

She looked a little older than I had imagined, but you could tell she had been attractive when she was younger. Her reddish hair was pulled back, and tiny lines were formed at the corner of her eyes. A little plump, she wore her blouse outside her jeans. "Are you Mr. Elliot?"

I stood up awkwardly with my knees bent under the table and extended my hand. "Yes, but please call me Sam."

She slid into the booth and laid her folder on the table. She didn't speak to me until after the waitress had taken her order for coffee and I rejected another cup. She looked straight into my eyes. "Do you have any identification?"

I showed her my driver's license which she studied for a moment and then returned. "Why are you interested in Dennis?"

I had rehearsed my reply. "I was actually looking

into the death of a friend–Bill Jenkins–the same one who Dennis was to meet in Mexico. Bill died in an airplane crash in 1964, and it occurred to me that his accident had some similarities to Dennis's."

She leaned forward, an interested look on her face. "Do you suspect foul play?"

"Perhaps. I have no proof at all. It's just that Bill's accident was attributed to impairment due to alcohol, and now there appears to be some doubt as to whether he was drinking at all. In addition, I spoke to a mechanic who says that Bill's airplane engine was mysteriously fouled–maybe intentionally."

"Why didn't you do anything then? That was a long time ago."

"Actually, I just talked to the mechanic for the first time a few days ago. Also, this isn't much evidence to go to the authorities with. I just couldn't let it go without checking to see if there were anything suspicious about Dennis's death as well."

We stopped talking when the waitress brought Rose her coffee. Rose bit her lower lip as she added cream and sweetener. She didn't look up as she stirred. "We did think something was wrong."

That got my attention. "How is that?"

She took a sip and placed both hands around her cup after she sat it down. "A few days after Dennis died, two men came to our house. They said they were from the State Bureau of Investigation of the State Police. Both were rough-looking men who fit my concept of detectives. They said it was just a routine visit and wanted to know if Dennis had discussed his work with us. We–my husband and I– assumed they meant his work with his law firm and talked about a recent court case. The two men seemed satisfied and left. We thought this was a little odd, but couldn't make anything of it. The very next day, a letter from the State Police came to Dennis's trailer. We opened it, and it was a check for $1,000. That was a whole lot of money back then. Ken called Mr. Tyler from Dennis's firm to let him know about the check to add to Dennis's succession. Also, we were curious as to why Dennis was receiving money from the State Police."

Rose opened the manila folder and produced a yellowed copy of the check. "We kept a file on the whole matter. Mr. Tyler called back and gave us the telephone number of someone at the State Police who could explain the check." She showed me a handwritten note with a number and the name of a Major Wilson. "Apparently the check was legit. I called Major Wilson who told me that the check was for some work that Dennis had done for the Bureau. I told him that explained why two of his men had been by to ask us if we knew anything about his work. Wilson seemed surprised. He said that he hadn't sent anyone to talk to us. He would do some checking and get back to me."

"The next day–I think it was the next day–Wilson called back to say that definitely no one from the Bureau had visited us. I was frightened and demanded to know what Dennis had been doing. Wilson seemed reluctant to tell me; but I said that I was involved now, and if I were in any danger I had a right to know. He then told me that Dennis had been undercover in an operation to expose some criminals in the Baton Rouge area. I asked him if he thought Dennis's death was anything but an accident. He said they were investigating that, but the only thing that seemed odd was that someone at the party thought there was somebody else in the car with Dennis before the accident."

Most of this was completely new to me. "What party was that?"

"This was a get-together of some lawyers at someone's plantation home out in the country. Mr. Tyler was at the same party and told us that he had heard the same story about someone else in the car with Dennis but couldn't confirm it."

"So what happened with the investigation?"

Rose was getting teary-eyed. "Nothing. Absolutely nothing." She waved her hand at the futility. "We called Major Wilson back a number of times, and he was sorry, but they couldn't find out anything more."

"Did you notice what kind of car the two men who visited you were driving?"

"No."

"Did they give you any identification?"

"No. I didn't think to ask. It all seemed so innocent. That's why I wanted to make sure who you were. I was so frightened at the time that I tried to get Ken to move away from Baton Rouge. We stayed in the area, and nothing more was said about the affair until you showed up. We did find three more deposits of $1,000 each in Dennis's bank account statements."

I tried to think of more questions. Rose had supplied some valuable information that seemed to justify some of my suspicions, and I didn't want to leave her if there was more to learn. "Who was Dennis investigating?"

She closed the file as if to end her contribution. "Wilson never told us. His investigation was at a dead end. He seemed satisfied that the two imposters had accomplished their mission, and that we were not in any danger. They were probably trying to find out if Dennis had talked to us about his undercover work. Wilson also said something about limiting our contact with him to insure that it stayed that way. He must have been right because nothing has happened in all these years. He promised to tell us if they found out any more about Dennis's death. Now, I've told you all that I know. What is it that you know that made you go to all this trouble?"

I tried to tell her everything I knew that had aroused my suspicions. She apparently knew nothing about Swifty.

When I got home, I gave Tommy a call. He answered right away, and I gave him a summary of my conversation with Rose. "Hey, this was a good lead. I think we have a good foundation for thinking there was some foul play involved in Dennis's death. His family obviously thought Dennis was a target because of some undercover work he was doing."

Tommy wanted to be more involved. "Look, I've got some contacts here that could help us. Why don't I try to dig up the old police reports? You seem to have had some luck with relatives. In the meantime, why don't you see if you can find some of Bill's kinfolk in Franklinton?"

I couldn't tell if Tommy was trying to get me out of the way so he could do his own thing, but I certainly didn't want to discourage him. "Sure. I'm a lot closer to Franklinton here. The only trouble is that the guy at the cemetery told me that there were no more Jenkinses in the area."

Tommy countered. "From what you told me, that guy may not be the most reliable source of information. Bill had a wife and a son didn't he?"

"Yes, but I don't remember the name of the son."

"Somebody in Franklinton should know where they are now. There are not many secrets in a small town like that."

I really didn't relish another trip to Franklinton, but Tommy was right, and I gave in. "Sure, I'll run over there in the morning."

The next morning, I took off for Franklinton again. When I got there, I parked near the courthouse again and went to the front where I found the same lady who had directed me to the Sheriff's office before. I tried to appear friendly. "Hi. My name is Elliot. Actually I'm looking for a family who lived here back in the 60's."

She smiled. "What was the family's name?"

"Jenkins. They were relatives of the man who owned Jenkins's Chevrolet."

"Well, there's lots of Jenkinses around here, but I don't remember Jenkins's Chevrolet. You say they lived here in the 1960's?"

"Yes. I had a friend in that family who died in 1964, so his kin may not even live around here anymore."

She picked up a slim telephone book. "You could try the parish phone directory. My guess is you'll find a lot of Jenkinses."

She was right–too many to start calling, and they were scattered around the parish. I closed the book and handed it back to her. "Thanks, that looks like a big job. Is there anyone here that might be knowledgeable about people who lived here forty years ago?"

"You might try Mr. Williams. He's the Administrative Officer and has been here a long time."

"Sure. Where could I find him?"

She made a half turn and pointed down the hall. "If he's in, he'd be in that office marked 'Administrative Officer' on the left. Mr. Williams is sort of our unofficial historian. I think it's his hobby. Once you get him started, it's hard to stop him."

A sign protruding from the wall was clear enough. "Thanks. Should I knock?"

"No. He has a secretary. Just walk right in."

I did as instructed. A black lady was typing on a computer and looked up as I came through the door. "Can I help you?"

"I'd like to see Mr. Williams."

"Do you have an appointment?"

She looked like the efficient type who would know for sure about every appointment, but I answered "No."

She picked up a phone. "Let me check. Who shall I say wants to see him?"

"My name is Elliot–Sam Elliot."

She looked away. "Mr. Williams? There is a gentleman here to see you. It's a Mr. Sam Elliot." Pause. "Sure." She put down the phone. "You can go right in." She gestured toward a door with an opaque glass insert.

Mr. Williams was a distinguished-looking black man with graying hair. He wore a plain tie with a short-sleeved white shirt and rose from behind his desk as I entered. He held out his hand across the desk, and said, "Hi. I'm Jerry Williams. What can I do for you?" He motioned me to sit down in a chair in front of the desk.

I shook his hand, stood for a moment and said, "I'm Sam Elliot. I understand you're the institutional memory here, and I wanted to pick your brains about a family that lived in the Franklinton area in the sixties."

He gestured at the chair again with his palm up. "Please."

I took the proffered chair and tried to think where to begin. "I'm looking for anyone that might have been related to the Jenkins family that used to own Jenkins Chevrolet here in town."

Mr. Williams put his thumbs under his chin and tapped his extended fingers together slowly. Then he dropped his hands and entwined his fingers on his chest. "I remember the Chevrolet place, but I'm trying to think of where the family went after it closed. There's a bunch of Jenkinses around, but I don't think any of them were related to the Chevrolet Jenkinses. I believe... believe that family lived up toward Oak Hill."

I leaned forward. "That's them. I was friends with the son, Bill, who was killed in a plane crash."

Mr. Williams made wrinkles in his chin and pursed his lips. "Yes, I remember the incident. I was about 27 when that happened and in the service out in California, just before Viet Nam heated up. I didn't come home before I shipped out, so I wasn't privy to the details–he was drinking, wasn't he?"

"That was the story. It's hard to tell exactly what happened way back then, but I would like to talk to the family to see what they have to say."

Williams cocked his head. "You mean to say you don't believe he was drinking?"

I hadn't meant to reveal this much. "I don't know for sure, but the story doesn't gibe with Bill's habits."

"How so?"

"Well, for one thing, eye witnesses claim there was a gin bottle in the cockpit, and Bill didn't–couldn't drink gin."

Williams smiled knowingly. "Not a whole lot to go on, is it?"

I had already given out more information than I had intended. Best not go too deep. This story was too complicated already. "You're right, but I still would like to talk to the family to ease my mind. Seems like he had a wife and a son, and I was hoping one of them would still be around."

"I take it you weren't living around here at the time of the accident."

"No. But I did live here in the forties when my father was at the CCC camp, and my mother and I came back again while he was overseas."

"Oh yes." Williams seemed interested. "Where did you live?"

I gestured in the direction I thought LA 10 ran. "Just a little out of downtown on the Bogalusa Highway. Right before a section they called the Hill."

Williams smiled again. "Ah yes, the Hill. I lived up there myself as a child."

I put one elbow on the chair arm and pushed on a front tooth with my thumb. I looked him in the eye. "Did you have a brother named Vincent?"

Williams looked surprised. "Why yes. How did you know that?"

"I think we used to play together for a while."

"No kidding. I think I remember that. If you are who I think you are, you were probably my first white playmate. What a coincidence! I'm glad to see you again." We shook hands again as if we were meeting for the first time.

"What's Vincent doing now?"

"Probably playing a harp up in Heaven. Vincent was a hero. He was a pilot and got shot down in 'Nam."

"I'm sorry to hear that."

"We were really proud of Vincent. He made major– quite a feat in those days."

"And your mother–Maw?"

"Long gone. She was a saint. She worked hard and

pushed us to grow up right. Sacrificed a lot so that Vincent and I could get good educations."

I wanted to acknowledge the prejudice that so recently existed in my home state. "Did you go to school up North?"

"No. We both toughed it out at LSU and went through the ROTC program. I went in the Army and Vincent opted for the Air Force a bit later. I credit that military experience with whatever success I've had when I came back here–to a somewhat hostile environment, I might add."

"You've been working in administration the whole time?"

"No. I was with the Sheriff's Department for a while. Came in not long after the first two African American deputies here were ambushed. One of them died."

This was skirting on something that interested me–crime in Washington Parish. "I don't believe I've heard that story."

Jerry was warming up to his role as historian. He leaned back in his chair and folded his fingers together on his abdomen. He rocked slowly. "This was back in June 1965. The deputies were Oneal Moore and Creed Rogers. They were patrolling around Varnado one night when a dark-colored pickup truck passed them and opened fire. Moore was hit in the back of the head, and Rogers was badly wounded."

I began to appreciate Williams' bravery in working in the Sheriff's Department. "Did they catch whoever did it?"

He stuck his jaw out and clenched his teeth before speaking, took a deep breath, and cocked his head to one side before speaking. "Not exactly. The Mississippi cops stopped a black pickup right over the border just after the incident. The truck had a Confederate decal on the bumper, just like Rogers reported on his radio."

"So they did catch someone."

"The charges were dropped within two weeks. The thought was that there were at least three people in the pickup, but no one has ever been tried for the murder."

"And that was the end of it?"

"Probably so. The next summer another black man named Clarence Triggs was murdered. They arrested some men, but they were found innocent. At that time, Bogalusa was thought to have one of the highest concentrations of Ku Klux Klanners in the country."

"And you joined the Sheriff's Department with all that going on?"

"Well, I thought I could do some good. My experiences in the Army were mostly positive, and I thought I could do anything when I came home. I was wrong. Just couldn't get enough evidence to solve either one of those murders. You know, some of these civil rights crimes still are being cracked, and the files are still open. It wouldn't surprise me if someone's conscience got the better of him before he dies, and he'll spill the beans on the real perpetrators. As for me, I drifted into administration with the Sheriff's Office and ended up here. Actually, people have been very supportive. I like working here and I like the people I work with. I'm sure there is a lot of talk behind my back because of my race, but no one says anything to my face. A while back, the Voters' League in Bogalusa was a high-profile civil rights organization that caught a lot of flak from the white population, but I've just tried to do my job, and things have quieted down quite a bit."

I appreciated the fact that he could be so candid with me. "Has Washington Parish had a long history of crime?"

"Early in its life it was pretty lawless. In the early 1800's, the area now in Louisiana from the Mississippi border just east of Bogalusa west to the Mississippi River was owned by Spain. There was a bit of confusion over who owned this territory after the Louisiana Purchase. Even today, that land south of Mississippi to Lake Pontchartrain is known as the Florida Parishes, because they were once an extension of Spain's Florida. A lot of the people who came here from the United States were actually people who sympathized with England during the Revolutionary War. Others were fleeing from the law or taking advantage of the fact that there was very little here in the way of law enforcement."

"In 1810 the settlers here actually rebelled, took a Spanish fort in Baton Rouge, and declared this area the independent Republic of West Florida. But probably our most famous crime happened here in 1980. They even made a book and a movie out of it. You've heard of *Dead Man Walking*?"

"Yes."

"Well, two of our locals killed a girl and left her body down in Frickies Cave, just below Franklinton. It's not really a cave, just some interesting formations the water has washed out."

This was getting a little too historical for my purposes, and I wanted to change the subject. "What about organized crime here–the Mafia for instance?"

"Not that I know of. Most of the Mafia stuff you hear of in Louisiana has been in the big cities. Some young Italian men killed a man in a bungled robbery over in Independence some time back that started rumors about the

Mafia, but that was just an *ad hoc* operation."

"How about the Dixie Mafia?"

"I believe they were headquartered mostly in Mobile. That was a rough bunch and probably not all that organized. Several murders were attributed to them, and some members have been convicted. They appeared to have some activity in Baton Rouge, and we are sort of in-between, but my guess is that they may have traveled back and forth on US 190 and later on Interstate 12. We're north of there." He thought for a few seconds. "I remember one possible incident that smacks of organization. Back in the sixties the Sheriff's Department found an abandoned pickup truck in a ditch on Louisiana 10. They towed it in, and found out the truck had been stolen in Mississippi. When they cracked open the tool box, it was completely full of marijuana. No one was implicated in the incident, and the theory was that the driver went off the road by accident and then ran away before he could recover the goods or get caught. Come to think of it, these routes through Washington Parish might be safer than trying to use the interstates south of here."

"Did the Dixie Mafia ever stage accidents to kill people?"

"Most of the time they used guns. I read one claim that they tried to kill the governor of Arkansas by sabotaging his plane. I can't vouch for the veracity of that article, though. Are you suggesting that might have happened to your friend?"

"I'm just reaching for straws I guess. My real purpose in talking to you was to find out what happened to Bill Jenkins's wife and son."

Williams smiled. "Sure, let me make a few calls. Somebody around here is bound to know." He picked up on a phone on his desk and dialed a number from memory. After a few rings, somebody evidently answered because he started talking. "Hello, Clarence? Just fine, and you? Glad to hear it. Listen, I'm trying the track down the daughter-in-law and grandson of the Jenkins that used to own Jenkins Chevrolet." He covered the mouthpiece of the phone with his left hand and asked me: "Was that 'Wild Bill' Jenkins' wife?"

I nodded.

He removed his hand. "Yes, that's the guy. Killed in a plane crash." He picked up a pencil, but didn't write anything. He just tapped the pencil on a pad. "How about the son?" Pause. "Okay. No, no problem. An old friend was trying to contact them. Thanks. No. I can't go tonight, Sarah and I are having the kids over for supper. I'll probably see you tomorrow and you can fill me in."

He put down the phone and turned to me. "Apparently the wife remarried after a while and moved away. My friend doesn't know where. But the son–his name is Dalton–worked for his grandfather at the dealership for a while when he grew up. They didn't get along real well, but the grandfather kept him on. Then the old man died, and the business closed down. My friend thinks Dalton is still selling used cars at the Chevrolet place in Bogalusa."

That sounded promising to me. The son ought to be easy to locate. I was surprised that Bill have failed to name his son "Grubb" after the *pilota* we met in Mexico. "About how far is it to Bogalusa?"

"About 20 miles or so. Louisiana 10 runs in front of the building here and goes straight to Bogalusa. Actually, you and I used to live right off the highway–if you could call it a highway back then."

I stood up and shook hands. "Thanks for the information. I'm glad to have seen you again. This is quite a coincidence."

He smiled. "Franklinton still isn't all that big. You might be surprised at all the people who are still around from the forties."

I tried to recognize landmarks as I drove out of town. Nearly everything had changed. The cotton gin building was recognizable by the railroad tracks, but the old movie theater had been converted into some kind of store. Fast food places were everywhere. The streams that seemed so large when I was young seemed paltry now. Either they had dried up, or my memory fooled me. So far, people in Franklinton had been very friendly and knowledgeable. I could probably live here again.

The trip to Bogalusa went quickly–mostly dairy farms and pastures. I intended to ask about the Chevrolet dealership when I hit town, but I spotted it on the main drag almost right away. I pulled into a parking place in front of the office and got out. A smiling young man immediately came out, shook my hand, gave me his name, and asked how he could help me. It wasn't Dalton. I looked past him. "No thanks, I'm looking for Dalton Jenkins."

The young man smiled through his disappointment. "Sure, hang on, I'll go get him."

He disappeared into the office and another young man emerged. He looked in his late 30's and was brushing his hands off as though he had been eating. He had curly blond hair and about a two-day stubble of beard–not what you would expect from a car salesman. He stuck out his hand. "I'm Dalton. What can I do for you?"

I looked into his green eyes, trying to see something of Wild Bill. "My name is Sam Elliot. I used to be a friend of your father's. I wasn't around when he died and I'm just trying to find out a little more of what happened."

Dalton cocked his head and frowned a bit. "Gee Mister, I was only four or five when he died. I don't believe I can help you."

I didn't want to give up after driving all the way to Bogalusa. "Maybe your mother then? How can I get in touch with her?"

He looked down. "She's living in Oklahoma and not in good health. I doubt if she can help you either. That was a long time ago."

I tried to catch his eye again. "Really. Anything you can remember."

His gaze wandered upward, obviously not much interested. "He must have been a good man. He tried to help out Mom and me."

"How so?"

"Well, he had a good insurance policy--for the time. Actually two policies, one for Mom and one for me. Mine went into a trust that kicked in when I was 18. It paid me a certain amount each year, but it's all gone now." He looked around at his environment as though times had been better.

I smiled. "Well, that's good. That is, I'm glad he could do that. Was your mother the executor?"

"No. The insurance agent, Adrian Brumfield was. He took something off the top for doing it."

"I guess Adrian is long gone now."

"No. He still hangs out in his office in Franklinton. He's a lawyer and an insurance agent. Guess he made a lot of money over the years–especially off of me, but he still pretends to work. Look, I got a lot of work to do myself."

Nobody else was in the lot. He probably wanted to get rid of me. I couldn't think of anything else to ask but wanted to keep the door open. "Say, do you have a card or something?"

He fished in his shirt pocket and handed me a business card. "Sure. Let me know when you're in the market for a car. We got some good deals."

As I drove back to Franklinton, I realized I should have asked directions to Adrian's office. I'm too old for this investigation business. I'm afraid I'll scare someone off if I get too aggressive. This whole venture reminded me of pursuing syphilis contacts in rural North Carolina. We couldn't reveal the real reason for investigations, but we still had to pump informants for locating information.

It seemed that I was doing a lot of running around for so little information. I noticed that I was doing over 60 and guessed the speed limit was more like 50, so I slowed down. No use getting a speeding ticket when I had so much time on my hands. The particulars about the accident was still eluding me, and the info I was getting was sounding more like my excuse for asking. Maybe I should be more direct. Also, it was getting harder to remember everything. It was probably time to write everything down. It would be easier to brief Tommy that way. I turned into the first gas station on the outskirts of Franklinton and asked the lady inside where Brumfield's Insurance office was.

She came outside to point. She didn't have to, but she did. She had a croaking voice. "You go to the second stoplight and take a right. Brumfield is in the middle of the first block."

It was a testimony to Franklinton's growth that they should have two traffic lights. I knew that directions were often faulty. "What does the office look like?"

She shielded her eyes and looked at me as if that information were not necessary. "It's got one big plate glass window. You can't miss it."

She was right. I followed her directions and spotted the office right away. There was no sign to proclaim it Brumfield's, but no other store front had a single plate glass window. I parked across the street and waited as two cars passed by. As I approached the door, I noticed a small hole about four feet high in the window as if from a gunshot. A man about my age was sitting behind a desk with his feet up. He wheeled around as I came in.

"Hi. I'm Sam Elliot. Are you Mr. Brumfield?"

He stood up to shake hands. "I'm Adrian. My daddy was Mr. Brumfield."

The location looked like the place that I used to get haircuts every Saturday in the forties–for twenty-five cents. "Did this place used to be a barber shop?"

Adrian sat back down and motioned me to a seat. "That it was, before my daddy bought it many years ago. How come you to know that?"

"I used to get haircuts here a long time ago. That hole was in the window back then."

He looked surprised. "You mean the bullet hole?"

"Actually I came in right after it happened. The barber told me that it wasn't a bullet hole at all. A car rolled over a rock in the street and pinched it so hard that it shot through the window and cracked a mirror in the back of the shop."

Adrian put his hand on the side of his head and looked disappointed. "Oh no, you've ruined a perfectly good story! I may have to get that thing fixed now."

I smiled. "Don't bother. I won't tell anyone."

He relaxed. "You didn't come in here just to destroy my best icebreaker."

"No. I wanted to talk to you about Bill Jenkins."

He tensed and put his hands on the arms of his chair. "Wild Bill?"

"Yes."

"Whatever for? Bill's been dead for years."

"Yes, I know."

Somehow he seemed to relax again as he eased back in his chair. "What is it you wanted to know?"

"Well, I was just over in Bogalusa, talking to Bill's son, Dalton."

Adrian broke in. "How's he doing?"

I welcomed the chance to keep my weak story going. "All right, I guess. He looked healthy. He told me that you were the executor of Bill's will."

"That's true. Why are you interested in Bill?"

"Bill and I were good friends when we were kids together here in Franklinton. We palled around together in college–even went to a summer semester in Mexico. We ran into each other in the service, and my wife and I were witnesses to his marriage before we got married ourselves. So I guess we were pretty close, but I wasn't here when he was killed. We moved back to Louisiana not too long ago, and I got to thinking about Bill and wanted to know more about his family and his death."

Some of the tension seemed to leave him. He put his elbows on the arms of his chair and put his extended fingers together under his chin. "So what are you doing now?"

"I'm retired and just enjoying myself."

"You're not here in some official capacity?"

"No. Not at all–just interested. Were you friends with Bill too?"

"Yes. Probably in between the times that you knew him. We went to high school together and got into trouble every now and then. I think he used to talk about you after college–especially that Mexico trip. Wild Bill was a good name for him. He would do anything. People around here know everybody else's business, and it was hard not to get caught when you got out of line."

"Like what? What did he do?"

"Well, one time, some of the good citizens decided to raise a Confederate flag in front of the local community house. It was mostly women who traced their backgrounds to Civil War soldiers. Bill rode up on a horse and cut down the flag with a sword. Not that he was against the Confederacy. His favorite guise was the southern gentleman. I think he was just interested in creating a ruckus, and he knew that he could offend a lot of people who wouldn't make a big fuss. The feelings around here sometimes run counter to political correctness. Not long ago, the government made us take down the 'Jesus is Lord over Franklinton' signs that greeted you as you came into town. People countered by putting up signs in their yards."

I smiled at the flag story. "But you said you got into trouble together."

Adrian shifted in his chair. "I suspect Bill was a bad influence on me. I'd go along with just about everything he thought up to do. One time he got a hold of a plastic woman that used to be a department store dummy. We dressed it up in a slip and put catsup on it like it was blood. Then we would put it on the side of the road and redirect traffic to side streets. We did this a couple of nights and figured that our luck would run out if we continued much more. We took the dummy and threw it off the Bogue Chitto River Bridge so that some passing cars would see us. Apparently someone recognized Bill, and the police arrested him the next day. He spent the day in the courthouse jail, but no charges were pressed and he got out that night. You know, he never ratted on me. I think the police knew I was with him, but he never told them. I'll always be indebted to Bill for not telling. My Pappy would have skinned me alive if he had found out. That could have changed my life. Funny, how little escapes like that can make you turn things around. If I had been more religious, I think I would have joined the born agains."

That story sounded like Bill. "You must have been good friends with Bill or he wouldn't have trusted you to take care of his family's insurance payouts."

"Yes. That was a job in itself. I had to identify his body."

"How come you instead of the family?"

"The insurance company made me do it. Besides, I wanted to spare the family of that chore. That was one of the worst things I ever had to do. He was burned beyond recognition."

"That I hadn't heard. I had the old coroner's record read to me, and it did say something about extensive burning. They even were able to do a blood alcohol measurement."

Adrian looked at me funny as though he hadn't expected me to go to such lengths. "Maybe that was because the fire wasn't the cause of death. Apparently the cockpit area caught fire after the crash."

"I'm sorry. If he was burned beyond recognition, how did you identify him?"

He shifted again. "I think his clothing helped. This was during his Caribbean period, and he was wearing an island shirt. Nobody around here would wear that. Also, they found his diamond ring. Besides, a kid had seen him take off just before the crash."

I tried to remember what the man in the cemetery

had told me. "You said the insurance company made you identify the body?"

"Yeah. They weren't real happy about paying that much money without proof. This is all probably public record. Bill had taken out an unusual policy connected to his will. His will had a complicated codicil that paid me to make sure that his son got half the proceeds. The kid's money went into a trust until he was 18, and I paid him every month until he was thirty."

I thought for a moment. "But if Bill didn't know when he was going to die, how could you figure out how much to pay each month?"

"It was in equal payments. The money was divided into the number of months were left for Dalton to turn thirty. Fortunately, it came out pretty even each month. Unfortunately, Dalton started drinking in high school and then gambling. I doubt if he had anything left when the payments stopped. I bet he lived high on the hog for a while. His grandfather tried to help him out with a job, but that never worked out well either."

"Why was the insurance company so concerned?"

"For starters, it was a half million dollar policy. On top of that, since Bill died in an accident, it was double indemnity. That meant a million dollar payout. Ruth got half, and Dalton got half–minus my fee, of course."

"You spoke of his 'Caribbean period.' What was that?"

He smiled. "Bill liked to assume different backgrounds. When he first went to college, he used a British accent–called people 'old chap'. When he was aggravated it was bloody this and bloody that."

I interrupted. "I remember that."

"Right. And there for a while, he was all southern

gentleman. He wore white suits with string ties and sometimes cord suits like a New Orleans lawyer. He drank mint juleps and pretended he had more money that he had. He took to referring to black people as 'darkies'. His wife told him that was demeaning, and I think he quit; but that was a blow to his fake persona. With all his tricks, people were down on him around here. I think he was uncomfortable living in Franklinton. I know he didn't like selling cars."

"And his Caribbean period? What was that?"

"That started not too long before he died. He must have gone to the islands. Sometimes he would take off in that plane of his and be gone for a week or more."

"But he couldn't get clearance to fly to another country without a lot of red tape."

"Probably not. Maybe he just flew down to south Florida and took a boat. I didn't see a lot of him during that time. I know that his wife, Ruth, used to worry about him. But he would always come back, tanned and cheerful. He switched to rum drinks and started using an island accent. He would say things like 'Hey Mon' and 'don't worry' whenever he could. I tried to talk to him about his trips, but he would put me off. Ruth was an awfully nice woman. Bill shouldn't have treated her that way."

Something was worrying me about the casual way Bill's body was identified. "I know that we didn't have DNA forensics back then, but didn't they try to match his dental records?"

Adrian looked me right in the eye and seemed a trifle annoyed. "I guess there was no need. We had a positive ID, and there was no crime committed."

"You said you identified the shirt but also that he was badly burned. How come the shirt didn't burn too?"

Adrian continued his annoyed look. "Part of it got torn off and was hanging outside the cockpit on another piece of the plane. Why all these questions?"

I didn't want to turn him off. "I don't know. I guess I felt a little guilty that I hadn't found out earlier. Since I don't live around here, I didn't want to come all the way here and then leave without finding out all I could. It sounds like you took good care of Bill's affairs. I know he and I used to take trips together. Did you ever do that?"

"Do what?"

"Take trips with Bill."

"Occasionally. We flew to Dallas once. Bill had some kind of business there. He set me up in a hotel while he took care of it, and we flew back the next day."

I couldn't think of any more questions. Adrian gave me one of his business cards. We shook hands, and I took off for Clear Creek.

CHAPTER TEN

When I got back to the house, Ellen came out of the house to meet me. She reached out to hold my arm, looking distraught. "Sam, Tommy's dead."

I wasn't expecting that at all. "Oh, no. Was it the cancer?"

"No, it was an accident. Jim Simpson called. The funeral's day after tomorrow."

"Did Jim know what kind of accident?"

"He said Tommy ran off the road near his house."

My stomach sank. That damn van! If I hadn't gotten him involved with this Bill business, Tommy wouldn't have bought the van--wouldn't be driving–wouldn't have died. I felt terrible. I gave Ellen a hug and walked up the steps to the house.

She sensed I was upset and tried to change the subject. "What did you learn today?"

We sat down by the kitchen table. "Actually, quite a lot. Do you want to go to the funeral with me?"

Ellen wanted to get my mind off of Tommy. "Sure. Tell me what you learned in Franklinton."

"More than I'll remember tomorrow. Maybe I ought to write it down."

Ellen got up and brought me a pen and notepad from around the phone without saying anything.

I wrote down the date. "Tell you what. I'll just write down the highlights while I talk and later, I can fill in the details. First of all, I met an old playmate, someone I hadn't seen in well over fifty years. He said that Bill's wife was long gone from there, but he put me on to Bill's son, who was selling cars in Bogalusa." I wrote down the heading, leaving space for details. "The son told me about an old friend of Bill's still living in Franklinton, so I went back there to meet him. The friend had administered Bill's estate and had actually identified Bill's body." I pulled out the calling cards I had collected to get the names right.

Ellen leaned forward. "Why did he have to do that? Wasn't Bill's family around?"

"Well, for one thing, the body was badly burned." I put down exactly what I had heard in quotes. "The other thing was that he was Bill's insurance agent, and the insurer wanted some proof that it was really him. Apparently, Bill had just taken out a big policy, and the company was a little reluctant to put out a lot of money. Bill's son seemed to think that the agent made a lot of money off the deal."

Ellen leaned back again. "I'm glad that Bill thought to take care of his family. He never impressed me as being very responsible."

I smiled. "You're mostly right. His friend told me that Bill used to take off in his plane and disappear for a week or so."

Ellen got up and kissed me on the forehead. "Your supper's in the fridge. Why don't I warm it up, you have something to eat, and then get some rest? I know you've had a long day."

The next morning, I called Jim Simpson in Baton Rouge to find out when and where the funeral was going to be. Jim didn't know any more about the accident except that Tommy apparently had missed a bridge going into his neighborhood and fell into a slough full of water. I spent a lot of time that day writing down what I had found over the course of the investigation. I finally realized I needed to put it on a word processor on the computer. It turned out to be easier to compose than long hand and was much easier to edit. I didn't want to include all the stuff that Tommy had written connected with the Kennedy assassination, but his e-mail included his statements on Lindsey Scott, so I pasted the whole e-mail in too. When I finished, I printed out my notes and put them in a folder. Writing things down and reading them over helped me implant facts in my memory.

Tommy's funeral was at the Rabenhorst Home in downtown Baton Rouge. I found it easily enough and parked in the back. Tommy's room was the first on the left. I signed the book for Ellen and me at the entrance and walked in, searching to see if I knew anyone in a somewhat sparse crowd. I was prepared not to recognize former friends and to be properly embarrassed. Fortunately, three people stood out immediately. Jim Simpson, Bat Slocum, and Johnny Ray Harrington were standing in the space between pews about midway on the right. Jim's red hair, Bat's protruding ears, and Johnny's perennial flat top haircut identified my old high school buddies right away. Jim was talking over the back of one row to the other two who had their backs to us. Jim saw us and came into the aisle to shake hands. He remembered Ellen and said something about how hard it would be to keep me in line. Bat and Johnny Ray seemed genuinely glad to see us after so many years. None of them had brought their wives, even though Bat had married a girl we went to school with.

We talked for a few minutes. They all wanted me to join them hunting in a few weeks on Jim's place near Clinton. We had hunted doves and squirrels there in high school and college, but high water had forced a number of deer on the property several years ago, and the animals had taken up permanent residence there and were reproducing.

I asked Jim to point out Tommy's wife, Evelyn, to

me so that I could give her my condolences. I didn't really want to approach the casket. She was up front, talking to some other people. I nervously waited for my turn, rehearsing what I would say. When I did get to talk to her, she immediately recognized my name and was most gracious.

"Sam, I want to thank you for instilling a little animation in Tommy before he died. He had been so despondent over the last few years. Apparently the project you and he were working on spiked his interest and he became more like the Tommy of old. He worked on the computer constantly, was cheerful, and bought that van so he could get around."

She made me feel better, but I had to say it. "But that van was what killed him."

She put her hand on my arm, probably realizing what I was thinking. "That van was one of his favorite things. You would have had to see the difference in him after he got it. Those few weeks of happiness were the only ones he had in a long, long time."

I was embarrassed. "Still, I feel a little guilty—"

She squeezed my arm tighter. "Don't even think that way. You should be proud of having reached him at last. He thought a lot of you."

I suppressed tearing up. We talked for a while until I realized other people were waiting to talk to her. I excused myself and went back to where Ellen and my friends were waiting. I remained standing as we all did. "She seems like a nice lady."

Johnny Ray spoke up. "I didn't really get to know her that well." He looked at his companions who shook their heads, indicating the same experience. "Tommy must have liked her—he married her. Come to think of it, none of us had seen much of Tommy lately either. He seemed pretty negative about everything, so it was hard to talk to him. Then, too, the place where they lived was pretty isolated. It surprised all of us that he was driving. Did you get to see him after you all moved back?"

I put my hands on the back of the pew. "Actually, I did. I talked to him on the phone and visited with him twice in the last few weeks. He and I were doing a little research into the deaths of Wild Bill Jenkins and Dennis Dawson. Tommy turned out to be very good at it."

Jim seemed to perk up. "What kind of research? We had heard that there was something fishy about the way Dennis was killed, but I never heard anything more about Wild Bill except he had been drinking–as expected." He looked at his two friends for confirmation.

I didn't want to go through the whole thing again. "Maybe he wasn't–drinking I mean. The doctor's report indicated that he wasn't drunk, and I talked to a mechanic who said there was some gunk in the plane engine that probably caused the crash,"

Jim responded. "Couldn't that have happened naturally? Bill wasn't one to maintain his stuff too well, as I remember."

I agreed with the latter. "Except that the mechanic had just serviced the plane's engine before the accident. His theory was someone put something in the gas tank."

Jim pursed his lips. "Wow! That's heavy. If you've got this much, why don't you go to the police?"

"Good question. One thing, we didn't have a heck of a lot more than that. The other thing is that it happened so long ago, I doubt if anyone is interested except family and friends. Even if we could prove anything, the perpetrators probably died many years ago." I gave Bat a

125

little hit on the arm. "None of us are too young ourselves anymore. I'd be a little embarrassed to go to the police at this stage."

Jim pursued the point. "With Tommy gone, haven't you lost your collaborator? Don't you know anyone else with investigative experience?"

"Not really. I enlisted Tommy's help because he was a lawyer and knew Dennis."

Jim bit his lip in thought. "How about the guy that bought your mother's house? Wasn't he a policeman?"

"Don? You're right, he's a policeman all right. I hadn't thought about him helping with this. But you know, that would be a lot to ask from someone who didn't know any of us. Let me think about that a little more."

After the funeral, Ellen, Jim, Bat and I got a bite to eat. Johnny Ray had to get back home. My old friends were funny. They kidded me unmercifully and discussed some of our old shenanigans that I had never revealed to Ellen. She enjoyed every minute of it, especially if it made me appear foolish. They filled me in on some of the people we all knew. They seemed to know a lot more than Tommy had known in our similar conversation. Through the years, Jim had kept me up to date on deaths through letters and the internet. Many of the people I inquired about were in ill health – neurologic problems, arthritis, and emphysema, confined to nursing homes. It was a revelation as to how our class was aging and to how fortunate our gang had been. Jim and Bat talked about the hunting trip as though it was a done deal that I would go.

CHAPTER ELEVEN

When we got home from the funeral, I was exhausted. Ellen changed clothes and went out to work in the garden. I took off my tie and shoes and sat down in the big arm chair with the last beer in the refrigerator. Accidents. It seemed as though my thoughts were full of these mishaps lately. This one was particularly hard, maybe because it was so recent, maybe because I still felt responsible for Tommy buying the van. His wife was thoughtfully quick to absolve me of any blame. Perhaps she had been dreading Tommy's inevitable decline and pain. People who have cared for terminal cancer patients have suffered too. Tommy's sudden death avoided much of that misery for both of them.

Accidents. In my whole life, I have been in only three automobile accidents as a passenger. All three were with Bill Jenkins. One was in Raleigh, North Carolina. One was somewhere in North Louisiana. And one was in San Luis Potosi, Mexico. The one in Raleigh wasn't Bill's fault.

Late in our second semester at LSU, Jim Simpson and I concluded that college was seriously interfering with our night life. We decided to join the Marine Corps. As I look back, that was a very good decision. At that time, the Corps was offering two-year enlistments with full benefits. Fortunately, I acquired a discipline that I had never had before. Afterwards, I received four undeserved years of financial aid for education under the GI Bill, and my parents were spared the anguish of seeing me flunk out of college entirely.

Jim and I took the oath in New Orleans and were herded onto a train bound for the recruit depot in San Diego via Chicago. We were guarded to keep us from escaping or harming the paying passengers. Other cars of recruits from Chicago and Detroit were added and similarly quarantined. Boot camp was a unique experience. We were beaten for any perceived infraction by any member of the platoon. We felt really mean when we got out. After three months of discipline and physical conditioning, I remained in San Diego to go to communications school, and Jim was shipped off to Japan. Unbeknownst to us, Wild Bill had joined the Corps also, but in Shreveport. I think he stayed with an uncle in North Louisiana from time to time--especially when he wasn't getting along with his parents. He went to boot camp in South Carolina. I don't know why Bill joined the Marines--maybe he heard Jim and I talking about it. Certainly, none of us were candidates for the Dean's List at LSU and going into the service was an attractive option to school.

Anyway, armed with a certificate as a trained teletype operator, I was sent to Camp Geiger, North Carolina to become the message center chief for the 2nd Combat Service Group. Two other experienced Marines were in the message center when I got there, but they didn't seem to mind that I was their chief. I rarely ever had to exercise my shaky authority. Duty was almost like civilian life. Seldom did I have to do military things other than an occasional overnight bivouac or inspection. When I made corporal, I took the initiative to lead the battalion in calisthenics (I could stop when I got tired) and then march them to breakfast in the mornings. That was a little scary at times because the four abreast columns stretched for blocks, and the column left command had to be timed perfectly to turn the troops into the mess hall sidewalk. I had visions of marching hundreds of people into the ditch.

As it turned out, several other of our classmates had joined the Marines as well, and I managed to make contact with them accidentally. We made frequent forays to the series of bars that shielded the law-abiding citizens in Jacksonville from the mayhem perpetrated by the Marines on liberty. One cold night, three of us were sitting around one of the inefficient oil heaters in a hut when I mentioned that I recently had seen a blue and white Chevy identical to the one Bill had driven in Baton Rouge. One of my companions said it would be easy enough to verify by calling the Provost Marshall's office for the combined Camp Geiger/Camp Lejeune complex. He put in the call, and sure enough, a William Jenkins from Louisiana was stationed over at Mainside. We were able to contact him the next day.

Bill was happy to see old friends, and I was happy to know someone with a car who could get me out of the immediate environs of the base. We made several trips that cold winter. Once Bill stopped on a road at the edge of a small airfield and told me he wanted to show me something. We walked over to the fence and he pointed out a small, one-engine plane parked on the tarmac.

"What is it?" I asked.

Bill smiled confidently and said "It's a Bellanca. That's the kind of plane I'm going to buy when I get out."

"What would you do with it?"

He dropped his cigarette on the ground without field stripping it and stepped on it. "I could go anywhere I want. I could even take cargo and pick up a little money."

That sounded a little bit ambitious for the Bill I knew. "What kind of cargo?"

"Anything at all. No. I wouldn't take bibles.

Anything but bibles though."

Bill and I had never talked about religion. I doubt if he was really against carrying bibles. Perhaps he was thinking about flights to other countries and was averse to messing with other people's cultural beliefs. Maybe he was just emphasizing his willingness to ferry anything–just an extension of the wild persona he wished to convey. Anyhow, I had plenty of exposures to that side of Bill and didn't want to get him started. He was just as likely to try to demonstrate his wildness on the spot. Besides, it was cold.

We got back in the car and drove into Raleigh. Downtown, we stopped at a stop light. The car behind us slammed into the rear of the Chevy with a loud crash. When we got out, I could see that the windshield on the passenger side was broken in a large spider web pattern where someone's head had hit it. Indeed, a woman got out of the car with blood streaming down her forehead. The police came immediately, and the woman and her companion said they had to go into a nearby drug store and get something for her head. The policeman wanted to call an ambulance, but the woman didn't want to wait. They took off down the street. We waited for a while, but they never came back. I never found out whether they fled because the driver was drinking or the car was stolen. Bill must have straightened it out somehow, but as I look back, it was strange that our first wreck wasn't even Bill's fault. Bill didn't seem upset that the couple disappeared. The way he talked, he was more impressed by the fact that they got away with it with the police standing right there.

Our second wreck was after we got out of the Marine Corps and was almost predictable. The whole episode started in Baton Rouge when we were drinking at

Swifty's one Friday night after my work at the bank. Bill was proud of his friendship with Swifty and would pick me up or I would meet him there fairly often. I would go just to drink the Kuhmbaker beer that Swifty stocked. It was expensive, eighty-five cents a bottle, which was four times what I might spend with my other friends. Bottled beer was usually twenty-five cents in 1956; but when I went out with Jimmy Simpson, we'd choose a place that charged only twenty cents–even if we had to drive a few more miles.

This particular night, Bill must have had a lot more to drink than usual because he was staggering and slurring his speech. Ordinarily, it was hard to tell if Bill was drunk or not. He was arguing with Mrs. Swifty and trying to grab something out of her hand. I thought they were just kidding around, but Bill was serious and angry. I turned away from my Kuhmbaker. "What's going on?"

Bill looked at me sort of bleary-eyed. "She won't let me have my keys."

Mrs. Swifty was insistent. "He's too soused to drive."

Bill headed out the door and we all followed him. I asked Mrs. Swifty, "Where does he want to go?"

She looked anxious. "He wants to go to North Louisiana and pick up his dog."

Bill picked up a chunk of concrete and reared back as if to smash the driver's side window on his car.

I grabbed his arm. "What's the matter, Bill? Can't you wait to go tomorrow?"

"No. I'm going right now, and nobody's going to stop me."

I could tell he was in that stubborn mood and meant to follow through on his intention. "Here. Wait a minute. What if I drive you?"

His head was hanging down, but he raised up at the idea. "Honest. You promise? You're not going to try anything tricky?"

"I promise, but you're going to have to show me the way. Where is the dog, and why is this so important to get him right now?" I didn't even know Bill had a dog.

He slouched again and talked to the ground. "He's at my uncle's. That dog is the only thing that loves me." He was supporting himself with one hand on the side of the car.

Now that statement was a surprise. Bill didn't seem to have any trouble with women although he leaned toward the commercial type most of the time. We rarely double-dated, mostly because I wasn't anxious to expose my dates to Bill's wildness. Whatever we did together involve alcohol. I suspected that this outburst may have been due to a bad experience with one of the coeds at LSU. He had rejoined the fraternity when he got out of the Marines and already had gained a reputation for craziness. It wasn't hard to believe that had turned somebody off, and Bill couldn't stand rejection. Any kind of rejection could set off a tirade.

I got behind the wheel of the blue and white Chevy and opened the passenger's door for Bill. He got in and leaned over in the seat.

I reminded him. "You need to tell me where to go."

He didn't sit up, but mumbled toward the floor. "Take 190 across the Mississippi River Bridge and then take a right on 71."

That made sense if we were going to North Louisiana. I backed the car up. "How far 'til we hit 71?"

He straightened up a little and put his hands on the dashboard. "Not far. No, a good ways."

That helped a lot. I decided to drive until I saw a

sign for Highway 71, then I would ask him again. It was always a little scary driving over the old Mississippi River Bridge at Baton Rouge. Not as scary when I was driving, but scary enough. Highway 71 turned out to be a good ways, especially since I kept looking for it every few miles. I took a right as instructed and shook Bill to wake him up. I thought about testing him to see if he remembered the purpose of our trip. If he had forgotten, I could turn back. "Where are we going Bill?"

He looked up at me as if I had forgotten. "Going to get my dog."

"Yes I know that. We've turned on 71 already and I need to know how far to go."

"Long ways."

"Is 'long ways' past Alexandria, past Nachitoches?"

"Past Nachitoches."

Shit. Nachitoches was a long ways. I had gotten myself into more than I wanted to. "Bill, this is going to take all night." He didn't answer, and I was getting a little perturbed that he was sleeping and I wasn't. It seemed like I drove forever. As we passed through Nachitoches, I woke him again. "Okay, we're going through Nachitoches. Where to now?"

He seemed to be a little more alert and sat up. "Go to Campti and take a right."

Highway 480 crossed the road at Campti and Bill directed me to his uncle's house. I thought it was getting light. Bill jumped out of the car and opened a gate in a cyclone fence. A large dog came bounding out, obviously glad to see his master. He knelt down and the dog licked him all over the face. Bill opened the back door of the car and the dog jumped in.

I felt like we weren't finished. "Aren't you going to

tell your uncle that you picked up the dog?"

Bill was leaning over to the back seat and roughing up the dog's ears. "Don't want to wake them up. I'll call him in the morning. Let's go back to Baton Rouge."

After driving for a while, I decided that I was doing all the work. Bill was playing with the dog, and I had been up all night. I asked him if he felt all right to drive. He said he was fine, and I pulled off to the side of the road. We traded seats and I lay back to try to get some sleep. The sun was coming up. Bill gunned the car and tried to pass the first pickup truck we encountered. Unfortunately, the truck was turning left, and we slammed into the side of the bed.

I got out to see if the driver was all right. He was, but neither vehicles could be driven. Before long, a beat-up wrecker and a police car arrived. Bill got a ticket and he arranged for the car to be towed. I walked across the railroad tracks that paralleled the highway to the little town, looking for some place to get out from under the rising sun and get something to eat. The town looked dilapidated. It could use some paint. Several of the stores had high false facades on the front, as though they had been built a long time ago. Nothing was stirring. A service station was on the left. It had a bold sign announcing 24 hour road service. That must be where the wrecker came from. Next to that was a grocery store. On my side was a drug store (closed), and next to it, a glass-fronted building with a crude sign announcing that it was both a café and a bar. I tried the door. It was open, but no one seemed to be inside.

On the left side of a large, open space was a wooden bar. Behind the bar were racks of bottles—mostly liquors I didn't recognize. The ceiling was high with two electric fans suspended and barely moving. The floor was concrete, unpainted and crisscrossed with cracks. Three small tables vainly tried to fill the space in the open area. Things didn't look too clean. Someone was rattling pans in the back, which I presumed was the kitchen. I called out, "Hello!"

A voice from the back answered, "Who's there?"

I looked around at the poorly swept floor and decided to give him a jolt. "It's the man from the health department."

The voice didn't sound too perturbed. "There's no money in the register. Just take a bottle off the bar."

That wasn't what I wanted. I shouted again. "Can I get something to eat?"

A man wiping his hands on his apron came through a door at the end of bar and looked me up and down. "You must be new."

I didn't want to tick him off. "I was just kidding. I'm not from the health department. Could I get some breakfast?"

He pushed his belly up to the back of the bar and wiped up some imaginary moisture from the wooden surface with a rag he produced from his side. "Sure. What do you want?"

"I'd like some eggs and toast and a cup of coffee if I could."

He wrote down my order on a slip of paper "How would you like them eggs?"

"Scrambled, if you please."

"How many?"

"Eggs? Two."

"Sure. Have a seat. Pour your own coffee. It should be done now. " He nodded toward a pot on a burner near the back wall. White porcelain cups were stacked up beside it on a table. Sugar and a bunch of creamers were there too.

I poured the coffee and hoped the creamers had not

been there too long. I selected the middle table and sat down. The coffee was not too bad. I needed something because I was getting sleepy.

The man came back shortly, carrying a dish of scrambled eggs and two pieces of toast.

He sat down at the table and watched me eat. "I knew you weren't from the health department. My brother-in-law is the sanitarian in this part of the Parish. I knew you couldn't be him. You don't look too good. What happened?"

I scooped up the last of the eggs. "Actually, I've been driving all night. We just got into a wreck, and now we're stuck. I'm so sleepy, I can't see straight."

The guy picked up my plate. "Tell you what. If you want, just put your head on the table and catch a few winks. Nobody's going to come in this morning, and, if they do, there's plenty of room for them to sit down. You said 'we.' Have you got friends?"

"I've got one. He should be looking for me pretty soon." I don't know if he answered me. I put my head down and went to sleep instantly. When I woke up, I had slobbered on the table. Bill was sitting at the table, drinking a cup of coffee and watching me. I swept the slobber off the table with the back of my hand and asked: "Have I been asleep long?"

Bill took a draw on his cigarette. "Most of the morning, I guess. The dog has a bowl of water." He gestured toward the dog, which was lapping up water from a metal bowl on the concrete floor. "But I guess we all need something to eat. Our partner behind the counter is fixing me a tuna fish sandwich." He leaned forward and almost whispered. "We have a couple of friends here... "He jerked his head toward the next table. "Who want us to give them a ride to Baton Rouge? Trouble is, I can't persuade someone to come pick us up. They can't fix my car today, and we need a ride to get back home. I've been calling at the pay phone at the grocery store, but no one at the frat house is willing to come. Have you got any ideas?"

I wiped my mouth but didn't look back at the next table. No use in encouraging anyone. "I could call a few people, if I have their numbers." I pulled out my wallet and found numbers for Jim Simpson, Tommy, and 'Bat' Slocum on the back of Tommy's calling card. "Do I need coins for the pay phone?"

Bill turned out his pockets. "All I have is bills."

The bartender said: "I can make change."

Bill warned me. "Baton Rouge is long distance. It'll cost more than a nickel."

I got two dollars' worth of coins to make sure and went out into the bright sunshine to look for the grocery store. It was still there. The telephone operator came on the line and instructed me as to how much money was needed for the calls. Jim wasn't home and Tommy's parents said he was at the law library. Bat seemed interested. He finally said he would come if we could pay for some gas. I obligated Bill and went back to the restaurant.

"Good news." I said. "We got a ride with Bat Slocum. He thinks it will be about two hours until he gets here. I told him you would pay for the gas."

Bill seemed uninterested. He tore off a piece of sandwich and tossed it to the dog on the floor. The dog ate it and promptly threw up. Bill jumped to his feet and exclaimed; "Jesus! Sam, would you clean this up?"

I looked at the disgusting mess. "Not on your life. It's your dog. You clean it up."

Bill whined. "My stomach is upset. I'd probably

throw up too."

I walked over to the bar, careful not to step in the dog puke. The bartender was laughing. I tried to focus in on the bottles behind the bar. "Gimme a glass of bourbon, straight up."

The bartender wanted to know my brand. I told him Old Crow was good enough. He pulled out one of those heavy, barrel-shaped glasses that they usually serve water in and filled it half way with the Old Crow. He probably thought I was a rube and would pay anything for a lot of bourbon like that. Determined to call his bluff, I laid a single dollar bill on the bar. He gave me thirty-five cents change. This wasn't such a bad place after all.

The bartender came from behind the bar with some pieces of cardboard for Bill to scoop up the mess. I noticed that Bill turned his head away from his task to avoid the fumes. Skirting around him, I looked at the couple at the other table for the first time. He was thin, with dark hair, sported a three-day growth of beard and wore a John Deere hat. The woman looked to be in her forties, with sagging breasts. She wore a dress that had the consistency of crepe. She smiled at me beguilingly. A large gap was evident between her two front teeth. I gave a small smile in return and sat down. I should not have acknowledged the smile, because they both moved their chairs closer to me.

The woman led off. "Your friend says that you're going to Baton Rouge."

I looked at their table to see if maybe Bill had bought them a drink. He hadn't. "We're trying to get a ride now."

She exposed her gap again. "Do you think we could tag along?"

I didn't want to be impolite. "That would have to be up to the guy who picks us up. But you have to know that there would be three of us and a dog. I doubt if my friend has a car big enough for two more people."

She heaved her ample breasts. "But you wouldn't have an objection if there is room?"

What could I say? "It really wouldn't be up to me." I sipped on my bourbon and winced as I regretted not asking for ice. If I continued to be macho, I'd probably have to drink the whole damn thing and burn my throat out. Maybe if I just sipped it. The couple continued to make small talk, and I answered as briefly as possible. Finally, I got through the glass of bourbon. Actually, it wasn't too bad, and I was feeling a warm glow. Bill found a piece of rope that he tied to the dog's collar and announced: "I'm going for a walk and try to find some dog food."

With some degree of malice, he left me alone with the couple, who seemed to be edging closer. I got up and went over to the bar with my empty glass. "I'd like another of these, but with some ice."

The barkeep obliged me by scooping up some ice in the glass from behind the counter before he added the bourbon. I guessed that was better than handling the ice with his hands. I gave it a sip and found it to be much more palatable. I was feeling pretty good. It really wasn't the custom for us to tip bartenders, but I laid a dollar bill on the bar and magnanimously waved off the change. As I weaved my way back to the table, I noticed that the woman must have tightened her bra straps and loosed a few buttons, because her breasts were much perkier now and she was showing some cleavage. I sat down and tried not to stare, but when I did look back at her, it was to note that the gap between her teeth had miraculously diminished. Very odd.

My eyes must have been playing tricks on me. I

tried to fix on the bar and not look at the woman if I could help it. Each time I looked back at her, the gap was less. I wondered if I could actually see the teeth move, but I didn't want to stare. The woman wasn't anywhere near as old as I had thought.

Bill came back by himself after a while. I asked him where the dog was, but had to repeat it when he didn't understand me. He said he had tied the dog to a bench outside. He saw that I still was drinking, so he went to the bar to get a beer. Bill wouldn't be outdone by anyone–especially if he could appear to be wild. When he came back to the table, I wanted to point out the woman's dental miracle but felt that might be impolite, seeing that they were close enough to overhear. We just sat there for a couple of hours except for a few trips to the bathroom. I wanted to be friends with the woman but had trouble making conversation.

Bill wasn't talking much either. I swirled the ice around in my drink and tried to start something. "Actually, this hasn't been such a bad trip." I was glowing.

Bill wasn't amused. "Easy for you to say. I'm stuck with all this mess."

Things didn't look too bad to me. "What do you mean?"

He took a slug of beer. "Well, for one thing, I'm stuck with that damn dog. There's no way I can keep him at the fraternity house." It looked like Bill had sobered up and was being rational.

I tried to avoid looking at him in his eyes. There was no way I was going to take care of the dog either. Best to change the subject. "What else?"

"What else? That guy in the pickup will probably sue me. My car is wrecked and I have to not only pay my deductible but also come get the car when it's ready. I wish I could just disappear and forget about all this."

I wasn't too sympathetic. "People can't just disappear."

He rejoined: "Harry Lime did."

"Who's Harry Lime?"

"He was the hero in a movie *The Third Man*."

I remembered. Good movie. "But he wasn't the hero. He wasn't even the main character. He didn't show up until the end of the movie. If I had to say, I'd say he was the villain. How did he disappear anyhow?"

"Everybody thought he was dead. He made his mistake by hanging around Vienna. He would have gotten away with it if he'd gone somewhere else. All his troubles would have been gone. His nosy buddy found him by accident."

I was ready for an argument. "How do you know he would have gotten away?"

He hung his head. "I just know."

That wasn't very convincing to me. "Bill, that movie was fiction. The author could have done anything he wanted to—magic, even. The action doesn't even have to be feasible. It's hard for someone just to disappear."

Bill had to have the last say. "If he wasn't the main character, how come they named the movie *The Third Man*.? There wouldn't have been a movie if Harry Lime hadn't pulled off a good ruse."

Finally, Bat showed up. I was happy to see him and to realize that I didn't have to go to work at the bank that night, because it was Saturday. Still, it was hard to leave the beautiful woman at the next table.

CHAPTER TWELVE

1958

Our last wreck together was a small part of a larger story, but the story provides considerable insight into Bill's personality. It all started with music. Dennis Dawson lived for a while in a trailer off Nicholson Drive just north of the LSU campus. Bill and I would visit with Dennis every now and then, drinking and listening to a first-rate stereo player that Dennis owned. I think it was a Pilot. Dennis mostly liked classical music, but Bill would bring records of bold music that spoke eloquently about Mexico. If I got bored, I would go out to a wire fence at the back of Denise's lot and talk to an old brown horse that lived in the field. As might be expected, we called the horse Brownie. I got up the nerve a couple of times to try to ride Brownie, but wasn't skilled enough to stay aboard very long. Not that Brownie was overly active, he (or she) would just walk around after I jumped on him from the fence. Just that gentle motion was enough to make me slowly slip and finally fall off in the tall grass. Not only that, Brownie's long hair was shedding and managed to get all over my suit. Back in those days we wore suits a lot, especially on dates and to football games.

Bill had two 78 rpm records in particular that he would like to play. He kept them at the trailer because he was afraid they would get broken at the fraternity house. One was an album by the Banda Taurina that performed in the bullfighting Plaza de Toros in Mexico City. The piece that I liked best was "La Virgen de Macarena" which was full of brass and drums and cymbals and very dramatic. Boom! Boom! The trailer would vibrate to the crashing sounds emanating from Dennis's large speakers. Just listening to it made one feel very brave. Enveloped in a cloud of alcoholic euphoria, I could imagine myself in the bullring. "El Gato Montez" swayed with each passing of the bull, and the crowd sounds built to a crescendo just as the bull slipped by the matador, signaling a successful feint with the cape. The plaintive sounds of the trumpet solo in "El Relicario" symbolized the mortal risks facing the toreadors at the very beginning of the drama.

The other record contained several mariachi or ranchero songs by an artist named Miguel Aceves Mejia. Miguel's songs were full of passion punctuated with shouts and crying. He was a master of falsetto which blended well with popular songs such as "Malagueña Salarosa". The song that Bill liked best was one called "La Cama de Piedra," which I think was about a guy in prison awaiting execution.

Bill would sit drinking a beer, mesmerized by the music. His eyes closed, his head would sway slightly to the beat. One evening I asked him: "Where did you acquire a taste for this kind of music? Have you ever been to Mexico?"

He didn't open his eyes. "A friend of mine went down last year and brought me the Mejia record. I've been across the border in Nueva Laredo a couple of times. It's great down there. You can do anything that you want." That was very much in keeping with Bill's concept of Utopia.

I thought for a few seconds. I had been taking a Spanish class but wasn't very good at understanding the language. My instructor had been promoting the department's special offerings. "Why don't we go to summer school in Mexico City? LSU has a program there

144

this year. The credits are straightforward, and the GI Bill pays just the same as it does here. I understand the cost of living is a lot cheaper too." I knew this from experience because I had gone to Mexico City College the first summer after I got out of the Marine Corps.

Bill perked up. He got up and actually turned down the volume on the phonograph. "Splendid idea, old chap! I'm game. Look into it for me."

That meant I should make all the arrangements. "Sure. I'll check with the department office on Monday. If we can get to Laredo, there's a train that goes all the way to Mexico City." My friends and I had made that trip on our way to summer school at the College. Our train had been 18 hours late getting into Mexico City. We didn't have sleepers and had to catch naps sitting on the slatted wooden benches that passed for seats. My cheapskate nature and poor Spanish skills had gotten us second class accommodations. The only thing that saved us was that I jumped off the train and purchased a tub of ice and some beer at one of our frequent stops. Not only did the beer furnish us with much needed hydration, but it made us the hit of our section of the train. I bought much too much. My impression was that the train stopped every time the engineer spotted someone walking beside the tracks in the desert. I still remember the heat.

Bill didn't like that idea. "No, no. I'll drive. I'll get a different car and make sure it's adjusted for the lower octane gas down there. That way we have a way to get around when we want to. I've driven to Laredo before. It's no big deal."

Remembering my experience with the train, this sounded like a much better plan. The next week, I did go to the Spanish department at school. The receptionist referred me to one of the professors who would be teaching the summer session in Mexico City. Professor Thompson was a portly gentleman with thinning gray hair. He looked down over his glasses at me as though to size me up but seemed very pleased that enrollment was reaching the point to make the class feasible. I believe he would have taken anyone even before analyzing my miserable grades. "If your friend signs up, we'll have enough students to make a go of it. We not only have people from LSU, but some students from Arizona who will join us. I would suggest that you stay with a Mexican family. That way, you'll learn the language and culture much better."

He seemed a bit disappointed that we had opted to drive down and rent our own apartment. He was right about the family, of course, but he was mistaken in his initial belief that we actually wanted to learn anything. I was delighted to hear that most of the students would be female. Professor Thompson was very helpful in setting up my enrollment. I just had to go to the Bursar's office to pay up and make the arrangements for my GI Bill payments. When I added up my obligations, I realized that I didn't really have enough money to live like I wanted. The first month would be tough. I told the office official that I would be back to pay later.

Since I would have to cancel my job for the summer, it seemed like the only way to bolster my finances was to gamble. I figured it would take just another $100 to get me started. If I won, the trip was on. If I lost, I would only be out the 10 dollars left in my pocket, and I could continue to work and save up for next year. Bill would be disappointed, but such was life. In those days, the only accessible gambling in Baton Rouge for college kids was the pinball machines. Every bar had one or several. A person could cash in the number of games won for a nickel a piece. The most popular gambling devices had a series of numbered holes running across the bed of the machine under a clear glass. Several rows of these holes progressed down the inclined bed to the bottom of the playing area. The object was to propel a metal ball to the top of the bed and try to make it fall in a particular hole that was predetermined each play. A player would get only one ball a game. Odds for settling in the winning hole were also displayed. The farther the ball would fall down the rows, the higher the odds would be for the payoff. After my previous (mostly losing) experiences with these machines, it became obvious that the odds were the most important aspect of the games. By dropping additional nickels in a slot, one could theoretically raise the odds. Theoretically, because additional nickels did not guarantee the odds would go up. Past a certain point, more money in the slot was a waste. I determined that the more games one won on a play, the less likely the odds would go up on the next play. The other odd thing about the odds was that they were expressed in odd numbers. That is, instead of displaying 100 games awarded for a large win, the next nearest odds were 96. What did that tell you? People were likely to strive for 100 games rounded off to win 5 dollars, but the machine was less likely to offer better odds if the player was winning already.

Armed with this knowledge, I decided to play one machine until I had won 96 games, cash in, and then go to another machine. I started on Highland Road on the town side of campus. The first bar had three of the gambling machines. I got a beer, a dollar's worth of nickels, and took a deep breath. I tried not to think about the importance of my mission. Perhaps I could earn the requisite hundred dollars without risking my last ten? No, not enough time.

Drinking beer probably wasn't a good idea for staying lucid. Slowly sipping was a good strategy.

I purposely wasted the first nickel to judge the tilt sensitivity of the machine. Between each of the holes was a small post. One could guide the path of the ball by hitting the rear of the machine with the palms of the hands just as it touched a post. It wasn't perfect, but a little skill could influence the descent by avoiding non-winning holes. Conversely, a sharp hit could propel the ball upwards toward a desired hole, even if it was a lesser payoff than one on a lower row. Winning anything was better than the alternative. Noting the degree of pull on the plunger that shot the ball into the playing area was also important. The payoff holes would be lined up vertically, and entering the maze at the right spot could increase the chances of hitting one. After the first launch, I kept hitting the back of the machine harder and harder until it lit up the "tilt" sign and stopped play.

My strategy was successful. After just a few minutes of play, the counter showed that I had won 96 games with a minimum investment of nickels. I called the bartender over and asked him to cash me in. He reached under the machine, punched a button to the remove the games on the counter, and gave me $4.80. While playing the adjacent machine, I smirked a bit as the kid playing my first machine had great difficulty raising the odds.

Over the next two days, I won $110–as much as I could have earned in a month at the bank. It was probably luck because I never did that well again after we got back from Mexico.

Wild Bill came through and paid his tuition. He arranged to meet me a full five days before the summer session was scheduled to begin so we would have time to drive to Mexico City and rent an apartment. He surprised me by driving up to my place in a late-model green Cadillac. As I loaded up what might be too much luggage, I remarked, "We won't get much gas mileage in this thing."

"Don't worry," he replied. "Gas is cheap in Mexico. We'll spend the night in Laredo."

"Isn't that a long way?"

"Nope. It's only 544 miles from here."

That figured to be at least 10 hours, stopping to eat and everything. On top of that, we were starting late at night. Bill must have had a hard night the previous day because he asked me to drive as soon as we hit the Texas border. He went to sleep immediately. After we cleared the cities, some of the Texas highways were straight as an arrow. I gunned the Caddy close to 100 through the desert during the night with no other cars on the highway. Up ahead, in the headlights, it looked like the highway was covered in something moving. Long-eared jackrabbits were all over the road. I braced myself for the impact, but they parted like the Red Sea, leaving a path before me. A lone cottontail, distinguished by his small size and short ears, panicked and ran in a big circle to come back directly in front of the car. Thonk! Silly bunny!

I was dead tired when we pulled into Laredo the next morning. The motel wouldn't let us check in until 1pm. Bill acted responsibly during our down time and went to the Sanborn's office to get maps and insurance. The Sanborn's office had a large sign proclaiming "Mexican Insurance" and "Yankee spoken here." After we got into the motel, Bill let me sleep for several hours before he got antsy to go again. He shook me awake. "Come on, old chap. I want to show you a place I know in Nuevo Laredo. I know you'll like it."

We paid twenty-five cents each and crossed over the bridge into Mexico. Bill drove up and down some dirt streets until he recognized the building we were looking for. "This is it!" he exclaimed. He was right. I did like it. It was a two-story adobe house with an entrance through a wall into a patio, and cooler than I would have guessed. Large banana trees bordered the patio and gave shade, as did a tile-roofed overhang that protected the bar. We walked through a door beside the bar. Inside was a dance floor with a few tables and a jukebox. Two young girls jumped up from where they were sitting with their heads on a table when they saw us come in out of the sunlight. They looked genuinely happy to see us, probably because they didn't expect customers so early in the morning.

The girls begged some American coins from Bill to play the jukebox. We selected some slow English-language songs and danced and drank Superior beer before we went upstairs. It was an altogether pleasant day. Maybe it was because we were the only people in the place that everything seemed so laid back. The girls laughed often, but in a soft way that didn't break the mood. It was obvious that they were having a good time too. Later, in the large communal shower on the roof, I noticed Bill's girl was pregnant.

Back in the car, I told Bill that this aspect of Mexico seemed pretty good but wondered if places like this could get rough late at night. I was looking at the neighborhood, with its poor houses and dirt streets. Bill was nonplused. "Sure, but we can handle ourselves. Look in the glove compartment."

I did and pulled out a pistol. "What is this?"

"It's a Colt .32 caliber pistol. One of my buddies in Washington Parish is a gun collector, and he loaned me this to take on the trip."

I turned the weapon over. "Is it loaded?"

Bill reached over to take it from me, but I pulled it away so he could concentrate on maneuvering around the tight corners. He looked back on the road. "It sure is. The bullets are in the clip, but I was going to show you how to get one in the magazine before it will fire."

I held the gun to the side, away from him. "Just tell me."

"Well, take your thumb and slide that little catch down on the left side above the grip."

I did. "Will it fire now?"

"No. You have to get one of the cartridges up. Hold on to the handle–but not on the trigger, and pull the whole top of the pistol back toward you. A spring in the clip will push the top cartridge up, and when you release the top, it pops back into place, and the cartridge slides into the chamber. It will fire every time you pull the trigger, and the spent shell casings will flip out to the side. Just like your M-1 did in the Marines."

"How many bullets in the clip?"

"Eight."

I didn't go through the motions and replaced the pistol in the glove compartment.

When we got back to the motel, Bill asked the desk to give us an early wake-up call. He seemed eager to get on with the trip. "I figure we can make another 500 miles and spend tonight in San Luis Potosi. With both of us driving, we can make that easy."

Our early wake-up didn't get us out of Nuevo Laredo as quickly as we thought. The bank wasn't open yet to exchange dollars for pesos. After the bridge, we followed the signs to a big government building on the right and parked in the rear. When we finally got inside, things went slowly. We both declared our religion was Catholic on our Tourist Card applications, thinking that would be of some help if we got stopped by the policia. I was a bit apprehensive about the officials discovering the pistol during the perfunctory search of the car, but they never opened the glove compartment. Finally, we were able to get out and skip the baggage inspection by distributing a few dollars. We got on the main drag and headed toward Monterrey. In about a half hour, we had to stop again for a Customs Check, but our papers seemed to be in order and we were waved on.

For over a half hour, we passed through the same-looking scenery. Then we passed over a narrow bridge over a river and began to climb. When we reached the top, the land stretched out flat like a tabletop. The terrain changed dramatically. Even the air seemed fresher up high. Cacti dotted the landscape just like a Mexican post card. We both shouted spontaneously in joy at the sight. We were really in Mexico!

Later on, the flat desert was crossed by deep cuts. Then, less than three hours out of Nuevo Laredo, we could see Saddleback Mountain in the distance, signaling that we were closing on Monterrey. Monterrey proved bigger than we thought, and we had a nice lunch in a hotel. The people there were very helpful, giving us directions to get some money exchanged and how to reach the road to Mexico City. Good thing too! Many streets were one-way in the wrong way. We probably would have missed our turns without some help. Fortunately, we flanked a river for a few blocks and crossed a bridge that put us back on Mexican Highway 85 heading south.

We began climbing again. Sometimes we would dip

a little, but mostly we were going up. Saltillo was considerably higher than Monterrey—over 4,000 feet higher but only about an hour away. We came into town and saw our first bull ring off to the right. Somehow, we missed our turn to Matehuala and started running into poor neighborhoods with dirt streets. Bill was driving and being very cautious. People on the streets looked a little hostile. We felt a little self-conscious driving an expensive car in an obviously depressed area. The map was of no help, but we knew that we needed to backtrack to get to our highway. Bill took three lefts, hoping to get to the road that got us where we were. With no sidewalks, the local residents were using the streets to get around. Bill hit a dog. My stomach sank. Everyone looked around at the yelping. We didn't dare stop. I thought we were going to be attacked, but people just stared at us as we made our way back to our missed turn. Finally, we saw a sign for Highway 57 and started back south again.

We stopped for gas right out of town because the map didn't show much in the way of settlements for the next three hours. Heeding the advice we had received at Sanborn's, we watched the attendant carefully and checked the meter on the pump before we paid. Everything seemed fine. Maybe we were being too cautious. We had run out of our U.S. cigarettes and bought Mexican Rialtos inside the station. I remembered that I didn't like them very much. It's probably just what an American is used to. My senses recalled how the Rialto smell had permeated the trains on my previous trip. Back in the car, the familiar smell came back, but we had to smoke.

Bill held his Rialto between his teeth as he was wont to do, and after a while, I noticed he was slowing down. Out my window on the right was the same desert landscape, and there was nothing on the highway. He turned left through the sand. An old adobe building with a high false front was sitting alone in the desolation in front of us, although I could detect some huts some distance in the back, and a power line ran beside the road. Hand-painted on the false front of the adobe building was the word "CANTINA." I had taught Bill the meaning of that word back in Nueva Laredo. He was smiling around his cigarette but managed to mumble through his teeth: "Come on, old chap. Let's see what a real Mexican bar looks like!"

It was blazing hot as we exited the air-conditioned car. Bill must have been right about the authenticity of the *cantina*. No touristy place here! The swinging half doors were a trifle askew and squeaked loudly as we passed through. The large room was lit with a single, naked light bulb hanging from the ceiling. The temperature seemed slightly cooler in the shade. Opposite the front doors through the back wall was a passage that may have led to a patio, but it was nearly blocked with equipment that looked like wooden plows. A short, crude bar lined the back wall to our right. Two handmade tables graced a floor that was indistinguishable from the sand outside. We blinked to get accustomed to the darkness of the interior. One table to our left was empty. The other table was occupied by three old gentlemen in white straw hats. They had no bottles or glasses in front of them. Their hair was mostly white and contrasted nicely with their brown, weather-worn faces. Their shirts and pajama-like trousers were white as well. We nodded to them, and they nodded back, respectfully. The bartender was dark-skinned and sported a large handlebar mustache. He looked to be about 40–some thirty years younger than his three old customers.

We strode up to the bar and ordered two Coronas in

Spanish and confirmed our request by holding up two fingers. The bartender fished them out of a chest below the counter and opened them for us. The chest must have had ice in it at some time, because the bottles were wet, but not very cold. I wondered how sanitary the water might be, but decided just to limit the contact between my mouth and the bottle. We wiped off the bottle tops with our shirts, sat down at the empty table, and tried to survey our surroundings. The mud-brick walls were completely blank, no advertisements or posters. The cantina was mostly open space. The light bulb was hanging on a thin cord which was looped along the high ceiling and disappeared through the wall beside the bar. The place looked like a set from a western movie

Every time we looked at the old men, they would smile and nod their heads reverently. After a couple of swigs of his Corona, Bill got up and went to the bar. Through gestures, he managed to buy three beers for the old gentlemen. The bartender delivered the bottles to their table. The bottles weren't clear like Coronas, so the bartender must have known what the old men liked.

We had made friends for life! They held up their beers in salute and gave us a loud *gracias*, displaying broad smiles that sometimes lacked teeth. After a minute one of the old men came over to our table. He took off his hat and gave us another *gracias*. With my poor Spanish, I tried to translate what he was saying for Bill. The man spoke slowly but seemed to think we could understand him. He wanted to know where we came from. We told him, but I don't think he understood "Louisiana." With his hat, he motioned toward the opening at the back of the cantina and swept his left hand repeatedly as though we should follow him. Bill got up and walked with the old man. Somehow, the bartender and one of the other men had produced two roosters inside the opening. Both birds had restraining cords around their necks. The roosters made loud cackling noises and tried to attack each other. They were ferocious and jumped into the air using their wings. The men held them back so they couldn't hurt each other, but I'm sure they would have fought to the death had they not been restrained. Bill said *"Gracias"* and pointed to the chickens in appreciation for the show.

He turned to me and asked how to tell the men that he liked ranchero music. I got up, pointed to my friend and slowly said something like: *"Le gusta la musica ranchera."* I wasn't really sure that they understood me, but they discussed something for a few minutes and two of them disappeared through the swinging doors. We sat down again and waited through an awkward silence, while the remaining old man smiled at us periodically. After a while, the other two men returned, carrying crude musical instruments–a small guitar, a large guitar, and a violin. I swear the violin looked as though it had been made out of a cigar box because the part below the neck was more rectangular than anything. After a bit of tuning, the men began to play. I was hoping for something fast, but their music was slow and not very melodic. However, it was preferable to their singing. Everyone sang the same notes, with no attempt at harmony. The violin player dropped his instrument from under his chin when he sang.

As they sang, they kept their eyes rolled upwards. On every high or particularly loud note, they would rise up on their sandaled toes. We had to admire their effort, and applauded loudly when we thought they had finished. They all had embarrassed smiles and started to pick up their instruments to play again. Bill tried to head them off before they began. "Tell them I like Miguel Aceves Mejia."

I used the same "*Le gusta*" phrase and guessed they would play something we knew. One of the men gathered together the instruments and disappeared again. Again we were left with an uncomfortable silence. When the man came back, he was carrying a small suitcase. He set it on our table and opened it up. It was a phonograph with one 78 rpm record on the turntable. He slid our table under the light source, stood on a chair, and unscrewed the light bulb. Then he inserted an outlet piece in the receptacle, attached a short extension cord, and plugged in the phonograph. He seemed pleased and a little surprised when the ancient phonograph began to function, the record was, indeed, by Miguel. He sang a scratchy version of *La Cama de Piedra* as the disk wobbled on the turn table. We were amazed and honored that these men went to such lengths to please us strangers. But it was time to go. We had a long way if we wanted to make San Luis Potosi that night.

Bill was in a zone when we got back in the car. "You know, I could live in a place like this. Someone could live like a king here with just a few dollars a month. If people are this nice all over rural Mexico, I'd be perfectly satisfied. Maybe a place nearer the water would be better. I wouldn't mind something isolated, like an island."

Even though he sounded serious, I doubted that Bill would have much patience in a place without the finer things of life. The road went up and down a bit and it was beginning to get dark. Trees were appearing out of the desert. Bill cut on his lights. Just around a curve we saw a line of men in white clothing, completely blocking the highway. One of them stepped out of the line toward us and signaled for us to stop. I spotted a paved road to our right, leading slightly upward. "Quick!" I yelled to Bill. "Turn right!"

He did, screeching the tires. To our dismay, the road ended in less than a hundred yards in a cul de sac—a deserted scenic overlook. The men must have planned it that way and meant to ambush us when we stopped. I yelled again: "Turn around and gun it. Don't stop for anything—even if you have to hit someone." Bill turned, but had to put it in reverse to gain enough room to change direction. I opened the glove compartment, pulled out the pistol, and jerked back the top of the gun to load a cartridge. Without thinking, I rolled down the window and leaned out. Sure enough, the men had re-formed a line across the side road, blocking us from the highway. I got off a shot over their heads, a metallic sound with sparks showering in the darkness. "Don't stop!" I feared opening the window was a mistake, and they would jump on the car and grab my gun arm. Fortunately, they parted like the jack rabbits, jumping out of the way at the last moment. I had visions of a lone cottontail getting in our way, but that didn't happen. I don't think we hit any of them, but I could see as we passed that they were just boys—teenagers. The only weapons I saw were machetes. Some of the boys wore big hats, some had no shirts, and most were barefooted.

Bill got back to the highway and took a sharp right. I looked back through the rear window. The group was hurrying back on the highway, but they would never catch us. I settled back and returned the pistol to the glove compartment. "Well, I guess we have seen two sides of the Mexicans today. Maybe this is why we were warned not to drive at night." I turned to Bill. "Do you think maybe that was just something innocent? Maybe they had a sick relative that they were trying to get to a doctor and just needed some help."

Bill didn't look at me. He was trying to light a cigarette with one hand while still steering the car. "Don't be an idiot. Why do you think they were carrying machetes? That was great! Let's go back and try again."

He was joking of course. I should have expected Bill to say something like that. The danger had excited him. The experience was like the matador letting the bull come close to him. The interior of the car glowed as he pulled hard on his cigarette. I almost could see him smiling in the semi-darkness.

I was still shaking from the experience. "What do you think would have happened if we had stopped the car? Do you think they would have cut us up with those machetes?"

Bill took the cigarette out of his mouth and gripped the steering wheel with both hands, the cigarette sticking out between his knuckles. "No. That would have been stupid. They would have killed us all right, but they would make it look like an accident. I believe they would have knocked us over the head, taken most everything of value, and run the car with us in it over one of these cliffs with us in it. He swerved the car to make the point.

That sounded plausible to me. "You mean our bodies would have burned in the crash, leaving no clues for the police?"

Bill pulled on his cigarette again. "Not unless those banditos did something to make the car burn. That business of cars crashing and burning every time is probably mostly Hollywood. I don't know exactly how they could start the fire, but if I had enough time, I wager I could figure it out."

He always pronounced "out" as though it were "oot." Bill wasn't very mechanical, to my knowledge (never worked and never will), but he was extremely confident in his mental abilities.

The rest of the trip to Matehuala was uneventful. We stopped for gas, and learned that San Luis Potosi was still 120 miles away. Although there were some nice places to stay in Matehuala, Bill wanted to push on. His schedule was to get to Potosi tonight and that was what we were going to do–even if we had to drive at night. I was getting a headache and didn't care much what we did. The headache got worse, even though I dozed off a few times. Finally, I could tell by the lights outside the car that we were entering a city. I cupped my hand on my forehead to shield my eyes from the lights as we stopped. "Are we at a motel?"

Bill was getting out of the car. "No. A cantina. I need a drink."

I was discouraged and lay my head against the door, thankful for the small coolness of the metal parts around the window. I either went to sleep or passed out from the pain, but I was awakened by a knocking on the glass. Two men were standing outside, obviously agitated. I rolled down the window part way, expecting a request for a handout or worse. One of the men was wearing a mechanic's jump suit, smeared with and smelling of oil.

"Señor. Come quick. Your friend is in trouble inside the cantina and will not leave."

I was still in pain. "What do you want me to do?"

"Come tell him to leave,"

"I can't come. I have a *dolor de cabeza*. You tell him I want him to come out."

They left, and I tried to get comfortable with my misery. A few minutes later, they came back. "Your friend has trouble. Bad man has the knife."

This did sound bad. Maybe they just wanted to get me out of the car. Nevertheless, I opened the door and gazed around hopelessly until the two men guided me to the door of the cantina. The light inside hurt my eyes. Bill was leaning on the bar with his back to me. I didn't see the bad man or at least didn't recognize him. I grabbed Bill by the arm. "Come on Bill, we need to get out of here."

Bill jerked his arm back. "No. Everything is fine. I'm staying."

I had to think quickly. "The police are coming to take you away. We'll never get to Mexico City."

Bill reluctantly took a final swig of beer, wiped off his mouth with his arm, and said angrily: "All right. All right. Let's go." He stalked out of the bar, jumped into the Cadillac, and slammed the door. I barely had time to get in before we shot off into the darkness. He was driving fast, reminding me of the time he wrecked in North Louisiana. Sure enough, we hit something hard and spun to the right side. The engine killed. Bill got the car started, but it wouldn't back up.

I got out to survey the damage. In the light of the one head lamp that was burning, I could see that we had hit a concrete block that supported a clock situated on the corner of a park of some sort. The front end of the Cadillac was bent in, probably binding the tires, which was the reason the car would not back up. I had been in a similar kind of jam before and knew that I should try to find the police before they found us. It always looks better if you pretend like you are seeking their help. A few people were gathering around. I hoped they hadn't come from the cantina, but guessed we had gone far enough to outdistance them. My headache was greatly lessened. I grabbed one of the bystanders by the arm. *"Donde esta la policia?"*

He led me for a few blocks where we encountered a distinguished-looking man in an expensive cowboy hat and a leather coat. He spoke perfect English and informed me that he was a sheriff. I told him my friend had missed a turn and hit something on the edge of the park. When we got back to the car, Bill was lying on the front seat. I thought I smelled gunpowder. Wonderful. That son of a bitch had shot himself and left me with this mess. I shook him violently, and, much to my relief, he stirred.

A car came and took us to a police station. While they were trying to talk to Bill, I went into a cell and lay down on a bench. I wasn't really sure where I was when I woke up the next morning. My headache was gone, but my neck had a serious crick from sleeping on the hard bench. I sat up and marveled that I hadn't rolled off the bench during the night. It must have been early, because I thought I heard a rooster crow. Since no one was around inside, I went through the open cell door and out into the yard in front of the police station. I stretched and turned my head from side to side to loosen up the crick.

Bill was there in the yard, standing with his arms folded while a crew attempted to pull the body of the car away from the front tires. They had tied the front bumper to a large stump and were pulling on the back of the car with a wrecker. The Cadillac almost came off the ground as the wrecker moved forward. However, the plan worked, and the tires were free from the fenders. The front end was a mess, with tears in the metal and a smashed headlamp.

I fished out a Rialto and walked up to Bill. "What now? Is the car drivable?" The Rialto was just as strong as I remembered. I had a nasty taste in my mouth and wanted to brush my teeth.

He sighed and pointed at the crew working on the car. "I think so. These chaps told me it started this morning and the only thing wrong was that the tires were bound.

They hauled it here with the wrecker. We can go on to Mexico City to get the body work done, but we can't drive at night because of the headlights."

I was surprised. "How about the law here?" I looked around the bare yard and the front of the police station.

Bill smiled. "Apparently we're all square. I've paid up what we needed to fix the clock or whatever we hit, and they say we can go. Actually everyone has been quite decent." He went up to the men from the wrecker crew and distributed a few pesos. "Come on. Hop in." He started the engine, pumped the gas pedal a few times, and backed up gingerly.

I settled in and threw my Rialto out the window. It was not very satisfying in the cool, damp air of the morning. "How do we get out of town?"

Bill pointed through the windshield. "Highway 57 is supposed to be just up there. We take a right, hit a circle, go out the other side, and head to Queretaro."

I wondered how he got that much information from the Spanish speakers, but apparently the directions were correct because we got out on the highway easily. A sign saying Queretaro confirmed our route. I pulled out our map. "Looks like it's around 250 miles or so to Mexico City. We can easily make it before dark. Without both headlights, we shouldn't drive at night at all."

Queretaro was no problem. About 40 miles out of town, we had to pay to ride on the toll road. Bill and I changed places and I drove on to Mexico City. When we finally got there, the traffic was really bad. I followed the signs for Reforma Centro, remembering that Reforma was the main drag and our hotel where we had reservations was like on a service road. Luckily, we spotted the Hotel Emporio before we got there and pulled up in front without a hitch. I had stayed there first on my previous trip and had visited its tiny bar many times, as our apartment had been just a short distance away past the Diana Statue. An attendant took our car after a little wrangling with Bill, who wasn't entirely comfortable with the idea. A bellboy took all our luggage, and we checked in, tired from our journey– especially from driving through the traffic. We had arranged to get our mail at the hotel before we left Louisiana, but nothing was waiting for us.

CHAPTER THIRTEEN

Our room in the Emporio was small, but comfortable. Bill tipped the bellboy, who asked what else he could do for us. Bill said we were fine, but I had a couple of requests. "Actually, we need to find a place to get our car fixed, and we need to find an apartment. We're staying the summer."

The bellboy gave a big smile. "I can do both things for you tomorrow. It's my day off, and I can make some inquiries this evening." He spoke perfect English.

Bill was relieved. "That would be great. What is your name?"

The bellboy seemed to be about our age–a little shorter and clean looking. "My name is Roberto Diaz, and I can be back here around eight o'clock in the morning."

We all shook hands awkwardly, and Bill suggested that nine might be better.

Roberto was right on time the next morning. We decided to look for the apartment first as that was the most pressing need and so we could drive on our search. I don't know how he did it, but Roberto led us to the perfect apartment on the first try. We went three quarters around the circle, got on Insurgentes South, and drove down almost to the Viaducto. We turned left on a little street that dead ended under the overpass. The street looked clean and safe with modern-looking, one-story buildings. We met an agent who showed us the apartment for rent. The front door of the building opened into a short hall that took a dogleg left. Our apartment was the first and on the left, but the door faced down the continuation of the hall. A dining table was lined up with the door. A couch was under the windows that looked out on the street. The furniture looked new, with two easy chairs and a glass-topped coffee table in front of the couch. Two bedrooms were to the right and a modern bath between. The apartment didn't come with a phone, but we could use a pay phone in a little grocery store down the block. We put down our deposit immediately.

We brought our luggage back from the hotel and deposited everything in our new abode, happy that this problem had been resolved so quickly. Roberto guided us to a body shop where the owner said he could make the repairs on the Cadillac within a week. Then we took the first of many taxis back to the apartment, had a drink, and took Roberto to lunch.

School turned out to be laid back. LSU had rented some space in a school that had shut down for the summer. The school was easy to find, but we were forced to use taxis until we could get the Cadillac back. Some of the girl students looked interesting, but they seemed too serious about learning Spanish. Everybody else was staying with a Mexican family. I should have taken advantage of the opportunity to learn more, but Bill and I were out to have a good time.

However, I was determined not to lose the credits and the GI Bill payments like I had the previous summer; so I did spend a little time studying. I also tried to go to school every school day. This was much easier this summer because the school was in Mexico City. The previous summer I had to take a bus to Toluca up in the mountains every day to the campus of Mexico City College. Some days I had to go twice a day, because one class was in the late afternoon. That afternoon class was my undoing, even though it was the most interesting. The professor who taught Mexican history was a renowned anthropologist and a real character. He had a pronounced British accent and wore spats to class. It was just too darn hard to go down the mountain, have lunch, and try to catch the only bus back later in the afternoon. Eventually, I quit going altogether and lost the whole thing because of non-attendance.

Bill couldn't get the cantina in the desert out of his mind and he asked Roberto where he could find a really old bar in Mexico City. Roberto had to work at the Emporio, but gave us the address of a place he thought we would like. In the middle of the day on Saturday, we took a taxi to a scruffy -looking section which the cab driver seemed to know very well. Bill got out of the taxi and stepped back to admire the tall adobe false front of the establishment. He spread his arms and waved his hands to indicate the whole place. "This is perfect."

Inside, the place was a little dark and dusty. Old photos lined the walls above rows of liquor bottles. We guessed the pictures were mostly portraits of famous people who had patronized the bar. We found a place to stand at the bar and summoned a somewhat surly bartender. I ordered a beer, but Bill wanted a straight shot of tequila. He tipped rather well and the bartender became friendlier. The old wooden bar counter looked like a scarred, but expensive antique, and the surroundings must have pre-dated the twentieth century. Bill downed his tequila, grimaced, and ordered another. I knew then this would be a marathon, so I slowed up on my beer to make the long run. He struck up a conversation with a man on the other side who spoke English and may very well have been an American. I sidled away from the bar and stood in back and between them so I could join in. This man had short brown hair on top of his head and what looked like a three-day growth of stubble on his face. Oddly, all the hair seemed to be of even length and did not appear to be unkempt. He must have been in the bar for some time, for his speech was slurred and he was a little unsteady on his feet. He said his name was John Grubb Davidson.

The bartender brought us all a little treat, telling Bill that it was free. He passed me a small container like an Old Fashion glass. I was happy to have something of sustenance, but the treat didn't look very appetizing. It contained a clear broth with a small fish at the bottom with the eyes still in it. Bill and his buddy downed their treats, fish and all without blinking an eye. I tried to rationalize that we routinely ate sardines whole, but this little fish froze me with its gaze and promised a bout of *touristas*. I drank some of the broth and returned the glass to the counter, hoping that Bill would not notice. His new friend was describing his personal philosophy. "Nothing is worth doing unless it is illegal."

That statement sounded strange to me. I guessed he might be a fugitive from somewhere. He pulled out a wallet-sized identification card written in Spanish. "See, I'm a pilota. I can fly anywhere for anybody. His ID confirmed the name he had given. He was beginning to sound unsavory, but Bill was fascinated. He seemed to be agreeing with the man's lifestyle. A few more drinks convinced me that we couldn't afford to stay there any longer, especially with Bill tipping and buying drinks for his friend. I interrupted, "Bill, we're about to run out of money. We better get back to the apartment."

Bill checked his pockets and surprisingly agreed. "You're right. I couldn't go another round, and we still have to pay a taxi. John Grubb, come on with us. We've got some beer and rum back at the apartment."

John agreed, and we flagged down a taxi in front of the bar. As we steered through masses of people in the streets, the *pilota* suddenly got suspicious. "Where are we going? Who are you guys anyway?" He opened the door and practically fell out of the cab. He got to feet and disappeared into the crowd.

Bill laughed. "I bet he thought we were CIA. That poor bastard thought were kidnapping him."

I agreed. "That must be tough, trying to live in a strange land and suspicious of everyone."

Bill became serious. "Yes, but think of the freedom. He can disappear now, and no one can find him. If he can pull in enough money through his nefarious schemes, he can live down here forever and do whatever he wants. A pilot can always earn money. Don't pity him. He's a free spirit and enjoying life. If I ever have a son, I'm going to name him Grubb."

The wait on the Cadillac turned out to be three weeks instead of one. Bill checked with the garage frequently and began to get irritated. Patience was not one of his virtues. Finally, the work was done. I was amazed. All the torn and crushed metal had been repaired, rather than replaced. I sighted down the fender and could not detect a wave in the metal of any kind. The repair work cost Bill about 50 American dollars. He was now ready to extend our travel area.

When the fourth of July came around, we got a chance to do some exploring. We got the week off and decided to go to Acapulco. Our checks hadn't come in yet, so we had to ask people at school to pay for gas for the transportation to the coast. Two of the Arizona girls took us up. We thought we were going to score, but it didn't turn out that way. The trip was really nice. The mountains were beautiful. I wanted to get out of the car and run down to some of the river valleys, but Bill said we needed to push on if we wanted to get to Acapulco before dark. I think he was still thinking about our previous experience with night driving. The hairpin curves were scary. The Arizona girls kept telling Bill to slow down. We did stop at Taxco to eat. I liked the colonial architecture and the cobblestone streets. We also had a tequila drink called a Berta on a second story veranda overlooking the square. The girls had orange Fantas, which disappointed us a bit and prophesied that we might not score on this trip. When we got to Acapulco, Bill and I got a room at the Papagayo Hotel and the girls went to the Del Pacifico Hotel where I had stayed during the previous Fourth of July break from Mexico City College. The girls were obviously trying to distance themselves from us, meaning we probably had gained somewhat of a reputation among the other students. No matter, Bill and I had a good time at the beach and especially in the hotel's saltwater pool. Very few other people used the pool, and one night we were there by ourselves. At night thousands of tiny creatures would luminance as we swirled our arms in the captured ocean water. The pool itself glowed blue in the reflection of the underwater lights and lent a calmness to the quiet night.

Bill, probably bored by the lack of action, stated his intention to dive off the high diving board. There were no girls around to impress, but he climbed the ladder anyway. At the top, he wiped some of the moisture off his trunks and walked to the end of the board, gently bouncing in spite of his gingerly steps. He stared down at the pool for a few seconds and then turned around slowly and came down the ladder. I was amused but didn't try to kid him about his loss of nerve. This was tantamount to refusing a dare, which was not in Bill's character. I could tell he was embarrassed by the incident, but it did impress me as something new about Bill. There was a limit to his recklessness. He wasn't willing to risk his life or well-being if he had time to think about it, even if he was drunk. He wanted to be known for his wildness, but his comfort came first. In Bill's mind, Bill was number one. I was beginning to understand that he really didn't care much about other people, but there did turn out to be some exceptions.

At the end of the week, we picked up the girls and ate some ceviche on the waterfront. We had to borrow some money from them to pay our hotel bill in addition to the gas money to get back to Mexico City. Money was more and more of a problem, and we tried to go cheap whenever we could. Bill, however, became disenchanted with the Rialto cigarettes and decided to smoke a more expensive brand. They were not only milder, but came in a stiff flat box hat gave Bill the impression he was using a sophisticated case. He even would tap a cigarette on the box before he would light it.

Roberto turned out to be a good friend and provided valuable information about Mexico City. He went with us on a number of our forays, but we could tell that he didn't have the money to keep up with us most of the time, even with my limited resources. The Mexican beer was good, and sometimes we would just sit around the apartment and drink. Wild Bill liked Mexican girls but asked Roberto where a good place to meet some American girls in Mexico City was. He suggested the Hotel Geneve, because a lot of foreigners stayed there. We dropped Roberto off at the Emporio and drove over to the Geneve, which was only a few blocks off the corner of Insurgentes and Reforma. We parked the car nearby and sprinted to the hotel entrance in a light rain.

The Geneve turned out to be a bit more luxurious than the Emporio. We staked out the bar and waited for something to happen. Sure enough, two American-looking girls came in carrying some shopping bags and sat down at a small table across the way that was half surrounded by a vinyl-covered bench seat. Bill said: "Bingo" and went over to meet them. I could see him talking to the two young ladies and pointing to me and our table. He seemed to have trouble communicating although the girls appeared to be smiling and attentive, pointing to themselves and talking to Bill.

"*Uh oh*," I thought. They're probably married or don't want to join us. Bill came back to our table but didn't sit down.

He leaned over to talk to me with one hand on the table and one on the back of my chair. "Look here, old chap," he motioned toward the girls with his head, "Those two young ladies don't speak English."

I looked past Bill and saw that the girls were still smiling. "What do they speak?" I asked.

"I think it's French, but I'm not sure. Come help me out."

I picked up my drink and walked over to the table with Bill. The girls were pretty. The girl with dark hair more so. The blond had curly hair and a bit of a Gaelic nose. I held up my glass and said: "Hello, my name is Sam." Smiley blank stares that followed my glass as though that was what I was talking about. I pointed at my chest and said clearly "Sam." I pointed to Bill and said "Bill." Then I pointed to the brunette and shrugged my shoulders to show it was a question.

She pointed to herself and said "Amelie." I pointed to the other girl. "Yvette."

I pointed to the bench they were sitting on and gave the shrug gesture again. Amelie looked at Yvette for confirmation and slid over to make room for me. Bill jumped in next to Yvette.

I wasn't sure where to start, but hesitantly tried about the only French I knew. *"Parlez vous* Francais?"

The girls looked delighted. "Oh! Oui! Oui!" They then proceeded to say something unintelligible in French.

I pointed to myself again and said, "No–non parle Francais." knowing full well that wasn't the way to say it.

Utter dejection. I was understood.

Just then, the waiter came up and asked what the girls wanted to drink. They ordered two gin and tonics in good Spanish.

I figured we may have a way to at least partially communicate. Their Spanish wasn't much better than mine, but it was better than nothing. It turned out that Amelie and Yvette were from Canada and had been in Mexico City for about a week. They were going back home on Monday. I suggested that we do something together tomorrow which was Saturday. Bill wanted to do something that evening. The girls said they were tired from shopping, but would be happy to do something Saturday evening. We made a date for 6:00 the next afternoon The Mexicans always seemed to eat dinner late–maybe 10 or so, but restaurants were open earlier, maybe for the tourists.

After the girls left for their room, we decided to go see Roberto at the Emporio for suggestions about what to do. Bill thought I had made a mistake by asking them out for Saturday. "We could have done something this evening. A couple of more gin and tonics and I could have nailed the blond one."

I felt a little indignant. "Bill, these are nice girls!"

He was reproachful. "You don't mind messing around with girls that aren't nice. Why do you divide up women into nice and not nice? Girls are girls!"

Roberto was very helpful. "Saturday evening, your lady friends would probably like to go to Tenampa and listen to all the mariachis in the square. You might be careful there. The pickpockets like to prey on the tourists. The square is close to Reforma and all the taxi drivers know it. Sunday, you could take them to the Thieves' Market in the morning and the bullfights in the afternoon."

This sounded like good advice. I wondered, "What is the Thieves' Market?"

Roberto smiled. "It's much like a flea market back in the States. Lots of different people come to sell whatever—sometimes putting their stuff out on blankets. You can find almost anything there. It's almost all been used before. Most people say that a lot of the stuff is stolen."

Bill sounded interested. "What time do the bullfights start?"

Roberto looked around the lobby to see if the manager could see he wasn't working. "I'm pretty sure they start around four o'clock, but you ought to get there early. Try to get a seat on the shady side of the ring. In the summer, the matadors are all novices, but it is interesting because they take chances."

Bill came back to his interest. "Does the band play?"

"Oh, yes. If you like bullfighting music, that is the place to hear it. And another thing, don't try to take your car to any of these places. Parking is hard to find, and people will try to rip you off. Take a taxi. The Thieves' Market is just off Reforma and the bull ring is close to Insurgentes South, past where you live.

We picked up Amelie and Yvette at the appointed

hour and had no trouble finding Tenampa. It looked like a tourist place because all the mariachis wore the stereotypical outfits–the decorated vests and broad brimmed sombreros. Some even sported crossed gun belts and pistols. But they were good. Good and loud too. At first we were too cheap to request songs that we knew we would have to pay for, but there were enough tourists around to keep the music going. After we ate, we continued to party and our defenses broke down. Bill started requesting ranchero music from his Mejia records. I even got up on a table and sang a very bad version of *La Cama de Piedra*. The mariachis didn't care because they were getting paid to please the gringos.

The girls knew more English than we thought initially. Maybe they had practiced or maybe the alcohol had softened their inhibitions about not being entirely correct. At any rate, they could make themselves understood more and more as the night wore on. Finally, the girls seem to have had enough drinking and asked us to give them a break. We went out in the square toward the taxi stand. Bill put his arm around Yvette's shoulders and coerced her into following his kick dance step. They strutted off in unison while he began the song: "We're off to see the Wizard, the wonderful Wizard of Oz."

Amelie and I joined in and we pranced around the square, four abreast. "They say he is a wiz of a wiz if ever a wiz there was." It surprised me to know that Wild Bill had embraced a child's song. What was even more surprising was the fact that two French-speaking girls had been impressed enough by the movie to remember the words. The mariachis had great difficulty in following our lead. It really was fun though, and we were all laughing when we piled into the cab. There wasn't enough room, so, happily,

Amelie had to sit on my lap in the front seat. Bill gave the cab driver the address of our apartment and we took off.

Amelie must have figured that it was only fair to switch languages. She pointed to herself and then to me. "I'll teach you the French song." She began to sing and motioned for me to join in. I had heard the song before, but wasn't sure of the words.

"Allouette, gentille Allouette

> Alouette je t' eplumerai
> Je t' eplumerai la tete
> Je t' eplumerai la tete
> Et la tete
> Et la tete
> Allouette
> Allouette
> O-o-o-o-oh
> Allouette--"

Amelie pointed to me when it was time for me to repeat the line. Bill and Yvette joined in from the back seat. It became apparent that some words of the song referred to parts of the body, and Amelie would point to the corresponding part as she sang. I really was learning some words in French although I would have been hard pressed to spell them.

> La tete - the head
> Le nez - the nose
> Les yeux - the eyes
> Le cou - the neck
> Les pattes - the legs

We prolonged the "o-o-o-oh" part between verses because that was what we knew the best. Finally, I began kissing the featured part of Amelie each time the word came around. I didn't know how I was to accomplish "Les pattes" in the cramped front seat, but we got to the apartment before I had to. Back at the apartment, I learned that acting out "Les pattes" was my favorite part of the song. After a while, Bill continued to sing, but pulled a willing Yvette back to his bedroom. Amelie hunched her shoulders and put her hand over her mouth in amused embarrassment as the song from the back bedroom began to include body parts I hadn't been taught as yet.

Amelie and Yvette refused to stay over. They insisted on going back to the Geneve, even after Bill refused to drive them home. They clearly wanted to change clothes for our excursions the next day. I didn't want to jeopardize our relations and drove them back in the Cadillac.

We started late on Sunday, giving everyone a chance to get some sleep. The Thieves Market was easy to find. A bored cab driver on Reforma took us all the way and deposited us at the edge of the Market. By the time we got there the market was in full swing. People were everywhere. Many of the vendors had spread their wares on blankets directly on the ground, while others had set up tables and had hung up blankets on ropes to form cubicles that shielded them from their neighbors and made their spaces more definite. I can't think of a used item that was not on display. We walked up and down the aisles, bending over now and them to inspect small objects of interest. Amelie wore a sleeveless dress and sandals that complemented her smooth white skin. She had wanted to wear a wide-brimmed sun hat but I had suggested that she return it to her room before we left the hotel to keep from losing it later in the crowded areas we were to visit.

Amelie and I held hands as we strolled around the mass of humanity, looking for paths that would lead us from one section to another. Periodically, she would lean her head on my shoulder as we stopped to view unusual displays. One area had large objects like baroque furniture that must have been difficult to steal if that was the way they were acquired. Standing in the midst of all these ornate items was a half-nude statue of a woman with a large clock imbedded in her abdomen. Complicated ornamental fountains were scattered about. There seemed to be a concentration of similar items in particular places that allowed the buyers to compare among different vendors. I bought two 78 rpm records with nearly new covers, *The Heart of the Piano Concerto* and Michel Legrand's *Castles in Spain*. Neither record seemed to have significant scratches. I tried to show off my bargaining skills to impress Amelie, but the price didn't change very much.

Several blanket vendors displayed large collections of false teeth. I shuddered to think how they must have been acquired. Amelie and I stopped and stared as people tried on different sets to see if they fit particular needs. A few got lucky and purchased dentures. Amelie didn't want to watch the fittings.

I noticed that some of the blanketed cubicles had some depth. That is, the back was covered by a hanging blanket as well. We lifted up the separations and ventured farther and farther into the private areas that could be found only by people who knew what they were seeking. We passed through quarters of barber chairs and operating tables. Finally, we reached a crowded space filled with shiny black equipment and gauges inscribed with white letters, apparently in German. Finally, I realized that one piece of equipment was a periscope. We were looking at the insides of a German submarine!

An agitated Mexican showed up and told us that if we didn't intend to buy, we should leave. We tried to retrace our steps through the maze of hanging blankets and finally reached an open aisle and the regular touristy display of wares. We saw an unusual amount of fine clothing at almost unbelievable prices, even before haggling. Amelie was looking for a hat since I had talked her out of bringing her own, but ladies' hats were not to be found. We finally encountered Bill and Yvette and set out to eat an early lunch.

The outside of the Plaza de Toros resembled LSU stadium on a game day. Hawkers were everywhere, selling mostly food items. Luckily, we had eaten already and did not risk the ingestion of exotic organisms from the street vendors. We found seats on the sunny side of the stands, in spite of Roberto's admonition to sit on the shady side. Bill looked around for the band and finally spotted it high to our left. Not as many instruments as we had guessed, but with plenty of fire power. They blasted out a familiar air as the parade of toreros began. Since we couldn't have known the difference between novices and the professionals of the high season, the pageantry was impressive. We watched as the men on horses wounded the first bull with lances. The girls were becoming squeamish and obviously sided with the bull. Then, more toreros on foot plunged barbed banderillas into the neck of the reeling animal. These men seemed bored, even as they scampered adroitly from the path of enraged bull. When the matador finally appeared, we guessed that the bull was severely hampered. The matador looked like a kid, but he doffed his cap and held it toward the crowd as he haughtily pirouetted without regard to the danger. The bull took this opportunity to charge at full speed and caught the matador fully in the back. The man went down like a shot as his helpers rushed to his aid. The girls didn't wait for the rescue but bolted

179

from our seats and rushed out of the stadium. We followed discreetly, trying to retain our manly demeanor as the ticket takers smirked at the girls' revulsion. No matter, Bill had heard the band, and we had a story to tell. Actually, we heard later on that the matador had not been killed. The bull's horns had passed on both sides of the slim youth's back, and he merely had been knocked out.

On the way back to the apartment, Bill told the taxi driver to stop at the Emporio so he could pick up his mail. We waited in the cab. After a few minutes, Bill staggered out of the hotel and sat down on the sidewalk with his back against the building between two tall windows. Something was obviously wrong. I told the girls to wait and went over to Bill to see what the matter was. He was waving a telegram in his right hand and periodically putting his head on his left forearm which was resting on his knees. He was almost sobbing. "Dennis is dead! Why couldn't it be someone else? He even named one of our friends as a candidate."

I chased down the waving telegram. It was from Swifty and said that Dennis was killed in a car wreck, and we shouldn't try to come back. I tried to get Bill to get up, but he refused. I went back to the car and told the girls what had happened. Yvette wanted to go and comfort Bill, but I felt like it would be fruitless. I sent the girls back to their hotel, mindlessly forgetting to get Amelie's address in Canada, as that would be the last time we ever saw them. I had never seen Bill like this before. He wasn't prone to great emotion, and this incident was counter to my impression that Bill did not care about other people. Dennis seemed a nice enough guy, but I couldn't understand why his death should have affected Bill so much. Dennis was scheduled to come see us in Mexico that summer. Bill had brought

Dennis's white yachtsman's cap with us, and we kept it on top of a radio in the living room. I actually don't remember Bill ever wearing the cap. I don't think he ever mentioned why he had it, although a plausible affectation would be Bill in a blue blazer posing as a rich man at a swanky yacht club.

After a few days Bill seemed to have forgotten about Dennis. We went to school as usual, and everything was back to normal, although Bill took to going out by himself in the evenings. Bill was fine enough to get along with as long as everything was going his way. He was used to having enough money to do pretty much whatever he wanted. Without that support, his irresponsibility and disregard for other people began to show. We were getting low on money toward the end of the month, and he took some of mine that I put in the refrigerator for safekeeping. It rains in Mexico City nearly every afternoon in the summer. Bill borrowed my Marine Corps raincoat for one of his forays and traded off my coat for a woman. I was pissed off, but he said he would recover the coat as soon as our checks came in. He never did. He said he couldn't find the place again.

One afternoon, while I was studying at the apartment, we heard a knock on the door. When I opened it, an attractive woman in her thirties nervously told me she lived down the hall and wanted to borrow a cup of sugar. It seemed like an excuse. Bill jumped up from the couch. He was immediately interested and greeted her in his most gentlemanly manner. When he wanted to impress a new girl, he would take her hand and bow politely as he introduced himself. The woman's name was Elena, and Bill made a habit of talking to her whenever he saw her. Not long afterwards, Bill skipped school one day. When I got home from school, Bill and Elena were sitting on the couch.

Bill had his arm around Helena's shoulders and made a point of jiggling her breast with that hand. I guessed that Bill was completely recovered.

Bill seemed content to spend most of his free time with Elena while I slogged along with school, determined not to lose the nine semester hours of credit which were almost guaranteed. Our shortage of cash continued. One evening, I stood in the doorway to the kitchen, complaining to Bill about our inability to go out or eat like we had before. I was next to the large bottle of purified water that we purchased for drinking and ice cubes. Bill didn't seem to pay much attention. He was sitting opposite me on the couch and waving his pistol around, aiming at imaginary targets in the air. I wanted him to listen to me. "Stop playing with that pistol!"

POW! The gun went off and punctured the water bottle. He had deliberately fired at the vessel. Luckily, the hole was near the top, and not much water spilled out onto the floor. I was furious. He could have seriously injured me or even killed me. Pistols are not that accurate, even over short distances. I jumped at him and grabbed his gun hand with both of my own, determined to take the gun away from him. He came off the couch, and we rolled on the floor. He was stronger than I thought. I jammed my right elbow under his chin to keep him from turning over and reaching the pistol with his left hand. He held onto the pistol but didn't put his finger inside the trigger guard. We turned over the chairs beside the table as we violently tussled on the floor. He tried to hit me on the back with his left fist, but he couldn't get enough leverage to do any harm. I had a fear that we would turn over the coffee table and break the glass top. Finally, I got my knees around Bill's chest and squeezed as hard as I could. I felt, rather than heard, a sensation of breaking a piece of glass tubing under water as we were instructed in chemistry class. Bill suddenly went limp and a white buck shoe crashed through the glass top of the coffee table. He let go of the pistol and lay on the floor, groaning.

I picked up the pistol and took it to my room to hide it. I figured Bill would find it eventually, but this would give me a little bit of time to let him cool off. He didn't seem too feisty when I went back into the living room. He was holding onto his ribs as he awkwardly levered himself back onto the couch. He laid his head back on the couch. "Why did you do that?"

I was still angry. "You idiot! You could have shot me in the leg!"

He didn't reply but kept his eyes closed. He was still there when I went to bed, but went to his room sometime during the night. He declined to get up the next morning when I tried to wake him to go to school.

When I got home after school, Bill was sitting in an easy chair without his shirt, wrapped around the chest in what looked like an ace bandage. He gasped: "I couldn't breathe, so I called Roberto and went to see his doctor. You broke two of my ribs!"

He didn't seem too upset and neither was I.

CHAPTER FOURTEEN

I explained at school that Bill had been injured. The professors were sympathetic and indicated that he could make up the time if he was able to come back. Bill wasn't too concerned but said he could return to school soon seeing as how he was feeling better. However, he said he had some business to attend to at the apartment. It seems as though Elena was not too pleased with Bill's inability to perform and had taken up with a Mexican actor. Bill was unhappy with this decision and blamed the Mexican actor. He definitely did not want to become upstaged even if Elena was not the focus of his attention. He told me he was going to shoot the actor. He arranged the dining room chairs so that he could lie down on them facing the open door. He had found his pistol by this time and aimed it down the hall by bracing his elbows on the chairs.

Somehow, I wasn't too concerned about this prospect of violence. First of all, I wasn't too convinced that Bill could pull it off, given the awkwardness of the situation. Also, I remembered his reluctance to jump off the high diving board and thought that the threat may be a bluff. Who he was trying to impress, I don't know, but I didn't want to give him any indication that I was worried. I left him uncomfortably poised on the chairs and went to bed. Later that night, I had to smile as I heard him roll off the chairs in his sleep and fall on his damaged ribs. His distressed outcry seemed to have been well deserved. I rolled over and went off to dream land.

The crisis seemed to pass, and we went on with school. I was pretty sure that I had passed the summer courses. Seems as though I picked up most of my credits in the summers. They were easier to attend because the classes were every day and the time passed quickly. Roberto said he wanted to go back to the States with us. He had gone to the U.S. a couple of times before and was confident he could find work in New Orleans as he had done previously. His strategy was to make some money and then turn himself into the immigration authorities. The first time he was arrested in the States, they held him for a few days and then put him on a plane back to Mexico City. In his mind, he got a free ride home. Unfortunately, the next time he turned himself in, they flew him to Merida on the Yucatan Peninsula and he had to hock all his clothes to get bus fare for the thousand or so miles he had to get back to Mexico City.

None of us had much money left. Bill suggested that we try to sell something. Roberto already had hocked his clothes again to make the trip. I was sarcastic. "If I still had my raincoat, I'd sell that. What about that fancy ring you wear? If those are real diamonds, you could get some money from that."

Bill was indignant. "Over my dead body, but I have an idea. Let's buy some marijuana to take back. We can sell it in the States and pay for the whole trip."

Roberto was adamant. "I'm not getting in the car if we are carrying any contraband."

I chimed in: "That wouldn't be worth it, no matter how much money we could make." At that point in my life, I probably wanted to be known as wild. My association with Wild Bill could only enhance that reputation. However, there were limits. I had my own high diving board. It wasn't just the fear of getting caught and risking the punishment. I wouldn't do anything that would harm someone else, for instance. Beyond that was the concept of doing something that was obviously wrong in a larger sense. Dealing with drugs was that line I was not willing to cross. The renegade Huck Finn lamented his transgression on the institution of slavery–an obvious right for the whites of his day. In my own limited culture of 1957, opposition to Communism and illegal drug use represented higher Truths that could not be transcended.

Bill was hard to convince. The only things that really dissuaded him were the facts that we didn't have enough money to buy anything beyond subsistence, and we didn't have enough time to hook up with someone who would trust us with a consignment.

In meager preparation, we bought some cheap Mexican sandwiches called tortas--hard bread, this time filled with hot peppers instead of meat and--took off.   I drove most of the way. Going through the mountains was a problem.   To conserve petrol, I would cut off the ignition and try to glide down the slopes. The difficulty with that was that the Cadillac was fully automatic and all the hydraulics ceased without the motor running.   Not only was it hard to steer, but the brakes needed extreme pressure to function at all. In spite of our poverty, Bill insisted that we stop at a roadside pulqueria to sample the only an alcoholic beverage we had missed on our trip. The pulque drink itself cost only a few cents, but the experience was not really pleasurable.   The thick white liquid was in a large vat, fully open to insects, which seemed to die on contact. Maybe the drink was palatable in other places, but the pulque in this particular establishment was horrid. Not only did it not taste good, it was stringy, reminiscent of nasal secretions. At least we could say we had tried it. We could have saved the few centavos we spent.

The trip back seemed much longer than the trip to Mexico City. We hurried to get to the border before our money ran out and didn't get to enjoy the same pleasant journey that got us there. Nearly every centavo went to buying petrol. We even dispensed with the air-conditioning to save on gas. When we finally got to Nuevo Laredo, we were tired, broke, and thirsty. Bill said he had a credit card we could use in the U.S. if we could get there. Idling in line to cross the border, we suddenly realized we didn't have the seventy-five cents we needed to get on the bridge. We dropped out of line and pulled out the seats of the car, looking for coins. Luckily, we found enough to pay our toll. In Laredo, Bill's credit card not only got us a tank of gas, we got cokes and peanut butter crackers as well. It was a wonderful meal. Bill seemed reluctant to use his card for food, but I had no compunctions, given his theft of my refrigerator money and the loss of my raincoat.

The wreck of the Caddie on this trip was the last of my auto accidents with Wild Bill. We had a number of other adventures in Mexico that are better left untold, but the incidents mentioned here serve to describe the character of Wild Bill Jenkins.

I lost track of Bill for a while after we got back– enough to truthfully tell Elena I didn't know where he was when she managed to reach me by telephone me in Baton Rouge.

CHAPTER FIFTEEN

1998

Jim's advice from the funeral about getting help from an experienced investigator was good. I called Don, and he was more than willing to help out. He was not entirely convinced we were not dealing with accidents but acknowledged that I had some pretty good circumstantial evidence to warrant further investigation. Fortunately, he had a day off the next Friday and volunteered to lead me around. His inside knowledge of police matters would be valuable. "Since we're dealing with apparent accidents, we ought to take advantage of the official reports. From what you have told me, two of these accidents occurred on roads outside municipalities. You could write away and purchase the reports from the Louisiana State Police if they still have them. The better plan would be to go to their headquarters and take a look at the files themselves. I'm not sure how they were formatted back in the '60s, but getting our hands on the files would ensure we got everything there is to get. I'm betting we would save over a week as well."

The next day I drove to my parents'–Don's–house and parked in the left-hand driveway. Don met me out front of the house. I wondered if he didn't want me to see how he had changed things. Don was a big man. I knew he had been much heavier at one time and was diligently trying to keep his weight down. He was wearing his uniform, which seemed tight. His cap was under his arm, and his short hair was wet. "I was just jogging around the neighborhood this morning, and took a shower." He explained, "I think we may have more leverage with my uniform. Have you ever been to State Police

Headquarters?"

"No. It's that big building at the corner of Florida and North Foster, right?"

He laughed. "You're right for the time being, but they are about to move. The new headquarters will be on Independence which begins at the end of Goodwood."

"I thought the small airport was at the end of Goodwood." I remembered taking free flying lessons there when I was in the Civil Air Patrol.

"It was, but that whole area is public land now. There's a botanical garden on the property and there will be a really nice police complex."

I was beginning to think that I didn't know much about the Baton Rouge of 1998. "Shall we take my truck?"

Don eyed the Toyota as if measuring the comfort of the ride. "No, let's take my car. I know the shortcuts." We got into his late model green Ford.

Don really did know streets that weren't even there when I lived in Baton Rouge. The traffic was terrible, even though we were well past the morning rush. Eventually, he turned right just before the heavy traffic of Florida Boulevard into the parking lot of the State Police Headquarters. We went around the lot twice, passing five empty spaces for disabled persons. At the front door, we went through a checkpoint like at the airports. Don pointed to a small elevator. "Let's take the lift. The file room is on the second floor. I called the duty clerk this morning, and luckily I know him."

On the second floor, we came on the door to the file room. Large letters on a sign said "Law Enforcement Personnel and Attorneys Only. Others see the duty clerk on first floor." Don turned to me. "Didn't you tell me that you were a sergeant in the Marine Corps?"

I didn't understand. "Yes, I was."

Don opened the door and strode in confidently. A uniformed officer was sitting behind a computer monitor on a large desk. Behind him, a low fence with a top rail separated the front area from a huge bank of filing cabinets. Two long tables were to our right. They had low, individual lamps like library study areas. Don stuck out his hand. "Hey there, Trosclair!" He gestured toward me. "You remember Sergeant Elliot, don't you?"

Trosclair stood up and shook my hand. "Sure." he lied. "What can I do for you gentleman?"

I tried to look official. "We're looking into a couple of traffic fatalities."

Trosclair smiled. "Sure. We have everything on the mainframe. Copies of the reports will cost you a dollar a page. Were these in the last couple of days? They may not have been entered yet."

"Actually," I answered, "they happened in 1958 and 1964."

The smile left. "In that case, the reports will be in the hard copy files." He gestured to the area beyond the fence. He shoved a log sheet toward me. "Fill out this request and I'll get them for you."

I filled out the log sheet as best I could. I knew the month of Dennis's death, but Tommy hadn't told me much about Lindsey's, other than it occurred near some deep water and was around the time that Bill died. The reason for asking for the files gave me pause. I finally put down "family inquiry." I handed the sheet back to Trosclair and asked him if that was enough to find the records.

He cocked his head as he looked at my writing. "I think so. We don't have the complete records in the computer, but we have cross-referenced the old ones and assigned them a file number. Somehow, Lindsey Scott rings a bell." He typed in some information and said, "Bingo! We have both of them in hard copy. Here's why Scott sounded familiar. Some guy came in just a few days ago to ask for the same records."

"Some guy?"

He put his finger on a line on the monitor screen. "Yes, a Thomas Freeman."

I wondered if it was someone with the same name as Tommy. "Was he an attorney in a wheel chair?"

"That's him. He sat at that table over there and paid for some photocopies. Let me go get the files for you." He copied down the file numbers and went back to the file cabinets. After a few minutes he came back and looked at the computer screen and at the numbers he had written down. Then he flipped through the log sheets and compared them again.

I had a sinking feeling. "Is there something wrong?"

Trosclair looked perplexed. "I can't find them again. I know I re-filed them." He showed us the log sheet line with Tommy's name and pointed to initials and the time under the column "re-filed." "See, when someone checks out a file, they can only look at it here, and then they return it to this basket." He pointed. "Every file has a log that tells how many pages and photographs it contains. I count the pages to verify that we got them all back and initial the daily log sheets after I re-file them. I don't make mistakes. I know I put these files back! I better call Lieutenant Boudreaux." He picked up the phone.

I wasn't happy about getting embroiled in anything else. "Why make a call?"

Trosclair had punched a button already. "Missing files are important. I'd get into trouble if I didn't report it right away. Also, Lieutenant Boudreaux may want to talk to you." He held up a finger and leaned away to let us know his connection went through. "Hello, Lieutenant? This is Trosclair. Look, I've got two officers here who were looking for some files, and those two files are missing. Yes. I'm sure I filed them correctly. Someone asked for the same files just a few days ago. Yes, I have their names on the log sheet." He shoved a blank sheet toward Don and made a writing gesture with his free hand to indicate that Don should write down his name. Then he listened on the phone for a few seconds.

He hung up the phone and turned to us. "Boudreaux doesn't need to see you, but he does need to have a way to contact you again. May I see your driver's licenses?"

He frowned a bit when he saw my address in Clear Creek but didn't comment. He wrote down the addresses and asked for our telephone numbers. "Is there anything more about this that I should know?"

Don stroked his chin. "I don't think so. We and the attorney were working on the same case, but we didn't know he had been here already. This was really just a long shot anyhow. Would you let me know when you do find the records? We may come back. And, Trosclair, thanks for your time. I hope we haven't caused you any trouble."

We shook hands and Trosclair mumbled something about this situation really being strange. Don and I didn't speak as we rode down the elevator and walked out into the parking lot. When we got into Don's car, he gripped the steering wheel with both hands. "What's your take on this?"

I tried to make sense of what had transpired. "Well, we know the records existed when Tommy was here. He evidently thought something was important or he wouldn't have had pages copied. I don't know what to make of the missing records. The fact that they had just been handled would make it seem as if they could have been misfiled. I'm sure Trosclair has a routine to follow when something like this happens. If he doesn't find the files in a few days, it could mean that someone else took them. I can't see Tommy taking them, especially since he had something copied. Supposing, just supposing, that someone else had an interest in those files, taking them would keep anyone else from looking at them. That would mean--" It began to dawn on me. "--that all the parties in these accidents slash murders may not have died; and someone is still trying to cover it up. Since we haven't been snooping around very long, it could also mean that Tommy's visit somehow triggered the response. This could be an inside job."

Don started the car. "I was afraid you would say that. It would pain me to think that someone connected with the police would have taken the files." He looked at me earnestly. "This still doesn't change things much. We don't know anything more than we did before. Tell you what. Let's go to the East Baton Rouge Sheriff's Department and see what we can find out about Swifty's death. They keep cold-case files on unsolved homicides. What was Swifty's last name?"

"Sheffield. James Sheffield. But everyone called him Swifty–among other things."

The Sheriff's office was on North Boulevard. We went through the same routine with the metal detector and went to an information desk. Don spoke to the uniformed officer on duty. "Hi. I'm Sergeant Carruthers with the BRCP. Who would we speak to about cold case homicides?"

"In the Parish?"

"Yes."

"Today that would be Lieutenant Campanelli in the Detective Division. Do you have an appointment?"

"No."

"Sign in the log, and I'll give him a call." The officer indicated a log book and punched a button on his phone. "Lieutenant Campanelli? This is the front desk. There are two gentlemen here to see you." He paused. "Okay." He turned to us. Campanelli can see you. He's in room 206, right off the elevator on the second floor." He pointed to a small elevator.

I was curious as we rode the one floor on the elevator. "The Sheriff's Department has detectives? How do they differ from the police department?"

Don opened the elevator door. "In the Parish and outside cities with police departments, it's easy. The Sheriff's Department has jurisdiction for criminal investigations. Inside the city...." He rocked his hand palm down to show there was no good finish to his sentence.

Campanelli seemed like a friendly man. He had dark, curly hair and shook our hands warmly like he was a politician. "I'm Detective Campanelli. Have a seat." He pointed to two chairs by his desk. Calling himself "Detective" seemed as though he was stressing the importance of his job. He wasn't just a file clerk. "What can I do for you?"

Don answered. "We're interested in a homicide that took place in 1961."

The lieutenant sat back down. "And who would the victim be?"

Don must have realized that he didn't remember Swifty's first name because he looked at me for the answer.

"A James Sheffield. Most people called him Swifty."

Campanelli leaned back in his chair and put his fingers together under his chin. "Doesn't sound familiar. Are you sure it's a cold case?"

I leaned forward. "Reasonably so. It was unsolved the last I heard, and a friend of mine didn't seem to know who did it. I understand Swifty was shot in the back of the head with a shotgun."

Campanelli smiled. "That ought to do it. Let me look it up." He turned to his computer and typed out the name with two fingers. "Yep, we got him. Why are you interested?"

I felt a little uncomfortable in answering this directly. We could look like idiots following up on such slim evidence. After all, I had shared my suspicions only with people I knew well up to this point. The missing State Police files might be the only clue as to a cover up, and that fact could easily be explained as accidental. I started slowly. "It's a long story."

Campanelli leaned back and put his hands behind his head as though anticipating a lengthy story. "I'm listening."

Summarizing our findings could be difficult. I wanted to eliminate any of my conclusions and stick to the facts. Chronological order would be best. "Back in 1958, a friend of mine named Bill Jenkins and I were going to summer school in Mexico. Bill got a telegram from this Swifty–we knew him through a bar he owned here in Baton Rouge–that another friend of ours, Dennis Dawson, had been killed in a car wreck. Swifty said not to come back, there was nothing we could do." I paused, wondering whether my chronology should be as things happened or when I found out about them. "I finished LSU and was working in Cleveland when Swifty called me to tell me that Bill had been killed in a plane crash. Several weeks ago, I met the mechanic who worked on the wrecked plane. He had suspicions that the engine had been sabotaged because he found some foreign material in the gas line."

Campanelli straightened up, pulled out a legal pad from a desk drawer, and made a note with a pencil. "Did he report his suspicions?"

"No. He probably felt guilty at the time because he was responsible for the maintenance of the plane. His feeling was that the sabotage occurred after his inspection and before the crash."

Campanelli continued writing. He made a check mark as though he wanted to come back to a point later. "I'm going to take some notes. Go on."

"I told one of my friends, who is a lawyer, about the coincidences with Swifty and he told me some more. One, that Swifty had been murdered, assassination style; and two that my friend had had a client who died in a car accident and who also had a connection to Swifty. My friend had some concerns about his client's death at the time because he was facing indictment and wanted to turn States evidence against Swifty in exchange for leniency. We don't know whether the client had informed Swifty about the opportunity to rat on him. The accident occurred about the same time as my friend Bill's plane crash."

"Was this wreck in East Baton Rouge?"

"I'm not sure. My friend, the lawyer, said the accident occurred near some deep water in a river because the car was submerged and the body was lost."

"What was his client's name?"

"Scott, Lindsey Scott. Well, anyway," I continued, "I recently contacted the sister of Dennis Dawson, the one who was killed in 1958. She had always been concerned about Dennis's death because of some eyewitnesses who stated that he was not alone in the car before the accident, but he was by himself when they found the wreck. She discovered that Dennis had been working undercover for the State Police. Not only that, but two men claiming to be with the State Police came to her house after the funeral and questioned her about what Dennis was doing. By accident, she found out that the men had to be imposters. Just now, "I nodded toward Don, "Don and I went to State Police Headquarters we were looking for the crash reports on Dennis Dawson and Lindsey Scott. The files were missing."

Campanelli looked up from his writing. "I don't doubt that. Those accidents were a long time ago."

I didn't much like the way he said "accidents." "But we did find that the files were there within the last few weeks. That lawyer friend of mine had looked at them then."

"And they're gone now?" He looked surprised.

"Yes. And the duty officer is certain that he re-filed them."

"Was that Trosclair?"

"You know Trosclair?"

"Yes. We collaborate quite a bit. We nose around in each other's files sometimes. He does a good job. Who is your lawyer friend?"

"His name is Thomas Freeman."

Campanelli smiled as though the problem was solved. "Surely Mr. Freeman would have noted if there was something unusual about the files."

Don piped up. "May have, except Freeman's dead now too."

Campanelli wrinkled his forehead and pointed to

his notes. "Is his death related to this?"

I felt like we were being asked too many questions, but the detective stood in the way of our getting Swifty's file. "Not that we know of. Freeman lost his legs in a car accident many years ago and was driving a specially equipped van when he lost control and went into a ravine by his home."

Campanelli drummed his cheek with his pencil. "I think I remember reading something about that, but I didn't remember the name. What else makes you want to see Mr. Sheffield's file?"

I looked at Don. "Nothing I can think of."

The deputy was perusing his notes. "What was the name of this airplane mechanic?"

I tried to remember. "Joe—Joe Varnado. He lives in Franklinton. That's where the plane crash was."

Campanelli turned to face us directly. "Well, I can certainly see why you might be concerned, seeing as how you knew two of these people. We have a number of coincidences here." He tapped the notes. "How do you think looking into Mr. Sheffield's death would shed any light on these other incidents?"

I was afraid he would ask that question and wanted to turn the responsibility around. "We wouldn't know until we find out what was in the file. My premise was that Swifty had something to do with these other deaths. Someone obviously killed Swifty. Maybe just finding out that Sheffield was involved in other violent criminal activities would show that he was capable of staging the accidents we're looking into." It was the only thing I could think of at the moment, but somehow that didn't sound convincing. I wasn't sure that Campanelli would buy the rationale.

The detective paused a few seconds, not looking at us directly. Then he got up suddenly. "Sure. Let's take a look at the files. Excuse me a minute." He unlocked a door behind him and disappeared into the evidence room. A few minutes later, he reappeared, holding a cardboard container a little larger than a shoe box. He blew some dust off the top of the box, placed it on his desk, and sat down. "Well, these files are still here." He placed his hands on top of the box, but didn't open it. "I'll try to read you what is on the summary sheet, and we'll decide what's worthwhile looking at. One thing, though: We usually hold out some piece of evidence that has not been disclosed to the public. That way, if we have a good suspect or someone confesses, we have something that only the killer could know about. Since unsolved homicides remain open forever, I wouldn't be able to share that particular piece of evidence with you."

He opened the box and pulled out a folder which he held in the air for us to see. "This contains all the written reports about the incident and the subsequent investigations. Let me take a look at the summary page." He opened the folder, leafing through the reports briefly before returning to the first page. Everything was bound together with a large clasp at the top. "Hello! Here's something that was added years later." He read for a minute and then turned to us. "I think you'll be interested in this. Here's a report that was added in 1986 by a detective who has since retired. I'll read you the parts that I can."

He cleared his throat. "This is dated May 7, 1986." He read from the report. "Yesterday, I received a call from a Father so and so of such and such church." Campanelli looked at us. "I'll skip some identifications for now if you don't mind." He continued reading without waiting for a response. "Father so and so said he might have some information about an unsolved homicide and wanted to talk to me in private. This morning, he came to my office and appeared a little nervous. He said he had heard a deathbed confession and was not really sure about the ethics of reporting it, but he was concerned that some innocent person might be accused of the crime if he didn't say something. His parishioner was adamant about not wanting the information to get out. I told him that I could not promise anything, but I would try to be discreet about what he had to tell me and that I was not obligated to go public with it. The priest had recently administered to a Mrs. Ethel Sheffield who was terminally ill with cancer. Mrs. Sheffield said that she had killed her husband, but no one knew about it."

Don and I looked at each other in disbelief. I choked. "Did this detective believe that story?

Campanelli read silently for a few seconds and then said: "I believe so. Mrs. Sheffield knew where the killer stood when the shot was fired and also what her husband was carrying when he died. Those facts were not disclosed to the public at the time. Apparently the motive was that her husband was forcing her to go cold turkey from a bad drug habit–maybe even something commendable on his part."

Don asked, "Why then is this still a cold case? Isn't there some prestige to the Department for resolving murders old and recent?"

Campanelli closed the file. "You're right, of course, but evidently this detective" he said pointing to the file, "thought that he should honor the priest's request and not officially close the case. It's also not conclusive. After all, this is second-hand information, and the presumed perpetrator is dead. I think I would have taken the same action–inaction–if I were in the same shoes as my predecessor. You know, I believe you two should act in the same way and be extremely careful with this information. I don't see how it could benefit anyone." He cleared his throat again. "This testimony doesn't seem to further your premise about Sheffield being involved in your accidents. My considered opinion is that you really don't have any information that would point to foul play in any of these incidents. The only things that might suggest outside culpability to my mind are the mechanic's assertion that the plane's engine contained sludge, and two people that may have impersonated State Police Officers. There are probably reasonable explanations for both. I can see why you could be concerned, but let me tell you, in my business, we run across more convincing coincidences every day. Just this week, I found someone in the files that had a name spelled very similarly to a prime suspect in a case. He had a similar MO as well. We pursued the lead to the hilt, thinking we had our man, only to find out he was incarcerated in Texas at the time of the crime. I wish I could be of more help." He turned to Don. "Why are your superiors asking you to follow up on these cases?"

Don stiffened slightly. "They're not really. I'm just trying to help a friend."

The detective nodded knowingly and waved a finger up and down, pointing to Don's torso. "But you are in uniform. Are you on duty?"

"No, just coming off a shift. As you know, we're always ready to follow up on something that might help the public."

The detective slid back in his chair. "Is there anything else I can do for you?"

I stood up. "Don, can you think of anything?" He

shook his head. I extended my hand to Campanelli. "Thank you so much for your help–and advice. This really was a surprise. I don't see any reason to disclose what we have learned."

As we walked out into the parking lot, I told Don: "I don't see how this changes anything. I'd still like to learn what was in those missing files at the State Police Headquarters."

Don looked at his watch. "Look, it's past my lunch time. Why don't we get a bite to eat and talk about it?"

My stomach had come to the same conclusion. "Fine with me. Where do you want to go?"

We got into the car, and Don started it. "Let's go to the Pastime. It's near here and they have good sandwiches."

The name was familiar to me, but its function was not. "Is that the same Pastime that used to be a lounge on Highland Road?"

Dan laughed. "I think it's probably the place you're thinking about, but most people go there to eat now."

The Pastime turned out to be the same location. The area where we used to bring dates and dance was now a kitchen. We stood in line and wrote down our orders on little sheets of paper and put down our first names. I picked up Don's check, and we found a table to wait until our names were called.

Don produced his cell phone. "Why don't we see if Freeman's widow has the photocopies that her husband made?"

"Good idea. I have their telephone number in my wallet. I hate to bug her, but she did mention to me at the funeral that she knew Tommy and I were working on something together." I took the phone and dialed the number. She could be at work, but maybe they gave her time off. "I need to get me one of these cell phones for myself. We got one for my wife, but didn't get one for me. I worry sometimes when she's driving by herself. They sure are handy." I was stalling while the phone was ringing. Luckily, someone picked up. "Mrs. Freeman?"

"This is she."

"This is Sam Elliot. We met at the funeral. How are you making out?"

"Pretty well. There's a lot of paperwork, with the insurance and such, but I've got some good help."

"I hate to bother you, but Tommy had some documents related to the project we were working on. They would have been in the form of photocopies from State Police Headquarters. Does that sound familiar, or do you have his briefcase?"

She paused for a few seconds. "I haven't seen anything like that to my memory, but I do have his briefcase. It's right here. The police returned it to me after the accident. Would you like for me to look in it?"

"That would be awfully good of you. Yes, I'd appreciate it if you would."

Another pause. "I see some papers in here. I can't tell if they are photocopies or not, reproduction technology is so good these days. These papers seem to be related to the Kennedy assassination. You guys weren't working on that, were you?"

I smiled but tried to get the thought out of my voice. "Gee, I hope not. Tommy told me about that aspect, but we decided that it wasn't pertinent to our project. No, what we are looking for had to do with a Dennis Dawson and a Lindsey Scott–probably accident reports."

A longer pause. "I've looked through everything

and I don't see anything like that. Of course, they could be imbedded in these lists from the Kennedy thing."

I was disappointed. "No. I suspect the papers we want would have the names right up front. Listen, you've been most kind. You still have the card I gave you at the funeral?"

"Yes, I do. And thank you for the flowers. I haven't had time to send out thank-you notes yet."

"Please give me a call if there is anything I can do, or if you should happen to run across those papers."

"Could you give me the names again?"

"Lindsey Scott and Dennis Dawson."

"I wrote the names by the phone, and I'll be sure and call you if I find anything."

I tried to think of something consoling to say, but I'm afraid I'm not very good at that sort of thing. Its times like this that I wish I were more religious. That would give me something to say automatically. "Well, thank you again. I can't tell you how sorry I am about Tommy."

I gave the cell phone back to Don. "That seems to be a dead end. Got any more ideas?"

He closed the phone and put it back in its holster. "Well, we could try to look at Freeman's wrecked van. There may be something in the glove compartment. If the accident occurred south of town, the wreck should be in Clyde Anderson's salvage yard. I know Clyde. We could take a look-see."

A lady called out our names, and we picked up our orders. The sandwiches were quite good, and the place was packed. It was easy to see why it was so popular. When we finished, we picked up our trash and went out to the lot in back to the car. The place was near to the ramps for the Interstate 10 bridge crossing the Mississippi, and the cars made a constant roar as they climbed up the structure. Don pressed the remote to unlock his car.

I got in the car. "I'm game for seeing Clyde. You're sure I'm not keeping you out too long on this?"

"No. It's getting interesting. Talking to the detectives on the force, they say they spend a hundred times more time following unproductive leads than they do with the successful ones. I think this has been par for the course. Let's go see Clyde. He's a closet mechanical engineer. Clyde went to the University of Michigan out of high school but decided to come back to Baton Rouge and help his dad with his wrecker company. Back then, it was unusual for a black man to be successful here. Under Clyde's guidance the business grew. I suspect he's a millionaire, but you'd never know it. You'll like him. And he does a good job."

Anderson's place had a large, well-kept wooden fence on the road side that kept his business from sight, and, probably, evildoers out. One of the double doors in the fence was open and we drove in on a crushed granite road past neat rows of vehicles in various states of demolition. Three towing trucks, some pickup trucks, and several trailers were parked by a substantial wooden building in the center of the lot although seemingly hundreds of wrecked vehicles stretched out past the building. A metal building sat toward the rear of the property, and several men could be seen outside working on portions of cars. Sparks showered out the door of the building. We parked in front of the wooden building and crunched our way through the gravel to the front door. Inside, a gray-haired man with light chocolate skin was sitting on a bar stool the other side of a long counter. He stopped looking at a computer monitor and got off the stool when he saw Don.

Don stuck out his hand. "How are you doing, old

man?"

Clyde shook hands. "Who you calling old? Haven't seen you in a long time. Does the uniform mean this is official business?'

Dan feigned deep thought and then looked up. "Guess not."

Clyde wiped his brow. "That's a relief. I was afraid one of those angry husbands turned me in again."

"You wish. Look, I want you to meet a friend of mine." He turned to me. "This is Sam Elliot. I bought my house from him."

Clyde shook my hand warmly. "Glad to meet you Sam. Can I interest you two in a cup of coffee?"

I knew a cup of Louisiana coffee would keep me up all night and I dreaded the idea. "Sure, where is it?"

Clyde opened a piece of the counter and let us through. "It's in the back. Come on." He called to another man to watch the front and led us through shelves stacked with car parts. Each shelf was labeled with the vehicle make and model and each part contained a tag showing the year and part number. The shelves stretched on forever. He looked back over his shoulder and waved at the shelves. "We just keep the small parts up here. Heavy stuff like engines and transmissions are in the building in the back of the lot." We came to a table with two coffee machines. "Would you prefer decaffeinated or high test?"

Relieved, I said, "Decaffeinated, please."

"Me, too," he replied, filling two large ceramic mugs. "Regular keeps me up all night. How 'bout you, Don?"

"Let me have some of your high test. Nothing keeps me from sleeping."

Clyde indicated a table with coffee fixings, and we

sat down. He looked at Don. "Looks like the diet is finally working some. Congratulations."

Don patted his abdomen. "I'm not there yet. It's not as easy as it looks."

I looked admiringly at the rows of parts and waved my hand. "You really have a large selection here. Has the business been good?"

Clyde took a sip of coffee. "Ever since we hooked up with a big clearing house, things really took off. People log into their website and type in what they want. Our inventory is on line to the clearing house, so they can see if we have the part. If so, we can ship directly from here. We have a shipping department behind this building, and United Parcel comes by twice a day to pick up the packages."

"Wow. I didn't realize these operations could be so big." On impulse I said, "Do you remember a salvage yard owned by a man named Swifty Sheffield?"

Clyde set down his cup. "Faintly. I wouldn't call it a full-fledged salvage yard, but my dad used to tell me stories about Swifty. He said Swifty could find almost any part someone could ask for. It just took him a few days." He chuckled. "My dad told me about a man who went to Swifty to get a fuel pump for his BMW that was in a mechanic's garage. In a week, Swifty had him a rebuilt fuel pump. The man went back to the mechanic and found that his car had been stolen. My dad thought that Swifty had the car stolen just to get the fuel pump. He probably didn't even know whose car it was."

This reinforced what Tommy had told me. "Seems like a lot of people knew about Swifty's practices. Why wasn't he ever arrested?"

Clyde swirled his coffee around in his cup. "He

never was arrested here, but somebody told me that Swifty might have served time up in New Jersey before he came here. At any rate, Swifty probably had some connections with the police or sheriff's departments. I know a lot of coppers hung around his bar at night."

Don seemed a little uncomfortable with the thought. "I sure hope things have changed since then. Listen, the real reason we came by was to look at a van you might have picked up. It was equipped with hand controls for a guy with no legs."

Clyde leaned back in his chair. "Oh, yeah. I think we have that van. Went off in a ravine just before a bridge, and the poor fellow drowned.

"That sounds like the one," I said. "I didn't really know how he died. He was a friend of mine."

Clyde's face got serious. "I'm sorry. We had a hell of a time getting that van out of there. The Sheriff's divers had gotten the body out somehow, but we had to use our heaviest tow truck to pull the van out. It's in the back of the lot if you'd like to see it."

Don said: "We can make our way back if you're busy."

Clyde held up his hands. "No, no. I don't mind. Drink up, and I'll show you."

We got into one of the double cab pickups, and Clyde drove us to the back of the lot, past the shipping department and the disassembly plant. I spotted the tan van before we stopped. It was still muddy but didn't look too broken up. A wave of sadness hit me, knowing that my friend had lost his life in this grimy shell.

As we got out, Don said, "We're really looking for some papers that the police might have missed. I'm going to look in the glove compartment and under the seats."

Clyde and I stood outside while Don searched the van. We could smell the mold growing on the damp carpets when he opened the door on the passenger side. I realized that this was actually the fourth fatal accident connected with our investigation. Even though the van was in front of me, it was hard to conjure up exactly what had transpired. I wasn't around to see the other vehicles, but here I was with perhaps the last chance to ascertain if foul play was involved. I turned to Clyde. "Can you tell if the brakes failed?"

He seemed mildly surprised. "I can tell right off if they didn't. The brake lines could have been ruptured during the crash, and it would be difficult to say if it happened before or after." He tried to open the driver's door. It was difficult, but finally opened with a screech. "I know they had to get in this side to get the body out. The wheelchair is gone. It looks like they cut the seat belts. Here's one way to check. I'll just pull the lever for the brakes. If there's a leak, the lever would depress all the way or slowly depress while it drains." He put one foot inside and worked the lever. "It feels like the right pressure. I think we're closing the calipers on the discs. I can do one more test to make sure we don't have a perfect crimp in the main line."

Don got out of the van. "It's clean. Clean of papers anyhow. I didn't see anything. What are you two doing?"

Clyde was getting a car jack out of the pickup. "We're going to see if the brakes work." He jacked up the van so that the back wheels were just off the ground, and then he turned the left wheel. He told me to spin the tire when he said to. Then he went back to the brake control. I spun the tire which stopped abruptly when Clyde applied pressure to the control. "Did it stop?"

Hoping to find something, I was mildly disappointed but also relieved that we didn't open another can of worms.

Clyde closed the door which creaked loudly. "I don't see how a crippled man could manage a door so bent up."

I tried it myself, and it was hard to open and shut. "But this happened during the accident, didn't it?"

Clyde ran his finger down a crease. "It looks like he had been in an accident before."

"How do you mean?"

He brushed off some more dirt from the side. "This is a pretty hard scar. See. There's some blue paint in the dent from the other vehicle."

I rubbed some dirt myself. "You mean he had been in a wreck before?"

Clyde dusted the dirt from his hands. "Yeah. A good wallop. I've seen these kind of injuries before. Somebody sideswiped him good."

I had a sinking feeling. "Enough to knock him off the road?"

"Oh yeah. Unless the car is parked, it's hard to maintain control with a whack like that." He cocked his head as he looked at me. "Are you thinking that this may have caused the accident?"

Don was looking over my shoulder. "Let's not mess with this anymore. Clyde, I'd appreciate it if you would leave the van where it is, and I'll try to get forensics over here to take a look. They can usually even tell what vehicle that paint came from."

I was stunned. "Oh shit. You're serious. You must be thinking someone could have deliberately knocked him into the ravine."

Don was serious. "It's a possibility. Maybe this is an opportunity to get someone officially looking into your suspicions."

I backed off to get a better look. "One thing I don't understand. Why would anyone be willing to commit murder to cover up something over thirty years old?"

Don scratched his head. "I dunno. Didn't you say that a kid was with your friend Bill at the airport in Franklinton? He could surely be alive today. Say he was nineteen or twenty at that time. What would that make him today?"

I'm not particularly good at math. "Let's see--Bill died in 1964. This is 1998. That's thirty-four years ago. If the young guy was twenty at the time, he'd be fifty-four now–if he's still around. That's young enough to be still worried. However, Dennis died in 1958. Maybe it's the same group, but not the same people. Clyde, is there anybody still around that was connected with Swifty?"

"Yes there is. Swifty's son, Tony, still runs his daddy's old bar although I don't think it's called Swifty's anymore. The way I know that is that Tony also runs a repair and parts place out Hooper Road, way up in North Baton Rouge toward the Comite River. I also got the idea that Tony is a rough character."

When we got back to Don's car, I shook hands with Clyde and got some directions to Swifty's old bar. I didn't go to the bar that afternoon but instead went back to my house in Clear Creek after Don took me back to the truck. For the next two days, I sanded and painted the front porch. The wood looked in good shape, it was just the paint that was peeling before. I put up a saw horse in front of the front steps with a sign to keep people from getting in the wet paint. As I stood back admiring my work, I could hear the phone ringing inside the house. Ellen was visiting with old friends in Baton Rouge. I ran as quickly as I could to the side door and managed to catch the phone before the answering machine kicked in.

It was Don. "Look. I'm sorry. No one here is interested in looking into Tommy's death very deeply. They tell me that there is an ongoing investigation to incidents like this, but it is mostly focused on the scene of the accident. They did use the word 'accident.' Nothing has been found yet that would point to foul play. I believe there is a little elitism going on here. They don't want some off-duty patrolman discovering a major crime or pointing out how some other guys missed something."

I was a little disappointed. "Did someone at least take a look at the van?"

"That they did. Someone from forensics came out right after you left. I wasn't there, but they took a sample of blue paint off the side of the van. They were able to analyze the sample right away using some new equipment. Apparently, the sample didn't match any car's factory paint. It was a common auto paint that could have been purchased anywhere."

I didn't want Don to feel bad. "Look. We did the best we could. You never know if someone else is going to follow up once we got their attention. At a minimum, someone will remember this if something else turns up. Tell you what. I'm going to come into Baton Rouge tomorrow and visit Swifty's old bar. Are you interested in coming?"

"No, I've got a long shift tomorrow. Let me know if you find out anything. You have my cell phone number."

"Okay. After tomorrow, I intend to go fishing. I deserve a little rest and relaxation."

"Well, enjoy. I'll be talking to you."

CHAPTER SIXTEEN

1998

The next afternoon, I drove out to Jefferson Highway following Clyde's directions and found the area where I remembered Swifty's old bar had been. Everything in that area was highly developed with commercial establishments stacked side by side. One building looked familiar. A yellow neon sign proclaiming "Tony's" dimly competed with its more modern neighbors for attention. It looked like the old Swifty's building–maybe a little larger. It had to be larger because most things from my past looked smaller to me these days. Two plate-glass windows set in a white cinder block structure glared with advertisements of different beers. A windowless addition off to the right gave the impression of growth. I just had time to make the left turn into the gravel parking lot. I hate making decisions at the last moment like that. The back end of the pickup slid to my right from the stress of the sudden stop and turn. Embarrassed, I looked around to see if anyone noticed my clumsiness. There were only two other cars in the parking lot although something was parked in the shadows along the side of the addition. I parked in front of the door and wondered if I really had a good reason to be here. I was here to see if anybody inside could tell me anything about Swifty's demise. Another wild shot, but something that would bug me if I didn't do it now. Could I stomach a beer in exchange for some information? Sure I could. Even if I had to drive back drowsily to Clear Creek.

I opened the door and went in. An old-fashioned jukebox in the annex was playing "Jambalaya," probably by Hank Williams. That part of the building contained tables and a small dance floor. The old Swifty's was only the bar before me with eight or so bar stools. A man was sitting to my far left, hunched over a beer and smoking a cigarette. I debated whether I could stand the smoke, but it was not even detectable from where I was standing. Another man was at the far right, sitting on a stool that was different from the others. It had arms. He was a bear of a man, with hairy arms resting on the arms of the bar stool. He was facing sideways with his back to the three feet or so that remained of the old right wall of Swifty's. His head was down and his eyes were hooded, as if he were listening to the music. Neither man acknowledged my entrance. A pretty woman in her 30's was behind the bar. She had dark hair and wore a low-cut peasant's blouse. She smiled sweetly and asked, "What can I get ya, handsome?"

I looked over my shoulder and pointed a finger at my chest. "You talking to me?"

"Ain't nobody else standing there?" She took a desultory rub at the bar with a rag.

I slid into a seat in the middle of the bar in front of the girl. "Got an Abita Amber?"

"Sure do. Want a glass?"

"Please."

She bent over and rummaged in the cold box beneath the counter. As she did so, her blouse drooped open, exposing her breasts and everything else down to her navel. I stared unabashedly at the two pink pears swinging gently as she searched for the Abita. I noticed that she was not paying too much attention to her search because she was looking at my chest. Did she think she could identify the beer by touch? Or was she deliberately teasing me with her well-proportioned bosom? After allowing enough time for the cold air from the box to harden her nipples, she rose up in triumph with the requested Abita and popped the cap. Her nipples were prominent through the thin blouse. She smiled a sweet smile and asked, "Anything else?" She dried off her wet hands with the towel and gave me a glass from the top of the cold box.

The guy to my left held up an empty bottle and slurred, "Another."

My temptress slid close the lid to the cold box and said. "Coming, handsome." I was crushed that the appellation was not specific to me alone. Perhaps she did not love me after all.

She repeated her provocative display for my fellow ogler down the bar as she fished for his beer. I wondered how long he had been there, probably drinking just for the show. She did return to her position in front of me most likely because that was where she usually sat on a bar stool in back of the bar. I began my spiel. "I used to come here when I was in school, but then the place was called Swifty's."

She wasn't interested. "Could be. Before my time." She was acknowledging the difference in our ages.

"Anybody around today that remembers that time?"

She tilted her head to point to the heavyset man to my right. "You might ask Tony. I think Swifty was his father."

"Thanks." I picked up my beer and walked over to Tony. I sat my beer down, wiped off my right hand on my trousers, and extended it to shake hands with Tony. "Hello, I'm Sam Elliot. I used to come here when Swifty owned this place."

Tony didn't look too pleased, but it's hard not to shake someone's hand when it's offered to you. His fingers were like sausages. I expected his grip to be strong, but he just brushed my hand. I tried to make conversation as I leaned my elbow on the bar. "I guess Swifty isn't around anymore."

Tony wasn't a conversationalist. "Nope."

It was up to me to keep it going. "How long has he been gone?"

"Long time."

I poured some more beer in my glass. "I hope I'm not intruding, but how did he die?"

Tony looked up at me, meeting my eyes for the first time. "Somebody blew his head off with a shotgun." Apparently, he didn't know or didn't want to say anything about his mother. His position was crouching, like he could spring on me any second.

I tried to look grieved. "Oh, no. Swifty was awfully good to me when I was in school. I liked coming out here." I took a swig of beer. "I guess they got the guy who did it."

Tony had enough of the chit-chat. He slid off the seat and went into the annex to select another record, muttering over his shoulder. "Nope, never did."

I guessed that was the end of the conversation. I settled up with the barmaid and left. Somehow, I didn't feel too safe. Tony looked like the kind of guy who didn't mind rough stuff. I backed the pickup away from the plate glass front in an effort to hide my license plate and headed back to Clear Creek.

CHAPTER SEVENTEEN

1998

When I got home, Ellen was sitting at the kitchen table, reading a magazine. She didn't look up as I walked in. "Our daughter Jennie called while you were out. You missed her."

I detected a little peeve in her voice. "I'm sorry. I stayed later than I thought I would. Is our little grandson still on the way?"

Ellen looked up. "Granddaughter. Jennie is due in two weeks. At least that's what the doctor says. I think the first one is always a little late." We had our last child, Jennie, when we were in our thirties, and now she was having her first in her thirties.

I sat down. "Are you worried about her?"

"No, not really. Charlie still has to go to work every day, and Jennie is alone in the house."

I touched her on the arm. "You are worried. Would you like to go to Mobile to be with her?"

She seemed relieved. "Yes. I think I would."

"Do you want me to go too?"

"It might be a little awkward. They only have that single bed in the guest bedroom, and you'd go nuts hanging around for a couple of weeks, especially if we're not sure exactly when the baby is coming. It may be better for me to go alone. I could drive the Camry. It's a straight shot down I-12 and I-10, and we have been there before. I could find their place with no problem. Besides, I'll take the cell phone with me in case I get lost or have car trouble."

"Okay. It's a done deal. Let's call Jennie back in the morning. I'll get the oil changed and the tires checked before you leave. It seems like Mobile is only about three hours away, so you could leave at noon and get there in plenty of time before dark."

Ellen was smiling again. "What would you do while I'm gone–paint some more maybe?"

"Maybe. I'd really like to do some fishing. I haven't had a chance to put the boat in the water since I bought it."

The next morning, I took the Camry to a quick oil change place near Hammond. They checked all the fluids and the tires and changed the oil and the filter. I felt better knowing Ellen would be safer on the road. When I got back to Clear Creek, we went out to lunch. Ellen had packed all her stuff already. She didn't leave much in the house. I loaded her up and sent her on her way. She stopped in the driveway as she was backing out, got out, came back and kissed me before she left. I felt a little lonely already as she drove toward the highway.

I spent the rest of the day lounging around and getting ready to go fishing the next morning. With the low water, I knew even my little boat couldn't navigate Clear Creek to get to the Tangiphoa River near the house. However, I was determined to get out and do a little fishing. The boat landing on the Bogue Falaya River in Covington was just a few miles away, and the light traffic on the route wouldn't pose much of a threat to my towing phobia. I searched through my two old tackle boxes and made one box of baits and accessories. I only found two swivels. Why were there never enough swivels? Maybe I could buy a few at the bait shop on the way. I needed some live bait anyhow. I decided to take the old single shot .22 for snake plunking. The box of cartridges must have been 40 years old, but they probably last forever. I poured a handful in my shirt pocket. There was something comforting about the old long-sleeved checkered shirt. Long sleeves would protect against mosquitoes and the sun.

The trip wasn't anywhere near as hazardous as I had imagined. The bait shop had a circular driveway, so one potential back-up was eliminated. No such luck with the boat ramp in Covington. I didn't want to embarrass myself in front of other people if I could help it. There was only one blue SUV behind me. It had followed me all the way from the bait shop, and I thought he was going to put in too. Now I could see he wasn't towing a boat. I waited for him to clear the area before attempting to back the trailer into the launch. The SUV pulled up at the other end of the parking lot where they could watch me. The windows were shaded so dark that no one was visible inside, but I knew they were watching. It took me three tries to get the boat in the water and two tries to back the empty trailer into a reasonable parking position. The SUV was still watching me. Thankfully, the little 15-horse motor started right away, and I headed down river. The people in the SUV had no more sport to watch and pulled away. I hope they enjoyed my ineptitude.

The little boat performed well. I had to slow down to prevent the wake from washing up on the beaches of the fine homes that lined the shores for the first mile or so. As I passed the boat rental marina, two men were trying to start an outboard. They didn't look dressed for fishing. As I rounded the bend, I thought I could spot the blue SUV in the marina parking lot. I passed the juncture of the Tchefuncta River and went under the I-12 bridge. The houses thinned out, and thick swampy woods came up to the banks on either side. Tall cypress trees marched out to the river and set fat roots in the soggy soil. Farther back grew mostly tupelo trees and dense underbrush separated by patches of stagnant water. A low, irregular natural levee separated the swamp from the river. Startled by my boat, a great blue heron gave a loud "gronk" and flew off from his perch on a downed pine tree. At a sufficiently isolated spot I cut the motor and let down the anchor as I neared the shore. I threaded one on the shiners on a hook, threw the line in the water, and sat back to relax. In a few minutes, two boats came down river. One held the two guys from the rental marina, and the other was a larger, better appointed boat with four kids in it. The smaller boat held up and let the larger one go by. If they were going somewhere, why did they let the other boat through? Something didn't look right. As the larger boat sped down toward Madisonville, I could see that the two non-fisherman were looking directly at me. I didn't like the feeling. The wake from the passing boat caused the back end of my boat to swing around and ground on the bank. I was a sitting duck if the two men were up to mischief. I picked up the .22 and jumped off into the woods, getting my feet muddy in the process. I ran along the only high ground in the swamp for about thirty-five yards and looked back from behind a tupelo tree. The other boat pulled up beside mine, and the two men got out. They took out a long tool box and removed two objects. My stomach sank as I could see that they were both now carrying revolvers. Not only that, the revolvers had round cylinders on the ends that I took to be silencers. I looked behind me to see if there was an escape route. There wasn't. Everything was swamp. I couldn't run through that muck. I chambered a .22 long into the single-shot and pulled the plunger that activated the firing pin. A .22 wasn't much of a defense against whatever the two mugs were carrying, but it was a lot more accurate at this distance. Could this be something innocent?

What if I shot a game warden or some legitimate person? Not likely. These guys were definitely after me. The two men hesitated, peering into the dark woods to find me. This wasn't a case of an expired license plate on my trailer. It had to do with Tommy's death. Still, I couldn't bring myself to try a head shot. I braced the rifle against the tree and aimed at the first guy's right shoulder. The shot made a loud "tat" sound and the man clutched his shoulder and dropped his gun.

He screamed. "I've been shot. Get me to a doctor!"

The other man wasn't sympathetic. "Hold on, we've got to get this bastard."

"Hold on hell. I'm bleeding to death. Let's get the hell out of here." He started back toward his boat. "You shoot it out with Elliot. I'm leaving." Even at this distance, I could see that he was grimacing in pain and hopping around a bit.

The second man bent over to present a smaller target. He was obviously torn between finishing his mission and getting the hell out of there. Then he picked up the first man's gun and ran stooped over to their boat. He made a motion as if to push my boat out into the water. I put another round into the side of their tool box to frighten him. He jerked away and then returned to pick up the box like it was hot. They both got wet as they clumsily tried to get the boat out while trying not to expose themselves. The motor started and they raced back toward the rental marina. The man who was shot rocked back and forth in pain while he clutched his shoulder.

I was trembling. What should I do? If I went back with my boat trailer to Covington, the two men could be waiting there for me. If I went down river to the next boat launch in Madisonville, I had no way of getting my boat out.

I crept back to the shore and looked up river. No sign of the other boat. I decided to take a chance and go back the way I had come. The man I shot evidently was intent on getting medical help. I pulled up my fishing line. Something had gotten my bait. I poured the rest of the shiners in the river and pulled up the anchor. I ran the boat slowly until I got to the marina. Then I swung wide to the other side of the river to take a look. The blue SUV was gone. I steered up to the dock as an old man with a beard came up to greet me.

I tried to be friendly. "How ya doing today?"

"'Bout the same." As if I knew how he was before.

"Say, did two men driving a blue SUV just dock here?"

"Sure did." The old man nodded toward a docked boat. "They was only out a few minutes, and this one fellow hurt his shoulder and had to come back. Do you know them?"

"No, but I saw them coming back and thought something must be wrong. Did they say where they were going?"

"No. I figured they was looking for a doctor, but they didn't ask me nothing. Must have known where they was going. They sure took off fast, probably to St. Tammany Hospital. Can I do you something?"

"No thanks. I was just worried about the man who hurt himself." I put the outboard in reverse and backed away. I waved as I turned up river. "See ya."

I was too frightened to think straight. The two mugs could still be waiting for me at the Covington boat launch, but I didn't know of another alternative but to go there. There were no blue SUVs parked at the launch when I got there, so I cautiously pulled up and got my truck. This time I was able to back up to my boat on the first try. I cranked the boat up on the trailer while keeping an eye out on the parking lot and a hand near the cocked .22. Even though it was small caliber, it was still better accuracy at a distance than the pistols any day. I didn't want to go home. The men obviously knew who I was and where I lived. If they were getting medical help, it surely would take a little time. I went home anyhow. There wasn't anywhere else to go. I put the boat trailer in back of the work shop and went into the house to pack. Anywhere else would be safer than the house. I threw together enough clothes to last a few days. I wish I owned a hand gun, but all I had were the .22 and an old 12-gauge pump. I put them both in the toolbox in the truck.

Where to go? I called Jim Simpson in Baton Rouge to tell him I needed a place to stay. He didn't hesitate and asked me to come on over to his house. He told me one option would be to go on up to his place in Clinton and wait for the rest of the hunters. I did take the time and trouble to open the computer and add part of this latest episode to the notes of the investigation. I printed out two copies of the notes to take with me with the idea that I might want to give it to Jim or mail a copy to someone as a backup.

On the way out I stopped by Walter's place and got some 12-gauge shells and a warm camouflage mask that I could pull over my face. He sold me number 6 shot because I wasn't sure exactly what I would be hunting, and 6's were good for a lot of different things, including squirrels. I also bought a powerful little flashlight to use in the woods. As Walter was bagging my purchases he asked if my cousin had found me all right. Apparently, the two men who tried to ambush me had missed me at the house and had asked Walter where I would be. This time I didn't tell him where I was going. I only stopped once more to get gas.

225

I had to tell Jim the whole story over dinner, telling him the findings without going very deeply into how I discovered them. He sat back and toyed with a fork on the dining room table. "You know, without this latest incident, I don't think you have much to go on. Even Tommy's death sounds like an accident. If you had come to me with this tale last week, I would have said everything you've told me is just a coincidence."

I've always liked Jim. His flaming red hair was much reduced now. He seemed to have kept in shape, though. He didn't have the gut that surrounded most of us of the same age. Jim had been a fighter in junior high school. We'd get to school early and play touch football in the school yard until the bell rang to start classes. By that time, we were usually all dirty and sometimes bloody. Jim didn't like people getting too rough with him. The honor code in fourteen-year-olds meant that a fist fight was the proper way to respond to affronts. Jim engaged in a lot of them. Most of the time it was a draw. All the boys would form a circle once the argument seemed capable of spawning a fight. After the circle was formed, there was no recourse except to fight. Much prestige was at stake. Fights were stylistic. You'd think that boys would wrestle on the ground and try to pin their opponents. Not so at our school. They would stand toe to toe and pound each other with their fists. This nearly always resulted in bloodshed. Fortunately, one of the coaches would notice the commotion and run onto the field to break up the fight. The two combatants would be forced to shake hands and make up. Apparently all was forgotten because usually we would resume our game. I suspect that the fighters counted heavily on the coaches to intercede.

Jim laid down the fork and looked me in the eye. "I

still think you ought to go to the police."

"You're probably right. I still don't have enough evidence to do anything. Maybe if they could find the guy I shot. Even then, who's the culprit? Maybe they'd charge me. "

"How about the guy who bought your house in Baton Rouge? Couldn't you trust him?"

"Don Carruthers? You suggested at the funeral that I should call him. That was a good idea. I did contact him, and he's actually been helping me out. He was the one who got me into the State Police and Sheriff's offices to find out about the records. I do worry a bit that if I told him about the shooting, he'd have to do something official. "

Jim said several sets of camouflage jump suits were in the closet at the cabin, so I didn't have to buy any more special clothing for the deer hunts that would begin the next weekend. I could even have the use of an old Mauser rifle that Jim showed me how to operate. He gave me ten of the special cartridges the Mauser used. Jim wrote out a detailed list of what I needed to do at the camp. Among other things, it told me how to turn on the water and electricity, how to open the doors, and how to operate the heating system. Don't wear any leather because the deer would avoid the smell. Likewise, I shouldn't relieve myself around the deer stands. I wasn't to shoot any deer until Saturday when the season opened, but I was instructed to shoot every fox, coyote, or hog that I could find. The foxes and coyotes were suspected of killing some of the game animals, particularly the turkeys, and the hogs were tearing up the roads and the feed plots for the deer. I was not to shoot any wildcats because they were protected animals. Besides hunting, the group of friends was expected to form work parties to clear the roads and improve the deer stands.

Everything seemed to be set up except for a pair of rubber boots, warm gloves (not leather), and groceries. I was able to obtain what I needed at a Walmart on the way out of town. Lately, Ellen and I had gotten into the habit of having a glass of wine with our dinner. I wondered how my old friends would react to wine drinking, so I bought a bottle of Wild Turkey bourbon instead. Wild Turkey sounded appropriately manly. Somehow, I felt a sense of freedom as I drove up to Clinton, knowing that I would be on my own for a while, but relishing the change. I called Ellen from a payphone in Clinton and told her what I was doing, but not about the shooting on the river. The trip simply was to meet some of my old friends and go hunting with them. Everyone was well in Mobile, and the pregnancy seemed to be progressing normally. Ellen called Jennie to the phone to assure me. I let them know that it would be hard to contact me, but that I would try to call periodically.

CHAPTER EIGHTEEN

I found the hunting camp without much trouble. I turned on the water at the meter on the road and drove back on a dirt road about a quarter mile to the house. The key was hidden under the porch. The bleeder valve on the water line in back of the house was spurting and had to be closed. Someone had forgotten to close the valve after draining the water from the house on the last trip. The refrigerator was running, and I put nearly all of my groceries inside it, even things that didn't need to be refrigerated. Jim had suggested that I do that because the box would guard foodstuffs from little critters that could get into the house. Thinking that the water heater had filled with water by then, I turned on the rest of the electricity at the breaker box and surveyed my surroundings

Jim had described the site of my temporary home well. The hunting camp in Clinton was a former tenant farmer's house. There were two bedrooms, a large living room, a kitchen, and a bath. The bedrooms were fitted with bunk beds to accommodate as many as six hunters. The living room had two sofa beds that would sleep two more. In overflow situations, folding cots could be set up in the kitchen and living room to bring the total stay-overs to ten. The one bathroom was a problem, but Jim assured me that most functions could be discharged in the woods. I really didn't remember the woods from my hunting days back in the fifties. The Simpson clan owned over 700 acres of some of the prettiest hardwoods imaginable. Large hickory trees abounded. The property was crisscrossed with a number of steep gullies that drained off into a large creek with gravel and sand beaches. The hunting buddies had built rather substantial bridges across the major gullies and had placed a dozen or so deer stands in strategic locations.

The family's big farmhouse had burned to the ground during the seventies. Jim's parents moved to Baton Rouge after the fire and had died about six years ago. Jim and a cousin who did very little hunting owned the property jointly but hadn't tried to divide it up as yet. I could stay as long as I liked, but the accommodations would have to be shared during hunting weekends. I probably should buy a cell phone because the cabin did not have a telephone. I decided to procrastinate on the cell phone for a bit because Ellen had our instrument in Mobile and I hated to sign another contract. The lack of a phone presented a little dilemma if I wanted to find out how the pregnancy was coming along.

I thought about exploring the woods a bit but decided instead to sit down and look at my printed notes first. The notes were pretty extensive but still incomplete. Most of the business of the shooting had to be added to the end in longhand because I had left out some things in my haste. Luckily, I had double-spaced everything, so I could make additions in the spaces and the margins. The more I thought about it, the more I remembered. I tried to quote what people said as best I could instead of making conclusions. After I finished one document, I had to enter the handwritten notes on the second copy. Then, after reading the whole thing through, I remembered even more facts that I had left out of the first draft.

Satisfied with what I had done, I walked out on the front porch. The shadows were getting longer and it was growing colder. The barred owls were calling, and either dogs or coyotes were howling in the distance. The owls were loud: "Hoo-hoo-to-hoo. Hoo-hoo-to-hooaw." Exploring this close to dark didn't seem like a good idea.

Inside, I picked out a couch to sleep on in the living room and unrolled my sleeping bag. I ate a light dinner and walked outside again. It was dark now and the sky was filled with stars. It had been a long time since I had seen such magnificence. Millions of sparkling stars dotted a black velvet sky unencumbered by the lights of civilization. The Milky Way lived up to its name, appearing almost solid with its stars tightly packed in enormous swirls. The sky looked completely different out here. I sighted along the end of the Big Dipper to find the North Star, but the visibility was so good several stars became candidates. A shooting star traced a line over half the sky. I poured a glass of bourbon and water inside, put on a coat, and sat back on the porch, taking in the sights and sounds of the country.

That night I had trouble sleeping. Mice were running up and down the floor, probably unaware that I was there. I moved my sleeping bag into one of the bedrooms and shut the door.

The next morning I ate breakfast, cleaned up, and took a copy of my notes into town. Helpful employees at the post office showed me how to package my notes to send to Don. Luckily, I had his address since he was in my parents' old home, but someone had to look up the zip code for me. They assured me that my package would arrive by Saturday or before. I bought a few more groceries and headed back. People on the side of the road waved to me as though I belonged there. Country people are like that. They would be embarrassed if they failed to recognize a neighbor.

Back at the house, I put on the rubber boots, picked up the .22, and headed out to explore. I wanted to scout out the deer stands so I could choose a spot for the weekend hunt. I brought along a salami sandwich and a can of Sprite in case I got too far away from the house. On the wall of the house, Jim had posted a large hand-drawn map of the property that showed the cleared roads, fields, woods, sloughs, bridges, ponds, and deer stands. I decided to try the right hand side of the map first from the back of the house. Fences ran throughout the property from the time the owners had leased out the fields to cattle owners, but the gates were all open. The roads were carved out with a bush hog and were relatively clear of vegetation–more like wide paths than roads. According to Jim, some of the regular hunters had all-terrain vehicles and could get around using the manufactured roads. Since I didn't know the property, I stuck to the roads.

The main road angled off to my right and skirted a small pond. The pond contained lots of vegetation and was overhung with large trees. Swirls in the water indicated feeding fish. If I had known the hunting camp had this kind of resource, I would have brought my fishing gear. Funny, I just had gone to a bunch of trouble to go fishing in the Bogue Falaya, and right here looked like the perfect spot to catch some good-sized bass. Some bass swam up to the bank in the clear water and were pursuing visible bait fish in the shallows. The overhanging trees would present a problem in casting, but numerous openings along the banks offered opportunities to get a bait out into deeper water. I made a mental note to check out the fishing possibilities when my friends came in for the weekend hunt.

Farther down the road, a break in the woods opened up to a large field. I paused on the edge of the field to look up and down the open space for sign of animals, but all I could see were buzzards circling some distance off, probably over someone else's property. Back in the plantation days, the field probably was planted with some type of crop but now was covered with foot-high grass. I checked out two deer stands that overlooked the field and even crawled up into one to see what it was like. The rifle caught in the camouflage netting and was hard to detach. That was good to remember when I had to get into one of the stands during the hunt. The elevation of the stand increased the visible area considerably, especially back into the woods where I could look over the nearby undergrowth. I walked along the edge of the field until I encountered the road leading away from it on the other side.

The trees looked larger on this side, with less undergrowth. After a few hundred feet, a tree was down over most of the road. I guessed this was a project to clear when the crew came in. Just off to the right a small noise alerted me to three white birds fleeing from me. The birds never gained any height and came out into the road ahead of me. Then I could see they weren't birds at all. What I was seeing were the tall, cottony tails of three doe deer. The deer stopped and looked at me. They made loud blowing sounds as if to frighten me. The deer were perfectly camouflaged to my eyes when they were in the woods. I could have walked right by them if they hadn't moved. I sat down on the fallen tree and didn't move as I watched the deer watch me. After a while one of the deer put her head down and ate some grass. Then they slowly moved off into the woods. I could still see them for a while, and then they vanished from my sight while I was still looking at them. Unless they moved, they were invisible.

I remained sitting on the downed tree for a few minutes, thinking how privileged I was to have seen such a thing. I've seen many small animals in the woods before–squirrels, rabbits, raccoons, possums, armadillos, etc., but I have never seen anything as large as a deer. It seems strange that animals that big can coexist with civilization. I was 62 years old and had never seen anything like that. Odd, I certainly didn't feel 62. I felt like I could do anything physically that I had done 30 years before. Maybe I could get another surprise if I actually tried to do those things. I jogged rather than ran now. It was easier to get out of breath. I quit playing league softball just a few years ago when I tore a calf muscle. Still, I felt young. At one time, 62 sounded very old. My father died at 73, which seemed about how long someone should live. How did I get to be this old?

I felt proud that I had made it this far. Wild Bill didn't do it. Jimmy Simmons didn't do it. Many of my friends from high school were gone now, and I was still going. One time, at a fraternity meeting in high school, a speaker had said solemnly that some of us may not make it through the Korean War, which was going on at the time. Several people looked around at me, as though I would be a good candidate for an early demise. Maybe they thought I was expendable, like the sidekicks in the movies. I had fooled them all. I have never had any major health problems. Was it luck, genes, taking care of myself?

I was lucky to have had a good career helping people but still earning enough for a more than comfortable retirement. I couldn't have wished for a better wife than Ellen–loving, smart, and practical. We were blessed with wonderful children who excelled in everything and were making families of their own. Ellen and I shared many of the same interests and were very comfortable with each other. We had been able to travel and see the world. Yes, things could have turned out much worse. If I were to die right now, I would have had a good life. Now I had rediscovered old friends, friends who welcomed me as though I had never gone. We were about to embark on new adventures with stories to tell and gaffs we could kid each other about. I looked up at the cloudless blue sky and realized that things were going very well.

My idyllic day continued as I walked down the road. A little chill crept into the midday air. A light breeze waved the tops of the trees as a cool front moved in, bringing a few high clouds. The woods were especially beautiful when the tree branches met above the road like a tunnel. The path seemed to follow the crest of a ridge, and I was careful not to stray far off the cleared areas. Some of the sloughs looked really deep with steep sides. Finally, I sat down on a stump and ate my sandwich and drank my drink. I didn't see any more deer, but a few squirrels were still out from their morning feed, retreating at a run to their den trees. Birds were everywhere. I located two more deer stands off the road which were marked with reflecting cloths nailed to the trees to indicate the branching paths. These stands seemed too far away to locate in the dark for the next morning, so I crossed them off my possibilities. I turned around, worked my way back to the house, and waited for the dark again. Even though my soul was at peace with the beauty of the place, loneliness began to creep in. I missed Ellen. My friends were not to arrive until the next afternoon, the Friday before the beginning of the deer season.

After eating, I repeated my actions of the day before and sat on the porch in the gathering cold, sipping on the bourbon. It was noticeably colder. Because of the few clouds, the stars were not as prominent as they were the night before. Had I not seen that dazzling display the previous night, I would have thought tonight's performance was the most beautiful ever. Life is like that– you don't know how good something is unless you have something to compare it with.   Probably because of the exercise, and certainly because of my seclusion from the little critters, I slept well that night.

CHAPTER NINETEEN

The next morning, I studied the wall map after breakfast and planned out a reconnaissance of the left side of the property. The weather had turned noticeably colder. An outdoor thermometer read 46 degrees. I put on one of the camouflage suits for extra warmth. I started to take the .22, but decided that the 12 gauge would be more effective against varmints. Even the .22 was cumbersome to carry in my hands the day before, so I searched around for something to use as a sling. A piece of rope did nicely, tied around the barrel and the stock of the shotgun. The left side of the map started with a field very similar to the one on the other side, but closer. Evidently, someone had mowed it a few weeks back and rolled the resulting hay into cylinders that were stacked at the end of the field. The field was easy to walk in, especially in the paths cut by the all-terrain vehicles.

I headed toward a spot where one of the roads hit the opposite side of the field. This path was not so easy to find because of the heavy woods that came right up to the edge of the field. Finally, I found the reflecting tape on a tree and marched off into the forest. The path crossed several shallow sloughs before reaching a deer stand on the immediate right. This was a tripod stand that overlooked a stretch of woods with very little undergrowth. It too was marked with reflecting tape. My guess was that it would be hard to find in the dark without the tape. I climbed up to look around. The vista up high stretched for hundreds of yards. Trees grew sporadically over a park-like area that offered unlimited shooting lanes. I could see squirrels shaking the branches of faraway trees. I climbed down and looked down the path.

According to the map, the narrow road continued on to two more deer stands, but I figured I had gone far enough and turned around. The slippery bottoms of the sloughs coming back convinced me that I should avoid the stands on this path in the dark until I was more accustomed to the area. I turned left when I reached the field again, looking for another stand that should be only a few yards into the woods. Again, reflecting tape alerted me to a narrow path that led to another stand. This one was a tree stand attached to some kind of straight oak. I climbed up again, fighting the camouflage netting that wanted to catch the shotgun on my back. This area around this stand was not as open as it was around the last one, but the access was easier. The ground dropped off about forty yards in front of the stand, and I could envision deer using this ridge as a highway. I started back to the house, confident that I had a place to go to in the morning. At the camp, I transferred the make-shift sling to the Mauser.

Jim was at the camp already. He had towed his ATV in a trailer, and I helped him unload it. Before long, the other guys started coming in. Bat brought an ATV as well. Johnny Ray came with his son, Billy Ray, who appeared to be in his late 30's. They were going to ride in an electric golf cart and had brought a charger to hook it up overnight. Chester Melancon, whom I hadn't seen since high school came and surprised me. I still recognized him. He had gone to college at Mississippi State and had worked until his retirement at the Michoud plant just across the border from Louisiana. He helped build space vehicles at Michoud and only recently moved back to Baton Rouge.

We all went inside and ate cold cuts and peanuts for lunch. Jim had filled them in as to why I was staying at the camp, but they all wanted me to tell them what I had found out. I had to repeat the whole story. Billy Ray thought I should contact the police through Don. Even though there may be a mole in the force, gunshot wounds are reportable and my would-be assassins would be outed and watched. My friends all felt like we had a clear case for foul play with Bill, but the events were too old to get serious follow-up by the authorities. Apparently, some people were concerned at the time that Dennis may have been murdered, but nothing ever came of it. Surprisingly, the hunters all wanted to see my .22. It was an antique, but we couldn't tell how old it was. I found it in my grandmother's house many years ago, and had used it as a teenager to go plinking in the swamps of South Baton Rouge.

After we cleared the fallen tree I found from the road, we sat around in the cold on the porch, waiting for the steaks and potatoes to cook. Everyone had a beer and the group taught me some things I needed to know about deer hunting. A successful hunter doesn't move in the stand. Deer can smell you a long way away if the wind is blowing in that direction. The best shot is right behind the front leg to hit the heart and lungs. Deer will run after they are shot. Don't come down off the stand, but note the direction the deer runs. If you get down too soon, the deer will spook and run again. The hunters can follow a blood trail a long distance. Does can be shot now at the beginning of the season but will be illegal later on. Try not to shoot a buck with fewer than six points on his antlers. Most of this advice may be wasted because this group only kills one or two deer a season. I didn't expect to see another one judging from the stories.

The steaks were delicious. Chester broke out a bottle of Cabernet Sauvignon for the group, so my hesitation about wine was unfounded. Our habits must have changed as we grew older. Surprising to me were the group's heavily entrenched Deep South attitudes. They seemed to get their information about current events from a few dedicated sources. These were good people, involved with church and charities. Even with their strong beliefs, they were tolerant of my feelings. I believe that is characteristic of one way of thinking–opposed to certain groups or ideas, but intensely caring for family and individuals. Later, everyone gathered around the wall map and chose their morning stands. We went to bed early because we had to get up at 4:30 the next morning. I moved out to the couch again after hearing jokes about the expected loud snoring. The mouse woke me up again several times, but I must have been asleep when Bat roused me before daybreak.

We had scrambled eggs for breakfast. With our self-imposed healthful meals, Ellen and I hadn't had scrambled eggs in years. Everyone dressed and hurried to get their stands before it got light. I followed the edge of the field using my flashlight until I found my stand. Getting past the netting hanging around the seat was still a problem. Everything was dark as I settled in. I rested the Mauser on the rail in front of me to be ready to shoot. Gradually, after what seemed like a long time, dark shapes emerged all around. As the sun rose almost directly in front of me, the shapes formed into trees and bushes. I could imagine deer everywhere, but as it grew lighter, all the forms turned into vegetation. The birds began to call, slowly at first, and then bursting into a cacophony of sound as they greeted the new day. Shaking the limbs, squirrels came from a distance to feed in the wild pecan tree beside the stand. One squirrel with a bright orange chest sat watching me as he ate his nut. I didn't move. Every sound in the leaves alerted me, and every sound turned out to be a squirrel or a bird. It was getting uncomfortable sitting in one place, but I didn't move.

It was cold. A slight breeze ran before the sun and exited the woods into the field behind me. A shiver went through me. The sun rose full, and still no deer. How long should I wait before heading back? No one had said how long we should hunt. I slowly sneaked a peek at my watch. It was 7:00. I heard shots coming from miles away, but nothing from Jim's property.

After what seemed like hours, I spotted something out of the corner of my eye, coming from my left. Feet moving at a good pace were coming toward me, barely visible under the higher brush. As the feet drew nearer, I could see that it was a doe deer. But it was moving too fast for me to attempt a shot. A small clearing was directly in front of me, about thirty yards away. The deer would have to pass through that clearing, but even though the deer was trotting slowly, I would be afraid to attempt a shot. Just as the deer reached the clearing, I shouted: "Hey!" The doe stopped in her tracks and faced me. I shot at her chest, just below her neck. She fell to the ground. From my briefing, I expected her to get up and run, but she remained still. My heart was pounding. What should I do now? I waited for a while and then got down to inspect the kill. It was a beautiful animal with a healthy coat. I tried to drag it toward the field, but it was very heavy. I sat down on a log and waited. Someone would have heard my shot.

I could hear the sound of an ATV after a bit, and Jim drove up. "Was that you that shot?"

I pointed to the dead deer. "Yes, I got a doe."

We field dressed the animal on the spot and hoisted her on the back of the ATV. I walked back to the camp behind Jim, steadying the carcass to keep it from falling off.

We decided to butcher the animal and divide up the meat since it was the first deer killed in the season. I couldn't use any meat because I was not planning on going home as yet. Sometimes the hunters would donate the deer to orphanages through a local butcher. We hoisted the deer by a cable through the hind legs and cut up the meat to be placed in ice chests. With the cold weather, everything would keep fresh in the backs of the vehicles. We were almost finished when the rest of the group came in from the woods. Only one other deer had been seen. Johnny Ray had passed on a doe, giving me the feeling that my friends really were concentrating on bucks.

We all went out on Saturday afternoon, but again, the only deer seen were does. I began to think maybe I shouldn't have shot the doe. That night, we relived old times by telling stories on one another. We listened to the LSU football game on the radio. All of us were fervent LSU fans except for Chester. Our football team capped off a horrendous season by having Notre Dame run back an interception 89 yards to win the game by three points.

Sunday morning, I decided to change stands and went to the one on the other side of the property that overlooked the woodsy bottom. I directed my gaze to the woods rather than the field, thinking that something would be easier to spot in the field. This time, the shapes in the early dawn began to move and revealed themselves to be several deer, albeit small ones. I guessed they were does or fawns because of their sizes, but it was still too dark to make them out. Then, out to my left, a larger shape loomed. This animal had its head close to the ground and was approaching the group of small deer. It must be a buck, although it was still too dark to make out antlers. Slowly he crept forward, not making a sound. He put his nose up to the back of one of the small deer. I was afraid he would get away if I waited too long. I aimed behind what I thought was the shoulder and pulled the trigger. He went down immediately and rolled back and forth with his feet up in the air. I could have shot again, but remembered that one shot had done it with the doe.

Smug that I had struck again, I settled back in the seat and waited as I had been told. As it got lighter, I could see where the deer had gone down but couldn't see the corpse. Finally, I climbed down and went to the spot. The deer must have rolled over into a small depression. No, it wasn't there either. I made a wide search but couldn't find any signs. Bat came up later and helped me look. He thought he found some blood but wasn't sure. I was sick. I could have shot again while the deer was rolling or I could have gotten down before it got away, but my chance was gone forever. Not only that, the deer was wounded and probably would die somewhere else. Not a very successful outcome.

We heard a shot about half a mile away and later learned that Billy Ray had shot a six point buck down the muddy path that I had decided to forgo on Friday. They took the animal into town to donate it to the orphanage. We cleaned up the camp, and I said my goodbyes to my old friends with the promise that we would get together later in the season. As I was left alone again, I wondered just how long this exile would last. I really didn't have any definite plans. The thought of the two hoods was frightening still. They knew who I was, but I knew nothing about them. I needed to talk to Don.

CHAPTER TWENTY

Monday morning, I went into Clinton and called Don's cell phone from the payphone in the pharmacy. He answered right away. "Sam! Good to hear from you. Got that material you sent me in the Saturday mail. It was great! I think you could be a very good investigator–very thorough. I feel like I'm getting to know this Wild Bill character pretty well. Who were his heroes? Who did he admire?"

"Probably no real people that I can think of. He wanted to live extravagantly, like the Great Gatsby."

Don probed further. "Did he like bad guys?"

"He didn't mind playing the villain when we were kids. Once he told me something odd about admiring Harry Lime."

"Who was Harry Lime?"

"He was a character in the book and movie 'The Third Man". Harry faked his own death to avoid prosecution for some pretty nasty dealings. Bill thought that was a neat trick and Harry should have gotten away with it."

"Interesting. That sort of fits my picture of your friend. Actually, we've had a break in the case that should help us considerably, and I've got some theories as to what really happened. I'd like to discuss them with you."

That sounded good to me. "Go ahead. Shoot."

"Actually, this could take some time, some back and forth. Too long for a telephone call, especially if you're paying. How about me meeting you in Jackson? That's right down the road. There's a good restaurant right on the main drag called Bear's Corners, or something like that. I could meet you for Tuesday lunch. They're closed on

Mondays."

Restaurant food was a good motivator. I had been eating well, but sitting down to a good meal was appealing. "Can do. What time?"

"Noon would be good. You can park right on Highway 10 that goes through town."

On Tuesday I put on the best clothes I brought and went into Jackson. A light rain was falling. Bear Corners was in the middle of town. I parked across the street. Inside, most people were dressed in blue jeans, so I shouldn't have worried about my clothes. I didn't see Don. I told the hostess that I'd like to wait for him at a table. Don came in before my ice tea arrived. He was carrying the documents I had sent him.

I was anxious to find out his news as we shook hands. "What was the break you talked about?"

"This was just blind luck. That guy you shot went to the ER at Baton Rouge General for treatment. The ER doc wanted him to stay overnight, but he left against orders. He claimed it was a hunting accident, but all gunshot wounds have to be reported. A friend of mine on the force interviewed the guys at the hospital, but everything they said sounded suspicious. He tailed them when they left– and where do you suppose they went?

"Where?"

"Directly to Tony's repair shop in North Baton Rouge! I read the whole report. The only bad thing is that the guy you shot used a fake ID at the hospital. Of course, my buddy didn't know that when he followed them. I asked him to hold off until we could find out more."

I thought that was great news because now we could link Tony to the two gunmen. Before this point, all we could say is that is that someone had obtained my name and whereabouts from our visits either to the State Police or the Sheriff's office. "You said you had some ideas about what happened."

Don seemed excited and launched directly into his presentation after he ordered a beer. "First of all, the two dummies that tried to do you in probably didn't connect you with Bill Jenkins. My guess is that they were alerted to our interest in Scott and Dawson by someone in the criminal justice system. That's how they got your address in Clear Creek. Tweedledum and Tweedledee are too young to have been around for the earlier murders. I'm calling them murders because that's probably the only crime that would not be affected by a statute of limitations. It also means that someone is still alive that could be implicated."

I interrupted. "They would also have your address. Wouldn't they be after you too?"

"I think they would like to get me out of the way, but that would be more difficult for them now. I took the liberty of copying your documents and giving them to a friend of mine to be opened only if something happened to me. They wouldn't know that necessarily, but I'd be a lot harder to take out simply because I'm a cop. My house has a sign out front that announces my security system. There's also a sign warning people about my big police dog. My car has a motion-sensitive alarm. These guys didn't think things through. They never should have gone after you. Even if they had succeeded, they would have drawn attention to themselves that would have been counterproductive to their aims–that is, to cover-up those old crimes. My guess is that their instructions were to do you in and make it look like there was no connection. Tweedledee and Tweedledum are working for someone else who, in all likelihood, is a lot smarter than they are, probably Tony from what we know now. His best bet is to back off and hope that we don't have a breakthrough on our investigation. He most likely doesn't know that my friend followed his henchmen from the hospital, but that ER visit has to be troubling to them. They've got to be worried at this point."

The waitress came and took our orders. Don stopped talking until she left.

"Let me shift to Bill Jenkins. That's where we have the most info anyhow and where your interest started. We can assume that Bill was involved in something shady. His lawyer friend in Franklinton must know that too. Judging by what he said, those trips in the plane probably had some tropical destination." Don tapped an index finger on the documents I had sent him. "The administrator in Franklinton mentioned a pickup filled with marijuana. Do you know when they found that truck?"

I thought for a second. "No. I don't remember him saying when that happened. He may have. I know he was just listing crimes that had happened in the area over a long period of time."

"Did Bill use marijuana or talk about peddling it?"

"He didn't use it as far as I know, but on one of our Mexico trips he did propose bringing some back to the U.S. and selling it. A friend of ours and I wouldn't have any of that. It took some persuading to talk Bill out of it. I suppose he was just thinking about the money and maybe the thrill of doing something wild."

"Do you remember Bill ever saying that he would use the plane for illegal purposes?"

Things were coming back to me. "I think he hinted at it even before he bought the plane. When we were in the service in North Carolina, he took me to see a plane like the one that crashed later on. I don't remember exactly what he said, but he suggested that he could make money carrying cargo. The plane really didn't look big enough to do very much."

Don continued. "Marijuana was just a guess. He could have been ferrying anything of value. The lawyer in Franklinton said he spent more money than he should have had. I've thought of three scenarios as to what could have happened to Bill. One is that the foreign guy might have been Tony Sheffield. He would have been about the right age and he's still wearing those tropical-looking shirts that the guy in the cemetery described. We also have evidence of his recent involvement. The word is that Tony has never reformed from some juvenile transgressions some time ago and could be dangerous. I looked up Swifty Sheffield's arrest record and found that he had spent some time in jail in New Jersey before he came to Louisiana. The charge was narcotics trafficking. I couldn't figure out from your notes when the foreign guy could have time to put something in the gas tank of the plane, but that really wouldn't take very long. He and Bill apparently were arguing, and Bill seems to have owed him something. The black car peeled out and left the area before the plane could develop motor trouble and crash."

I agreed. "Actually, I had thought of something like that. After seeing Tony the other day, I wouldn't like to be in a dark alley with him. You said you had other theories."

"Actually, theory may not be a good word. That would imply some factual basis. What I have are more like guesses or possibilities about what could have happened. Bill obviously wanted to provide for his family. He must have known his life was in some sort of jeopardy. What if he took his own life?"

I frowned. "If that were true, why would there be gunk in the gas lines, enough to cause the engine to fail?"

Don smiled a 'gotcha' smile. "Mainly because he had a double indemnity policy. If he died in an accident, his policy would pay double. If it were a proven suicide, it wouldn't. He would have to have something to back up the accident, even if it pointed to murder. As it happened, no one but the mechanic knew about the gunk until you found out. Making sure that the engine would fail could take some of the decision out of crashing the plane when it came to crunch time. Things may have been closing in on him; the argument at the airfield would indicate that. Do you think he was capable of suicide? Was he afraid to die?"

"I don't know. He pretended he wasn't afraid of anything, but I remember him backing off a high diving board in Mexico. He almost drowned when we were real young and he seemed nonchalant about the near miss. He said something about we all have to go sometime. One time, I thought maybe he had committed suicide after a wreck down in Mexico, but as it turned out, he'd just passed out on the seat of the car."

"Was he religious?"

"We never discussed it <u>per se.</u> He seemed uncomfortable around churches when we went to weddings, and he did say one time that he wouldn't carry bibles in his plane. You said you could think of three possibilities."

"Right. Your notes said that Bill gave the foreign kid something at the air field. What do you think that was?"

"Something small. Didn't the guy put it in his pocket?"

"That he did. It had to be something valuable."

I thought for a second. "Money, maybe?"

"Possibly. The cemetery guy might have recognized that, if it were large enough to be bills. The foreign kid didn't seem to think it was enough, anyhow."

"A ring? Bill used to sport an expensive-looking ring."

"Could very well be. Bill wanted the kid to have whatever it was but the kid wasn't satisfied with it. He would have been satisfied if he had asked for it specifically to cover the obligation. Of course, your cemetery guy would have to have been very observant to pick up on all that body language."

I wasn't sure where this was going. "Wait a minute. They found a ring belonging to Bill in the plane."

"Exactly. What if Bill had given the ring or the ring and the key to the plane to the foreign kid? The plane surely had to be worth a lot."

I wasn't convinced. "What you are saying is that maybe it wasn't Bill in the plane at all, but probably the foreign kid–who couldn't have been Tony because he is still alive. The problem with that is that they would have been able to identify the body, especially if the plane had not burned after the crash."

"Unless Bill did something that would guarantee that the plane would burn. From what you have said, Bill didn't seem like the type that could figure out how to rig up a contraption to do that. Can you think of anything at all that would make Bill capable of pulling something off like that? Did he talk about plane crashes?"

I thought for a few seconds. "No. He never talked about plane crashes, to my recollection. Wait a minute. There was an incident that could touch on that. It wasn't about a plane, though. Once in Mexico, we had a close call with some kids who blocked our way on a lonely stretch of road. Bill seemed to think that they would have killed us if they had been able to stop us. He thought they would have gotten away with it if they pushed our car over a cliff and made it burn with us inside. Guaranteeing that it would burn was the problem because Bill didn't think burning was bound to happen. He thought most Hollywood car crashes were stereotyped. Bill said he could figure out how to do it with enough time–or something like that."

The waitress came with our meals. We both quit talking and leaned back as though we didn't want people to know what we were talking about.

Don finished off his beer. "See. He did think about the problem. Do you think he was capable of leaving his family and escaping to some other country?"

I thought for a moment. "Perhaps. He loved the freedom he found in Mexico. Once we found a little cantina in the desert, and he remarked that he could live there. No. I think he said he would prefer a seashore or something like that. I couldn't imagine him living in the desert in the middle of poverty. He once admired a guy in Mexico City who appeared to be a fugitive and could get himself lost in the crowds. His feelings did seem a little unusual at the time, but I thought he was just spouting off." Nevertheless, Don's last scenario still didn't seem plausible to me. "You're forgetting about one thing."

Don pushed his glass away. "What's that?"

"There was a body in the plane. If it wasn't Bill, it had to be someone else. And if so, people would looking for him. There wasn't anybody else."

"Yes there was."

"Who?"

"Lindsey Scott. Tommy put in his e-mail to you that he thought Scott was killed about the same time as Bill–but they couldn't find his body. Did you reread that e-mail before you pasted it into your narrative about our investigation?"

I was a little embarrassed. "Not thoroughly."

"Do you remember what Scott did for a living?"

"No. Not really."

Dan delivered the clincher. "He worked for an oil company, flying bigwigs around to meetings. Lindsey Scott was a pilot! Besides, we know he had worked for Swifty."

I tried to get out of this line of reasoning. "Someone still had to identify the body."

"Right. But wouldn't it be nice to have your best friend perform that task, someone who would profit from your insurance for years to come?"

There may have been other arguments against this set of conjectures, but I had a feeling that Don would have answers for everything. It was obvious that he had studied the documents more than I had and had thought deeply about this problem. "So what if any of these possibilities were true? What could we do about it?"

Don hesitated and bit on his lower lip before answering. "Probably nothing. At least nothing concerning Bill Jenkins. Since my superiors seem unwilling to do so, I think we should concentrate on Tommy's supposed accident. What physical evidence do you think we could find now?"

I was quick to respond. "I'd like to look at that blue SUV."

"I would too. Until you gave me these documents, I didn't know there was a blue SUV. It's very likely that the blue paint smear on Tommy's van came from the same vehicle that you saw near the Bogue Falaya River. If you were in this gang and had this repainted SUV that might be incriminating, what would you do?"

"I'd probably get rid of it or change its appearance."

"I would too. Given the fact that Tony owns a repair shop, my guess is that they would try to fix whatever damage occurred to the SUV and to repaint it to another color. We probably have to catch them in the midst of doing that. If so, we may be too late already. We should move quickly. Can you meet me at the repair place tomorrow night?"

That caught me unaware. "Why tomorrow night?"

"Because I have to work tonight and I want to take a look inside of the place when there is no one around."

I gulped. This sounded more like a cloak and dagger stunt that Wild Bill would suggest, but I couldn't back out. "Sure. What time?"

"Let's meet at 7:30. Have you got a highway map?"

"Yes. In the truck. It's got a blowup of Baton Rouge, if that helps."

"It might. There's a back way in from Clinton that might save you some time. Otherwise you might have to go all the way into St. Francisville and turn south on Highway 61. That would make you go way far west than you need to. Do you want me to walk you through the route or show it to you on the map?"

"I'll get the map."

When I got outside, it was pouring down rain. The map was easy to find. I shook off some of the wet in the doorway and went to the table. "Here's the map, but it's raining cats and dogs outside. Will this affect our mission?"

"No. The weather station says this rain will stop around tomorrow afternoon." He spread out the map, and pointed to an intersection. "Here. Highway 67 meets Highway 10 in Clinton. If you just go south, 67 turns into

Plank Road. Just past the airport, you take a left on Hooper Road. Then you drive to about here." He put a small x on my map. "You'll see a car seat place on your left. Tony's repair place is the next driveway up a hill. I've scouted this out. He's got a gate across the road a bit farther up the hill, so we'll have to park right there and walk around the gate. There's no fence. The shop is a big metal building with garage doors in the front. Think you can find it?"

I looked at the map. "I think so. It may be harder in the dark."

"Oh. There's a sign that says 'body work' right where you turn in."

My worries persisted. "Don, won't we be guilty of breaking and entering? Even if we do find something, would it be admissible in court without a warrant?"

"Well, for one thing, we won't be breaking in. That might be a crime. This place has some windows although they are higher up. Oh! Remember to bring a flashlight. You're right, we couldn't use anything we found in court without a warrant nor could we go back and rediscover something that was discovered without a warrant. I'm going to explore this business about a warrant tomorrow with a judge I know.

There are several things in our favor. Someone in the criminal justice system probably tampered with evidence and fingered Tommy. We risk alerting the mole if we make this an official investigation. We have the fact that thugs who knew your name and whereabouts tried to do you in when your only connection with Tommy were your inquiries about the files. This means we can't publicize our intent and end up warning Tony through his contact with the police. Judges take it into consideration when the element of surprise may be compromised. We have the time constraint that could allow Tony to destroy evidence if we wait too long. I'm going to tell this judge the whole story and see if he will issue a warrant to gain evidence without the permission of the suspects based on reasonable cause. The reasonable cause of course is the blue SUV itself, which is now mentioned in a filed police report. The vehicle most likely was used in the commission of a felony even without a connection to Tommy. We should be able to get warrants issued on hearsay. In other instances that's been done before simply on the basis of an anonymous phone call. In this case, you reported the attempted murder incident to me. Plus, we have evidence that the dummies lied about the gunshot wound in an official report. I'm pretty sure we can get a specific warrant that will allow me to look inside the repair shop. If the SUV is there, we–that is the police–can go in and inspect the place officially. I'm not mentioning to the judge that you are going with me tomorrow."

When we finished eating, we paid up and walked outside and stood in the doorway. I shivered a bit. "It's still chilly."

Don looked up at the rain clouds. "It's supposed to get warmer with this low pressure system. All our weather seems to come from the south and west. Every time we get moisture, it warms up. That's why we hardly ever get snow. Whenever it's cold enough, we don't have the moisture in the air. By the way, what was all that stuff in your documents about the Kennedy assassination?"

I had forgotten about that. "Oh, that was Tommy. I just pasted in his whole e-mail. On his own, he was researching incidents of people killed in plane crashes in Louisiana. The internet mainly had info on famous people. One thing led to another, and he uncovered a whole pile of likely accidents. I was surprised to see how many Louisiana notables were killed in plane crashes. Not at any point did I ever entertain the possibility that our accidents had anything to do with the Kennedy case."

"Good. That would have been a can of worms beyond anything we should get involved in."

We said goodbye and sprinted for our vehicles.

CHAPTER TWENTY-ONE

The heavy rain had ceased before I drove down the road toward Tony's repair shop. I had to assume that Don had obtained the warrant. If not, we could abort this mission when we met at our destination. I was hoping he had failed because this operation was getting scary. No other cars were in sight on Hooper Road, and no other lights were on in businesses or houses for well over a mile. As I approached the driveway to the garage, I could see a faint light up on the hill. Someone must be in the shop. It seemed like my car was making too much noise and my headlights must have been visible for some distance. Some sneak! I turned off the lights and tried to slow down. The clouds from the recent rain dimmed the light from the moon, and it was very difficult to see. I almost missed the turnoff and made more noise as I skidded to a stop before turning. Slowly, I made my way up the hill, not knowing how far I should drive before stopping. Suddenly, I spotted Don's car almost out of sight on the left side of the driveway. He had backed his car off the driveway with the front end pointing out as if to be ready for a quick getaway. That seemed like a good idea. I tried to back in beside Don's car, but I'm not very skillful at it and had to pause and take my time, making several attempts to get straight. At last, my truck seemed to be parallel and I gave it some gas to park. Something gave way under my back tires, and the front end of the truck raised up in the air. I tried to pull forward again, but the truck slid farther backwards, even taking a slight slide sideways. I opened the door to the truck and had to jump down. Damn! I used the flashlight, but I had to be careful or I would give away my position. Don was either in his car or up the hill, probably laughing at my awkward attempts and wondering how he could pull me out of whatever hole I was in. He wasn't in his car. I flashed the light briefly inside and could see the ignition keys were gone and the glove compartment was open. I felt my way to the back of the truck and saw that the bank to a drainage ditch had given way, and my truck was hopelessly mired in the mud. The water was flowing through the ditch still. I wished I had the .22 now. At least that would be something. Don, being a policeman, must be armed. No use spinning tires and making more noise. Better to make my way up the hill and find Don.

The first obstacle was a long metal cattle gate across the driveway, firmly padlocked. Don must be somewhere on the other side. I tried to climb the gate, but it creaked under my weight. I found a space where an angled piece left a gap between the horizontal slats and slithered clumsily through. When I looked back, I realized there was no fence, and I could have walked around the gate in the mushy soil. My shoes and clothes were muddy wet already. I was out of breath and still had to trudge up the hill. If someone was inside the garage, he would surely hear me if I called out Don's name. The metal building had a large roll-up garage door on the right, lined up with the driveway. Three windows to the left of the door cast their impressions in light on the ground outside. On the left, a small, room with a door stuck out towards me. The room was attached to the main building almost like an afterthought. A small glow like a flashlight lay on the ground. A low groan emanated from the dark space between the building and the lights. "Don?" I whispered.

"Sam!" It was a loud, hoarse whisper. "Over here!"

He was huddled against the side of the building next to a gas meter pipe. Both arms were hanging from the top of the regulator. I lifted his head. "Are you still here, buddy?"

He groaned. "Just barely. My leg is broken. The bastard snuck up behind me and hit me with something." Don stopped to catch his breath. He didn't look good. He tried to move his leg with his free hand. "Can't get comfortable. I was standing on top of these pipes to look inside when he hit me from behind. He cuffed me to the pipes with my own cuffs." He pointed his chin towards his waist. "Get my cuff keys. They're in my watch pocket."

"Where is he now?"

Don couldn't lift his head but replied with his chin on his chest. "Gone inside. I passed out for a minute, but I could hear him. He said I would tell him what I was here for when I woke up. He took my gun. Guess he can't risk the noise of a shot. Get those goddamn keys!"

I reached inside the watch pocket and found two tiny keys on a ring. Then I reached over and managed to fit a key into a handcuff lock that freed Don's hands from the pipes. He slumped to the ground with a groan. I tried to lift him up. He gasped. "Don't move me!"

"How the hell am I going to get you out of here if I don't move you?"

"Don't move me."

I looked as his leg. He had a compound fracture and was bleeding. I took off my belt and made a crude tourniquet. I know I hurt him again, but maybe that would slow down the bleeding. I didn't know what to do. "Have you got a cell phone?"

"No. That bastard took it. Get this other cuff off me."

"What do you think I should do?"

"First, get this damned cuff off." He held up his

right hand.

I unlocked the other side of the handcuff that was dangling from his wrist. I didn't know what to do with them, so I stuffed them in my pocket. "I hate to tell you this, but my truck is stuck in the mud beside your car. Do you have your keys? I can go get help."

He felt for his pockets, but they were turned out. "No, he's got my wallet and everything." Don looked like he was fading away, but he mumbled "That room," he pointed his head backwards, "is an office. There's a phone inside. I saw him use it once when I was sneaking up. Now go inside and call 911. You don't even need to answer. Just dial and get out. " He paused to gather strength. "Watch out. He's got my gun." He pushed the words out as if he didn't have the breath to form the words properly.

"Who's he? How many people are inside?"

"Just one person. I think its Tony—big fella."

I crept over to the office door, but it was locked, and I couldn't open it. Dimly, I could see a desk and a phone through a window in the door. The office opened into the large, open space that comprised most of the garage. I crept back to Don. "The outside door is locked." He just groaned. I looked at the garage. A regular door was ajar on the other side of the roll-up door, but I didn't want to use it. "How can I get past him to the phone?"

Don was breathing hard and barely got the words out. "I looked inside before I climbed up the pipes. The office is in the front corner and he's working in the back of the building. I think you can get to the phone before he sees you." His head fell back, but he pushed himself half up with one arm again. "Hurry!" he gasped.

"Look, maybe I'd better get to a phone down the road."

"No. That bastard said he'd come back to see if I was ready to tell him why I'm here. He'll hurt me or kill me, I know. Hurry!"

Against my better judgment I went over to the half-open door and bent down to look inside.

It wasn't dark enough for me. A shop light was burning in the middle of the garage, and I could hear someone rummaging through tools and throwing some aside. A blue SUV was parked below the light, but maybe twenty yards away from the front wall. Brown paper was covering the windows of the SUV, obviously in preparation for painting. A pickup truck was parked inside in front of the closed garage door and close to me. The office area was situated in the opposite side of the building on my side. The phone was there if I could get to it. The trouble was that I would have to pass almost the length of the garage along the front wall in order to get there. A compressor kicked in and startled me with the sudden noise, but I figured it provided me with some background cover. I began sliding with my back to the front wall of the garage and keeping as low as I could. A row of solid-looking packing cases were stacked up a few feet away from and paralleling the wall, forming a little island between me and the SUV, and I tried to slip behind them. They could offer a little cover at least. A metal tool box for a pickup truck formed part of the packing case wall. The tool box was shaped like a fat "T" so that the wings on either side could be fitted over the sides of the truck. One of the wings of the tool box left a shadowed hole that I could see through without being very visible from where Tony was. I had to bend over even more to look through the hole. In doing so, I almost knocked over a shovel that was leaning against the wall. I caught it before it fell, but not before it made a slight sound. I froze. The compressor sound stopped and Tony's voice growled "Who's there?"

The only weapon I had was the shovel, and I was trapped behind the boxes. As I tried to make my way back to the door, I could see that I would expose myself before I could get behind the pickup truck and out the door. Turning back to my peephole, I could see that Tony was creeping toward me like a big buck deer, picking his way through the underbrush. He held an ugly-looking crowbar raised in his right hand and a revolver in this left. It was like I was on my deer stand. I couldn't move or he would see me. He needed to get closer for me to swing the shovel. I shifted it in my hands so that the small side would be the leading edge when I swung it down like an ax but I was afraid to take my eyes off Tony. He stopped a few feet away and listened. *Maybe I could reach him now. No. Be patient.* My heart was pounding, but I had to keep calm. I only had one chance, and it had to count. He took a step and stopped again. He called out before he got to the pickup truck, using my pile of boxes to shield himself from view of the door. He must have guessed that the sound of the shovel had come from the door area. "Is that you, copper? You're not supposed to move."

Then he was right in front of me. *Please don't look this way.* I stood up and swung the shovel as hard as I could and hit Tony squarely on top of the head with the flat of the blade. He turned around to react to the sound of me standing up, and I could see the whites of his eyes. He wasn't quick enough to respond and went down with a loud groan. I couldn't see him on the floor behind the boxes, and I knew I had to make sure he didn't get up and attack me. My ankle turned as I ran around the end of the boxes, causing me to fall to my knees, but I hobbled to my feet before Tony could move. I remembered the deer and my failure to finish him off. That wasn't going to happen again. The shovel was still in my hand. Tony was struggling to get up, but he couldn't. With all my strength, I hit him in the head again. I didn't care if I killed him. My life was on the line. He went limp without a sound.

What to do now? I should call, but what if Tony got up again? I still had the handcuffs in my pocket, but I didn't want to touch him. If he got those burly arms on me, he could crush me. Better do it quickly. I could only get his right arm free, the other was underneath him, and he was too heavy to turn over quickly. I clamped the cuff on his free wrist and dragged him slowly past the pickup and over to the metal runner that guided the garage door open. It was like pulling an elephant. The cuff just reached, and I clamped it shut over the runner. He would have to pull the whole apparatus down to get loose. Then I limped around him to the office. The dial tone on the phone was a welcome relief. I dialed 911. As soon as the dispatcher answered, I said, "I need paramedics and police at Tony's Garage on Hooper Road." Then I pronounced the magic words that would insure a quick response. "An officer is down."

I needed to get back and help Don. I hobbled around the boxes, away from Tony to keep my distance from him. When I reached his end of the boxes, I peered around cautiously to see if Tony was awake. There was a flash and a loud report as a bullet whizzed by my head. I had forgotten about the revolver. Tony must have still had it in his left hand when he fell on it. I had dragged the gun along with Tony. I retreated and froze, sitting on the ground with my back on the pile of boxes.

Tony must have been delirious. He shouted crazily. "Come and get it you bastard!"

I wasn't about to get in the open again, and it didn't seem prudent to answer him. I had this vision of him tearing out the side of the garage like King Kong. I couldn't see any other way out of the garage, so I sat tight, thinking the police would respond soon.

After a moment of silence, Tony must have cleared his head somewhat. He shouted. "Who the hell are you anyhow?"

I pondered answering but could see no reason why not. If he was still cuffed, he couldn't get at me. My position shouldn't matter. For some reason, I wanted him to know who I was. "Sam Elliot."

"Elliot? Why the hell are you on my back? I didn't do anything to you."

I massaged my ankle and thought if I should reply. I decided to try Don's possibility number one. "It all started a long time ago when you put something in the gas tank of a plane in Franklinton."

There was a silence. "Jenkins? Is all this about that shit Jenkins? He tried to pull a fast one with us and deserved everything he got."

For the first time, I had a connection. At no time before did I ever know for sure that this man who sat cuffed on the other side of the box pile was implicated in Bill's death. I hadn't been positive that it was actually Bill in that plane. Now I felt I knew for sure. All the little coincidences fit together, and Tommy's efforts were not in vain. Sometimes it's the first and simplest answer that's right. I leaned back and waited smugly, confident that we had some closure. In a little bit, blue lights began to flash outside the garage. Someone came to the door and flattened himself against the wall outside.

"Watch out!" I warned. "He's got a gun."

Tony responded immediately. The gun skidded across the concrete floor toward the door. "No, I don't. See, the gun is gone."

A figure in a flak jacket rotated in with a pistol leveled at Tony, and it was all over.

EPILOGUE

It wasn't hard to ID Tweedledum and Tweedledee-
-especially since one paid for treatment for his wound
infection with a credit card at a second emergency room.
Tony's henchmen sang like songbirds to reduce their
sentences as accessories. Apparently, they had been
ordered to kill me in my home and to make it look like a
botched robbery. They took it on their own to follow me
out to the Bogue Falaya. At the trial, they implicated Tony
completely as the one who caused Tommy's crash. They
also squealed on the rest of the car chop/narcotics gang
which turned out to be much smaller and more loosely
connected than the group in Swifty's day. The District
Attorney put the case together in record time. The forensics
sealed the deal. Tony got life without the possibility of
parole. I didn't care that we couldn't connect him with the
murders of forty years ago. He couldn't get more than life.
Those atrocities occurred too long ago, and the links were
too tenacious to try to prove in a court room. At the time of
his conviction, we didn't know what was in those missing
police documents. They contained something that caused
Tony to panic. It was enough to know that he would be put
away, and that it would not have happened except for his
actions over three decades previous. As yet, we still didn't
know who pilfered those documents and notified Tony
about Tommy and me. I figured that was law enforcement's
problem now.

Tony never talked about the old murders. He
vehemently denied ever being in Franklinton even though
he seemed to admit as much when I confronted him in the
repair shop. He said he didn't even know Bill personally,
but had heard that Bill had stolen a fortune from the gang.

Would Tommy still be alive if we had not meddled in these long-ago mysteries? He knew he didn't have long to live anyway, but I would not have traded Tommy's premature death for the satisfaction of bringing Tony to justice.

We persuaded detectives to interview Tweedledum while he was in jail on his various charges. He was too young to have been involved with those old homicides. The airplane crash was unknown to him as was the Lindsey Scott incident, but he did remember now-deceased gang members bragging about "whacking" some lawyer who was about to pull the plug on the group. They even revealed how they had staged the car wreck in the country. Tony was furious with his two henchman for bungling their mission to do me in. He took away their privilege to use the van and even denied them the knowledge of what the van would look like after the transformation.

Dennis's sister was glad to hear that there had been at least some partial resolution to her brother's death. I think she felt safer now knowing that the culprits were gone, plus she began procedures to get some kind of formal recognition for Dennis' service. It was very satisfying to see her reaction and sense her relief when she heard the news.

The internal affairs group with the State Police worked overtime to discover who took the documents that Tommy had copied. They raked poor old Trosclair over the coals before deciding that he was innocent. Finally, after some time, they interrogated Tweedledum and Tweedledee again and found that Trosclairs's supervisor, Lieutenant Boudreaux, had been a frequent customer at Tony's bar. When the investigators confronted Boudreaux with that allegation, he agreed to talk in exchange for retaining his pension for his family. It seems that on the day in question he rode down the elevator at State Police Headquarter with

Tommy, who told him what he had found. The lieutenant followed Tommy out to the van and told him that since he was not representing a client when he copied the documents, he lost his attorney's privilege to work in the records room. No matter, there was a procedure for private citizens to obtain the documents. Boudreaux confiscated the copies and told Tommy that he could complete the paper work himself and send Tommy the copies within a week. Later, Boudreaux removed the originals and gave the copies to Tony.

Boudreaux had retained the originals as insurance and surrendered them to the internal affairs people. He swore he would have returned the documents to the records room as soon as he got the chance, but he never bargained on someone else asking for the same records so soon. As it turned out, the documents contained material that could have heightened suspicion at the time. What they showed was that Dennis was investigating Swifty for the State Police and that Scott had inquired about turning states evidence against Swifty. By themselves, those two facts didn't mean much, but at the time, no one had connected the two cases. Both files mentioned young Tony by name and conjectured about some of the gang's methods that are still being used, but could not be proved with 1960s technologies. The cases were reviewed by two different assistant DAs who decided not to prosecute because neither Dennis nor Scott was available to testify. With modern forensics and universal use of VINs, another look at Tony's operation could have uncovered the stolen car scheme.

I know that Bill had not been entirely innocent. He clearly had been involved with some shady characters. Probably he had been using his plane to transport illegal cargo or people for the gang back in Baton Rouge. I'd like to think that he got involved because he was desperate to provide for his family and had asked Swifty for advice. Swifty would have suggested that Bill use his plane to expand the illicit business, which, based on his statements at the airfield in North Carolina, would have appealed to Bill. Somewhere along the line, Bill had pocketed a large sum of the mob's money. Tony continued the family tradition and evidently took over the crime business at an early age after his father's death.

After two operations, Don's leg seemed to be mending nicely. With all the evidence we had now, he conceded that it had to be Tony that killed Bill even if Tony would not admit it. Don still had a question. "One of the things that bothered me was the gin bottle. Why didn't his wife or friends smell something fishy when they found it in the plane?"

I smiled. "Maybe it was because nobody knew about Bill's allergy but me. For some strange reason he thought it could injure his persona if other people knew and made me swear I wouldn't tell anybody about it. Tony couldn't have known or he wouldn't have planted the bottle. Unless of course--" I didn't finish what I started to say in jest--that Bill wanted to leave a sign for the only person in the world who knew about his allergy. Unfortunately, that thought might have started Don pursuing his theories again. Enough is enough. All that happened long ago and is behind us now.

I found the little graveyard in Oakville. The tombstone said simply, "William E. Jenkins–1935-1964." With a bit of sadness, I felt like I finally had done my duty as I slowly poured a bottle of Chivas Regal over the grave. Everyone had to assume that it was Bill in that grave, but it was tempting to think that he still might be at some seaside site in the tropics, living the fantasies he had always talked about and earning money flying. It would take some elaborate planning, but he had a long time to put all the pieces together. His role model had to be that renegade pilot we met in a bar in Mexico long ago. Bill could afford to disappear and start over again. After all, he must have fleeced Swifty's gang for enough undocumented dough to grubstake him for years.